Stickup

Boy

STICKUP BOY

BOY

Young Hustler

www.BeastAuthor.com

Black Queer Radical Books

ISBN-13: 978-0692420461
ISBN-10: 0692420460

DEDICATION

For my readers. The constant support from those that took a chance on my work is what helped me plow through page after page of this novel. Writing is something coupled with joy and distress. Staring at a blank page can be a hard thing. That's until I get messages from those who have read my work asking when the next story will be coming out. For that, I am eternally grateful.

Chapter 1

"Naw son," Romeo yelled. His face twisted in anger as he jumped up from the corner of the bed and yanked off his PlayStation head set. Romeo tossed his controller to the ground and looked down at Jamal as if the boy had stolen something. His hands balled into fists. "What the fuck you doing?"

Jamal glanced up at his best friend and shook his head dismissively. "Damn nigga, go ahead and play your little game." He wasn't the least bit bothered by Romeo's little tantrum. He ignored Romeo's posturing and slipped the second Air Jordan sneaker on his foot. He tucked in the loose laces and looked down at the shoes, admiring how they looked on his feet. Jamal's face beamed with satisfaction.

Jamal took his time primping the shoes and cuffing his jeans to get the exact look he wanted. He knew Romeo was watching. He didn't care. Jamal savored every moment of the torture he was putting his boy through. He got a sort of perverse pleasure from tormenting Romeo.

Finally, he looked up at his best friend with a smug grin on his face. Jamal looked at Romeo's fists, noting how they turned red from him digging his finger nails in his palms. He looked back up at Romeo's face with a *'what the fuck do you want'* expression.

"Jamal, my moms just got me those fucking shoes," Romeo explained. His voice sounded more like a whine. "I aint even worn them yet. Come on. Take 'em off."

Jamal waved him off. "You be alright, nigga. Your moms always buying your ass some shit you don't never wear. Those blue Air Forces been sitting in your closet for the last month, still in the box. All I know is, I'm bout to rock these motherfuckers today," Jamal said. His voice was raw as a Pit Bull's bark. He looked from the shoes back up to Romeo with a taunting grin. "They look good, right?"

Romeo's soft, brown eyes narrowed to a vicious scowl. His fists pumped on his sides and his left eye began to twitch. Sweat pearled on his forehead as his brow frowned. Romeo looked like he was about to explode. Jamal leaned back on the bed on his elbows, unfazed by the display.

It took all of Jamal's strength not to burst out into laughter. If Jamal knew anything about his childhood friend it was that Romeo was more bark than bite and even the bark wasn't much to be concerned with. Romeo just wasn't the fighting type. He lacked heart. He didn't have that survival instinct that made other cats ready to rip another man's throat out. Romeo wasn't built like that.

All throughout high school Romeo tried to put on a

rough-neck, thug façade but it just wasn't him. Watching Romeo try to go hard had always been funny to Jamal. Sometimes it was hard to watch because Romeo looked so pitiful trying to be something he obviously wasn't. It was like watching a car wreck over and over again. You knew it was bad but pulling your eyes away was damn near impossible.

At a little more than six feet tall and weighing about a buck fifty, Romeo was a slim, pretty faced, light-skinned dude. Despite his lean, athletic build, dudes in the neighborhood would punk him as soon as they saw the thick, bushy eyebrows, the clean corn rolls winding down to his shoulders and the deep dimples kissing his cheeks. He looked soft.

The one upside to Romeo's appearance was that the females loved him. They wooed when they saw him. He had a bright, white smile that shined in sync with his sparkling brown eyes. It got the ladies every time. The tragic part was when he opened his mouth.

As quickly as his looks hooked them, his mouth would have them cringing and sprinting in the opposite direction. Romeo couldn't spit game if his life depended on it. All he ever talked about was PlayStation and basketball.

Romeo always got his ass kicked on the games online but he was a pretty good baller in real life. Jamal and Romeo did almost everything together except for play on the same basketball team, even just in a pickup game. The boy had been a notorious ball hog since junior high. Romeo was one of the best power forwards in the state and he knew it.

It didn't matter though; no coach wanted him on their team anyways. They'd sooner take Jamal and he was mediocre at best. For that reason and his horrible grades, Romeo was eighteen years old and still living with his mom in the projects instead of going off to college on an athletic scholarship.

But despite all his flaws, Jamal looked at Romeo like the little brother he never had. They had been close since elementary school. Even back then Jamal didn't take shit from anyone.

Once, he saved Romeo from a fifth grader trying to take his leather jacket that his absentee father had given him. The two of them were in the third grade when it happened. They'd been boys ever since. But like any big brother, Jamal punked Romeo every so often. That was just the nature of their relationship.

Slowly, Jamal stood up from the bed. He was eye level to Romeo's lips. Although Jamal was shorter than Romeo, he still had the physical advantage. He was stocky. Jamal had the build of a college linebacker and the hands of a golden glove boxer.

Jamal glared up at Romeo and tilted his head. His eyes traveled up and down, sizing Romeo up as if he were only two inches tall. Romeo gritted his teeth and flexed his fists again. It was a fight or flight moment and Jamal never backed down from a fight. The two had play fought before. Jamal never hurt Romeo too badly but he made sure his boy knew he meant business when his fists flew.

After a minute of standing there, Jamal balled up his fists, too. His nostrils flared as he stared down Romeo. The line had been drawn in the sand. Romeo's eyes jumped nervously from Jamal's face to his hands and back. Doubt filled his eyes. The fire in his belly had been squelched by fear.

With a loud sigh of defeat, Romeo backed up and flopped down onto his bed, his head hung low. Jamal grinned, enjoying the moment. He shook his head as Romeo grabbed his controller and turned back on his game. Part of Jamal wished Romeo had at least put up a fight. Sure, he would have lost but at least he would have shown he had some heart for once.

Jamal walked over to the closet and opened the door. He looked at himself in the mirror hooked on the inside. Jamal heard the game going but he felt Romeo's eyes on him and the Air Jordan's on his feet. Jamal looked over his shoulder nonchalantly. Romeo sucked his teeth when their eyes met.

"Damn, Jamal. I aint even get a chance to take those bitches out the box," Romeo said, mumbling the words. "Ol' grimy ass nigga."

The disdain and hurt in Romeo's voice held no sway over Jamal. *Yea, I'm rocking these motherfuckers today*, Jamal thought. *A nigga look fly as shit*. He closed the closet and looked at Romeo.

"Aye, what you got up for the day, shawty?"

"Shit," Romeo answered. He shrugged his shoulders and put his headset back on. "Might ask my moms for the truck when she gets off work so I can ride up to the mall and scoop me a female."

"Really?" Jamal asked. Disgust lingered on the tip of his tongue. "The only thing you looking forward to is pulling bitches in your mom's truck?" Jamal shook his head and sucked his teeth loudly. "Nigga, don't you want your own shit? Don't you want your own dough in your pockets? Don't you want to push your own whip?"

Romeo shrugged and kept playing his game. Jamal walked over and stood in front of the flat screen, blocking the game. He crossed his arms over his chest and cocked his head.

"You need to come with me and make this money, nigga," Jamal said. "Sitting here playing this dumb ass game waiting for your moms so you can ride and find some pussy. That shit is weak, even for you."

"Whatever. Move, nigga," Romeo squealed and nudged Jamal out the way with his long arm.

Jamal grinned and pulled a blunt from behind his ear. He lit it, took a long drag and blew the smoke right in Romeo's face. Romeo's eyes shot wide open. He jumped up, flailing his arms in the air.

"What the fuck?! You know my moms don't like that shit in the house. You trying to get me in trouble? She already don't want you in the house after she caught us smoking last time. Damn, nigga!"

Jamal took another hard puff and passed the blunt to Romeo. "Then why the fuck we still in the house?" He was out the door before Romeo could offer an answer to the rhetorical question.

Jamal didn't have to look back. He knew Romeo would chase behind him, especially if given the chance to get high. Jamal waited at the foot of the front steps as he heard Romeo coughing the weed smoke from his lungs and locking the front door.

"Here," Romeo said, passing the blunt back. He smiled. "That's some good shit."

"If it aint some exotic I don't fuck with it. That right there is some Loud. I can't even fucks with Reggie or Mid. Can't put that dirt in my lungs no more. It don't get me high no more."

"Since when you got money to only smoke Loud?" Romeo asked. "You was smoking 'dirt' with me last Friday.

Ol' flexing ass boy."

"What can I say," Jamal teased, shrugging his shoulders nonchalantly. "I'm a hustler. I makes my money. Feel me?"

Romeo sucked his teeth. "Whatever nigga. So where we going?"

"The corner store," Jamal said, pointing down the street. "I'm thirsty as fuck."

"Naw, I meant, where we going to make this money?'"

Jamal looked at Romeo like he was stupid. "How else? We going to rob some niggas."

Romeo stopped in his tracks as Jamal pushed into the corner store. Jamal took a perverse pleasure from rattling Romeo's cage. He knew the off cuff remark would shock the shit out of Romeo. Jamal liked unnerving his best friend. It made life more interesting.

Jamal bought a pack of Cigarillos and two forties. The store owner didn't even look up when he set the bottles on the counter. Jamal had one of the bottles turned up before he stepped back outside. He handed Romeo the other forty and started walking. Romeo was right on his heels.

"Who you talking bout robbing, Jamal?" Romeo asked. His voice was shaky. "I aint trying to do some stupid shit, man."

"Damn nigga. Why you sounding all scared and shit like we aint never robbed some niggas. If you don't want to make no money then take your pussy ass home. I don't need no scared, bitch nigga watching my back."

"I aint scared and I aint a bitch nigga," Romeo said defiantly. "And stop calling me a pussy, Jamal. That shit aint cool. Just tell me what the plan is. We taking some niggas sneakers again?"

"Naw, that's some light shit. We going for some heavy weight. Make some real fucking money," Jamal said. He looked at Romeo, savoring the curious anxiety written all over his boy's face. "There some niggas from North Carolina that just set up shop down off Cascade. I figured we welcome the niggas to the ATL properly."

"You want to rob some drug dealers?" Romeo asked and then laughed nervously. "Wait. You serious aint you? Nigga, you crazy or just got a death wish? Or both?"

"Neither. I'm bout making that bread and I aint scared to take it. You in or what?"

"Fuck naw. That shit sounds crazy as fuck. Besides, how we gonna rob some drug dealers and we aint got no guns?"

Jamal grinned and pulled up his shirt, brandishing two Glock 9s. Romeo stumbled back and gawked at the steel tucked in Jamal's pants. He pointed at the guns like they were snakes ready to strike.

"Where'd you get those?"

"Nigga, why it matter? We got guns. So come on. All we need now is a car."

Romeo shook his head. His mouth hung open as he stared at the guns. "You know my moms took my car after I picked up that misdemeanor. And if I get caught wiring another car she said she was going to let me sit in jail next time instead of posting bail." Romeo finally pulled his eyes away from Jamal's hip. "I aint trying to sit in DeKalb County Jail, Jamal. That shit aint for me."

"We couldn't use your car no way. Why would we rob some dope boys in your car and they recognize that shit, dumb ass?" Jamal said. He shook his head and looked at his boy like he was a deaf/mute. Jamal pulled his shirt back over the guns. "Naw, we gotta steal a car. Aint no other way. We going to rob them niggas and ditch the ride. Could take it to Billy's chop shop if we wanted to."

Romeo frowned. "Why not just steal a couple of cars and take them to Billy? I won't get caught if you got the lookout."

Jamal knew Romeo would try to just steal some cars. Jacking cars was the one thing Romeo was good at. He could get any car, even the newer ones with all the hi-tech security features on them. The only reason he got caught last time was because he was trying to flex and took a Bentley to the club. Either way, boosting cars wasn't on Jamal's radar today.

"Cause I'm tired of robbing cars and shit. You just said you aint want to be in the county jail. Stealing a bunch of cars gonna land your ass there. And you know Billy don't be giving fair prices on them cars. Besides, we rob them niggas and they can't do or say shit to nobody. They aint going to the cops talking bout some niggas stole they stash and dope money, feel me?"

Romeo scratched his head and looked at Jamal for a long moment. "Fine. Fine. So we going up to the Underground garage to get a car?"

"Yep, hop on this Marta and get this shit poppin," Jamal confirmed. He looked at Romeo wondering if his boy had the heart to carry out what he had planned. Ready or not, they were about to be some stickup boys.

Chapter 2

The train ride up to Five Points station didn't take long but it felt like an eternity for Jamal. He knew he was ready to get that money but he wasn't sure if Romeo could handle what they were about to do. Jamal needed someone to watch his back. He needed someone who would blast a nigga if their lives were threatened.

His 'ol pretty boy ass might drop the damn gun instead of shooting it, Jamal thought. Fuck!

Jamal watched Romeo as he eagerly scanned the sea of black, brown and yellow bodies milling around the Underground and up and down Peachtree Street. The boy looked like a dog in heat, ready to jump and hunch on anything that moved.

Jamal couldn't blame him. They were in the dead heat of summer and most of the females had damn near nothing on.

All the shops and peddlers were open but flesh was the unsaid commodity on display.

"Damn, these females is out today," Romeo said. His excitement annoyed Jamal just as much as the cheesy grin on his face. He rubbed his hands together as if plotting on which one to grab first as if his game was that tight. "Come on, Jamal. Tell me you don't some dime pieces."

"Yea, they out here." Jamal nudged his friend in the side. It was time to focus and make that money. "Come on, aint got time for no sightseeing. We need a car."

The two of them headed to the parking deck across from the Underground and went straight up to the fifth level. Romeo spotted a car first. It was a dark Impala with tinted windows and rims. Romeo went to work on the car without saying a word. Jamal didn't argue. It was as good as any car they could get and it had tinted windows. Romeo popped the lock in less than a minute.

"Go ahead, get in," Romeo said, his voice giddy. He was busy working on hot-wiring the car before Jamal even got in on the passenger side. He pulled and crossed wires like a pro. Romeo looked up and over at Jamal as he worked.

"You know how many females we could pull in this shit?"

Jamal shook his head. "See, that's how you dumb niggas get caught and locked the fuck up looking at years under some prison. Be trying to get your dick wet and make money at the same time. Bitches get you caught up. You don't mix bitches or chasing bitches with work. You hustle and then get pussy, stupid ass boy. Get your fucking mind right, damn!"

"I'm saying. After we make this run we can come back through and pull some females, right?"

"Naw nigga," Jamal shouted. "We get rid of this fucking

car. If you want to ride back here on the Marta to get some pussy then do what you do. Why you want to keep a hot ass car all fucking day? Don't you think whoever car it is gonna report the shit stolen by the time we done? And you want to bring it back here?" Jamal frowned. "You got to think, man."

The car revved up, ending the conversation. Romeo grinned like a fat kid with a table full of candy and cakes as he gripped the steering wheel. It was like the chiding he had just received never happened. He was in his zone.

"Alright. Where we going?"

"Nigga, I'm driving," Jamal said. "Move your ass."

Without argument, Romeo stepped out and walked around to the passenger side as Jamal climbed over. Jamal pulled out the garage and headed straight down Peachtree Street towards the Westend Mall. Getting to Cascade from the Underground didn't take long.

The tension in the car became more and more palpable as they neared the neighborhood. Romeo couldn't sit still. He fidgeted in his seat like a crack fiend needing a hit. Even Jamal's nerves were rattled. But anxiety wasn't the beast he dealt with. It was his adrenaline.

Jamal turned down one of the streets with a lot of abandoned houses. It was the perfect place for a trap house. Jamal parked behind some cars on the curb and pointed over at a two-story, white house about fifty yards away. He nodded his head and smiled as he spoke.

"That's the house right there."

"You sure?" Romeo asked, more fear than doubt in his voice. "You know niggas be switching up houses and shit. Hell, most of these bitches look bout the same to me."

"Naw, these niggas is comfortable. They set up shop and

stayed. I been watching they asses for a good minute. They in there." Jamal pulled one of the guns from his waist and handed it to Romeo along with a black ski mask. "Here."

"Wait, we're going in right now? In the middle of the day?"

"Yea nigga, why the fuck you think we here for? If we wait until dark then all the dope fiends going to be all over the place. The sun be going down in a couple hour. These niggas done got they re-up. It's the best time to hit."

Jamal didn't wait for an answer. He put the Impala in drive and pulled up right in front of the house. Jamal pulled his ski mask over his face and looked over at Romeo.

"And make sure the fucking safety is off."

Jamal snapped the car in park and jumped out as Romeo fumbled with the gun. Like a thief in the night, Jamal quietly made his way up the stairs to the door. He pressed his shoulder against the frame of the door as he looked back at Romeo. He stood there and waited until Romeo flanked him on his left side. The two shared a look. Jamal nodded despite the fear in the boy's eyes. He didn't care.

Little nigga got to man up sooner or later, Jamal thought.

With a low grunt, Jamal pushed off the frame and faced the door squarely. He brought his foot up and slammed it against the door with all the strength he could muster. The old frame buckled against the force and the door came crashing down. Jamal held his gun up and ran into the house like he was SWAT. Romeo was right behind him.

Jamal's chest beat quicker and harder with each step he took. His breath was sharp and quick as he scanned the living room on the left and the den on the right. Adrenaline surged through his body like a torrent. He felt high as fuck and he liked it.

The butterflies tormenting his stomach from the second he stepped out the car until he stood in front of the door were gone. He had an iron gut. Jamal felt like a soldier on a mission and he was ready to get his money. Fuck all the casualties.

Jamal and Romeo trotted down the hallway towards the sound of chairs sliding against the ground. Whoever was in the back definitely heard the door come down. But Jamal and Romeo were too quick for them. The pair caught the would-be dope boys with their pants down... literally.

"Oh shit, ya'll got some ol' freak shit going on in this bitch," Jamal said, pointing his gun at the group. "Sit ya'll asses down on that couch! Over there! Sit the fuck down! And you two can finish pulling your pants up. Just don't try no bullshit. I aint got no problem putting a bullet in that ass. Motherfucker, try me."

Before anyone moved, Romeo stumbled into what looked like a family room off the kitchen and bumped into Jamal. His head snapped back in disbelief at what he saw going on in the room. Romeo leaned in towards Jamal.

"Why these niggas got they dicks out?"

Jamal shrugged and motioned for the two bull-necked, muscular guys that looked like brothers with their draws and jeans bunched at their knees to pull up their clothes. The two, dirty crack-head females on their knees looked up at Jamal and Romeo, scared to move. Jamal motioned for them to sit on the couch. He waited for the guys to cloth themselves. They were still brick hard despite having guns leveled at them.

The other two guys in the room watched Jamal and

Romeo intently, waiting for an opportunity. One was sitting on the recliner in the corner with a burning blunt in his hand. The other had a cell phone in his hand with the flash still on. Jamal figured he was the self-appointed video recorder. His other hand was down the front of his pants. Jamal walked over to him.

"Give me the gun or I'll put a bullet right through your head, little nigga."

The videographer looked up at Jamal with a steely gaze and sucked his teeth. He flipped up his shirt, revealing the Berretta tucked in the front of his pants. Jamal snatch the gun and tucked it in the back of his pants.

Jamal glanced back at Romeo. He smiled as his boy held his gun with two hands, pointed at the two guys that had been getting head. Jamal walked back over to Romeo's side, watching the brothers the whole time. He shook his head, disgusted.

The two females that were sucking their dicks were some far gone crack-heads; skinny as shit with the black sores all over their skin and nappy heads. Jamal couldn't imagine putting his dick anywhere near something that look so trifling.

What niggas will do to get they dick wet, Jamal thought. Bitches look like walking STDs.

Jamal leveled his gaze and gun on the would-be cameraman. The boy couldn't have been more than sixteen years-old. That's why Jamal chose him. He stepped up to the boy and pressed the barrel of the gun against the kid's chest. Jamal waited, savoring how the boy steeled his body and clenched his teeth, willing himself to be hard. Jamal wondered how far the boy would go with the gun at his chest.

"Tell me where the stash and the money at," Jamal said. "If you don't, I'll just blow your fucking chest away and ask the next nigga."

The boy clenched his eyes shut for a second and took a deep breath. He pressed his lips together defiantly and looked Jamal in the eyes. Contempt, anger and fear swirled in the kid's eyes. Jamal laughed heartedly at the gesture. Everyone in the room, including Romeo, recoiled in fear. Jamal looked and sounded like a madman.

"Look at this little nigga trying to go hard," Jamal said looking over the small group. He began to nod approvingly. "I respect that. Trying to stand up and be a man. That shit is admirable." Jamal looked back at the kid. "I hope you realize what it means to be a man in this profession, hmm?"

The boy narrowed his gaze. Jamal saw the fear behind the bravery in the boy's eyes. In a swift, fluid motion, Jamal slammed the butt of the gun on the bridge of the boy's nose. He yelled out in pain and fell to the ground. Blood flowed freely down his face. Romeo jumped back, shocked by Jamal's outburst. Jamal ignored his friend's reaction.

"Now you pissing me off, little nigga. Obviously you don't understand how this works," Jamal said, his voice teetering to a whisper. He leaned in towards the boy until he was only inches from the kid's face. Jamal pressed the gun against the boy's side as he spoke. "See, I point this gun here, full of bullets, at you, ask you a question and you tell me what I want to know. When that happens, everyone walks away still alive and your heart still beats. Come on, it's only money. Live to make more. Shit, you probably making money for another nigga anyways. You ready to die for him?"

The boy's eyes were blood shot as he looked away from

Jamal and stared at the wall. Blood still flowed from his face. His lips quivered but words didn't cross them. Jamal shook his head and grinned. With one quick move, Jamal kicked the boy in the chest just as hard as he had kicked the door. The impact sent the kid sprawling back to the couch. He desperately gasped for air as soon as he hit the couch.

The women screamed in terror. Jamal pointed his gun in their direction until they covered their mouths and quieted down, tears streaming down their faces. The boy squirmed and clenched at his chest, struggling to breath. Jamal motioned towards Romeo.

"Hold his hand down on the arm of the couch and make sure to spread his fingers apart."

Romeo looked at Jamal and frowned. The ski mask hid the expression. Jamal stared at his friend, waiting, until he finally did as he was told and held the boy's hand down. A devilish grin spread on Jamal's face as he stepped towards the boy. He reached in his pocket and pulled out the cigar cutter he had stolen a week ago from a tobacco shop. Jamal didn't like cigars and had hoped he would find some other reason to use his new prize. Now he did.

Jamal reached down and laced the cutter around the boy's small thumb. Romeo stepped back in horror, realizing what was about to happen; what Jamal was about to do. The boy clenched the couch with his other hand. Jamal loved every second of the impending torture.

"There we go," Jamal said. "Right at the joint. Perfect for a clean, bloody cut."

Jamal positioned the bottom of the cutter on the arm of the couch. All he had to do was bring the butt of the gun down like a hammer to slice through the kid's flesh, leaving him with nine fingers. Jamal looked the boy in the eyes.

"Now, I don't know about you but I like my thumbs," Jamal said, looking around at the scared and angry faces in the room. The women were crying. "I'm pretty sure everyone in here likes their thumbs, too. If you want to keep your thumb, you better tell me where the shit is, and I mean right now."

Jamal watched as the boy's face contorted and twisted, struggling with whether or not to say where the stash and money was or risk losing his thumb. Jamal shook his head and raised the gun over his head. The boy clenched his eyes shut. His body went rigid.

A shot rang through the small room. Jamal reeled back on his heels. His body snapped like a python toward the origin of the shot, his gun leveled. Jamal was eye to eye with Romeo. He took a deep breath and put his gun down.

"What the fuck you doing!?"

Romeo looked shook as he pointed to the weed head on the other end of the couch. "He was reaching in the couch cushion."

Jamal looked over at the man. He was clenching his inner thigh, where Romeo had shot him. Blood poured freely from the wound. Jamal motioned towards the man.

"Move your ass to the ground."

The man mustered as much hate in his eyes as possible as he looked up at Jamal before inching down to the ground. Jamal went to where the man was sitting and thrust his hand down the inside of the couch. He pulled out a sawed off shotgun. Jamal looked at the gun and back down at the man. Anger boiled in his veins.

"You were going to try and kill me, hunh?" An odd grin

spread on the man's face. Jamal leaned in. "You done fucked up, nigga."

Jamal wailed on the man, pounding away at his face over and over again until the man was barely recognizable. Jamal stood up and pointed the gun at the man's head. He pulled the gun's hammer back.

"It's in the bathrooms!"

Jamal looked back in the direction of the voice. It was a female. One of the crack-heads. Jamal barreled towards the women. Both of them flinched. Jamal looked from one to the other. The one in the dirty, purple t-shirt pointed towards the bathroom, her arm shaking.

"Look in the bathrooms," she said, her head hung low. "In the toilets."

Jamal smiled at the woman and motioned for Romeo to go and check the bathrooms. It wasn't long before Romeo came back with four large, dripping wet plastic bags filled with crack and coke. They'd hit the jackpot. Jamal walked up to the woman and pressed his gun against her kneecap.

"Now, where's the money."

Tears filled the woman's eyes. Her gaze shifted towards the kitchen. Jamal told Romeo to check the kitchen. He came back with a couple stacks of hundreds and twenties wrapped in rubber bands. It wasn't much but it was enough for an established trap house to start operations.

Jamal poked a hole in one of the bags and pulled out a vile of coke. He walked over to the woman that had told him where the stash and cash were. He popped the vile top and held it to her nose.

"Here, go ahead and get you a bump."

The woman didn't hesitate. She inhaled deeply, emptying

the vile. Jamal saw the wanting glare in the other woman's eyes. She wanted a hit too. Jamal ignored her. *Should have spoke up, bitch*, Jamal thought.

Jamal packed the plastic bags in a duffle bag and backed out of the room towards the door. Jamal and Romeo held their guns on the men on the couch until they were out of sight. Jamal backed out of the house and crossed the door threshold. He was about to break out into a full-fledged sprint for the car but the sound of a cocking gun at the back of his head made him freeze in place.

Jamal dropped the bag and put his hands in the air as he slowly turned and came face to face with the barrel of the gun. The large bald headed man holding the pistol raised his arm and slammed the butt of the weapon on the side of Jamal's head. The world went black.

Chapter 3

The heavy strike across Jamal's jaw jolted him awake from unconsciousness. A stinging pain burned the side of his face. His eyes shot wide open from the mind numbing pain. Instinctively, his muscles tensed and flexed as he tried to snap back at whoever it was that struck him. Yet, Jamal's balled fist held steady at his side. His wrists were tied to the chair he sat in. He quickly realized that he wasn't going anywhere.

Fear and anger danced in Jamal's eyes like kindles of fire. His hazy sight cleared. He looked up at the lanky, brown skinned man standing over him. Jamal's eyes shifted to the man's boney hand adorned with a number of gaudy gold rings. He was sure he had felt each one of them on the side of his face. The man bent at his hip until he was at eye level with Jamal.

"Bitch ass kid," he said, searching Jamal's face and

frowning. "You don't even know who the fuck I am, do you?"

Jamal didn't speak. He had no idea who the man was. Until a minute ago, he'd never laid an eye on him. Jamal averted his gaze and looked down. The man's face twisted in anger. Then a sinister smirk spread on his face, revealing a gold tooth, as if he'd just had an epiphany. In his peripheral, Jamal saw the backhand coming this time. He braced himself for the strike.

Blood and spit dripped from the corner of Jamal's mouth. His face was already numb from the first strike. The second wasn't as jarring but it still hurt. The man shook his head, turned and walked towards what looked like a bar. Jamal glanced around the room to gain his bearing. He hoped he could figure out where he was and find a way out.

There was only one bar in the room. Half a dozen pool tables were sprawled uniformly in the small space. Four small round tables with cheap, faux leather chairs covered the rest of the room. There was only a very small open space between the tables and pool tables. Jamal realized very quickly that he was in a pool hall; a very cheap looking pool hall. Jamal's gaze shifted back to the man who had struck him twice and had him tied down.

The man was about the same height as Romeo; brown-skinned and well groomed, a little too well groomed. He reminded Jamal of a pimp with all his gaudy jewelry and gold tooth but without the overdone perm and bright suit. He was dressed casually in a pair of slacks and collar shirt. But he seemed to be very attentive to his appearance. The gator shoes were a testament to that.

Jamal looked around again, searching for Romeo. His boy

was nowhere to be found. Concern surged through Jamal's body as he twisted around to look behind himself and search for his best friend. The man eyed Jamal and chuckled. He reached behind the bar, pulled out a glass and poured himself a drink. He took a sip as he watched Jamal.

"You might want to worry yourself, little man," the pimp warned. "You may have found yourself in situation with a very unpleasant ending. A final ending."

Jamal's eyes narrowed on the man. The well-dressed pimp downed his drink and slammed the glass down on the counter. He walked back over to Jamal with a haunting look of controlled rage in his eyes. Jamal saw how the man's eyes glazed over. He wasn't one to fear any man but the look on the pimp's face almost made Jamal piss himself.

"So let's try this again," the man said as he pulled out a pocket knife and snapped the blade open. He moved closer and pressed the blade against the middle of Jamal's throat. "Do you know who I am?"

Slowly, Jamal shook his head, his eyes looking down at the blade that was just out of his sight. The man hadn't hesitated to hit him. Jamal doubted he would hesitate to cut him. The man moved in close enough for Jamal to feel his hot breath on his ear and smell the liquor seeping from his pores. That hadn't been his first drink.

"See, that's what fucking amazes me. If you don't know who I am, then what the *FUCK* made you think you could steal from me?"

Jamal looked up into the man's eyes. They were cold. An eerie resolve lingered on his face. Jamal didn't have an answer to the man's question; at least not one that would offer any chance of not getting cut. So Jamal didn't say a word. He figured there was no point. He closed his eyes and prepared his mind for the impending pain.

"Hey, Slim!"

Jamal opened his eyes and turned his head towards the deep, husky voice. He recognized the man. It was the same bullnecked, bald headed man that had caught him at the door of the trap house; the same one that had knocked him out. He was holding Romeo with one hand like a rag doll.

"You want this one? He's awake."

"Why not? Go ahead and sit him next to his partner in crime here," Slim said, waving the bald headed man over. "Young ass dudes always trying to go hard but be fainting and shit when they have to deal with some real shit. We got us a new breed of niggas, Bricks. They aint got no intestinal fortitude."

Bricks nodded his large, bald head and grinned as he dragged Romeo towards Jamal and set him down in the chair. Jamal's eyes darted over to Romeo. The room was somewhat dark but Jamal could still see the cut just below Romeo's right eye and the bruise on his left cheek. Besides that and the fear washed all over Romeo's face, he looked fine. But Jamal knew that they could have beaten his boy's body. There was no telling without asking.

"You alright?" Jamal asked, whispering. "Did they hurt you?"

Romeo shook his head over and over again. His eyes stayed glued on Slim and Bricks. The two of them were huddled over at the bar, speaking in hushed tones. Jamal couldn't hear them. Every so often they would glance over at Jamal and Romeo. Romeo visibly flinched each time they looked. Jamal kicked Romeo's foot to get his attention.

"I knew I shouldn't have did this shit," Romeo said. He looked at Jamal from the corner of his eyes. "Now we bout to die because of your stupid ass, stickup boy bullshit."

Jamal cringed at the sound of anger mixed with fear in Romeo's voice. His childhood friend was right. Because of him, they were at the mercy of a couple of drug dealers they knew nothing about. Jamal and Romeo both knew what was going to happen. They were going to die.

Slim got up and slid one of the tables and a chair across from Jamal and Romeo. He sat down as his bald headed partner remained standing, flanking his right side. It was clear who was in charge.

"Tasha! Come on out here, baby girl!"

A pretty, chestnut complexioned woman with a bad weave, a skin tight red spandex pants and a spaghetti strap shirt came in the room. Jamal thought she might be a stripper or maybe a hooker. Everything from her cleavage, to her face and walk screamed sex; raunchy, nasty sex.

"Yes Daddy?" Tasha purred.

Slim handed her the glass he had poured a drink in earlier. "Mix me a drink. I tried but it wasn't nearly as good as when you make it."

"Of course, daddy."

Slim's eyes were glued to the woman's large, curvy backside as she walked over to the bar and leaned over the banister for the liquor. Her cheeks parted perfectly when she bent over. Her pussy lips pressed through the fabric of her pants and were hard to miss. Slim shook his head, visibly forcing himself to look away. The drug dealer's gaze settled back on Jamal.

"Jamal. You don't mind if I call you Jamal, do you?" He

asked. He didn't wait for an answer. "Why did you try to rob me? Why did you run up in one of my spots and try to take all my dope and all my cash? What did I do to make you want to take from me?"

Jamal's mind raced. He made sure not to carry any ID before he left the house. He knew he was going to try and rob the trap house that morning. The only way Slim could have known his name was if Romeo had told it to him. And if that was the case, there was no telling what else Romeo had said to their captors. Slim walked back over to Jamal.

"You feel that, Jamal?" Slim asked, leaning in as he pressed the blade against Jamal's jugular. "That's your adrenaline ramping up. It's supposed to help you fend off an attack, but right now it's only guaranteeing that you die that much quicker. Your heart is beating faster. The blood is flowing quicker. In the end you'll bleed to death more quickly."

"We tried to rob you because we figured it be an easy hit," Jamal said plainly. "I don't know who you are. I just knew that the niggas at the trap house was slipping."

Slim smiled. He brought the knife down to the plastic zip ties holding Jamal's wrist down to the arm of the chair and cut him loose. Slim walked back to the table and sipped his drink.

"The sad thing is your right. I was an easy hit. Them young cats in the trap house were slipping. Getting bop from a couple of crack heads right with the goods in the house." Slim took another sip and looked over at the bald headed man. "Guess it's a southern thing, hunh Bricks?"

"Must be," the bull of a man agreed. "We aint see no shit like this until we moved into Virginia. Just got worst in the

Carolinas and now here."

"You know what. You right. One of them boys in Richmond got stuck up in one of the alleys near the trap house. And the motherfucker was coming from a sale run to the basers. Motherfucking hit cost me four stacks."

Bricks chuckled. "Cost him a little more."

Slim laughed too. "Yea, it sure did."

Jamal shifted his weight in his chair and wringed his wrists. It was becoming more and more apparent that they weren't going to kill the two of them. Jamal was sure they had something worse in mind. Slim focused his attention back on Jamal.

"You know, your friend here is quite the talker when properly motivated. It may be a good idea, at least in this situation, to do the same." Jamal narrowed his eyes, looked to Romeo and nodded. "Good. You know you almost walked out with almost $15,000 in product and cash. $15,000 of *my* product, *my* cash."

"I figured it was a lot," Jamal said.

"And with your boy here popping off, had the police all over the place. Not only scaring off my customers but forcing me to make another bribe to a bunch of cops. Now I have to find and set up a new trap house. That's at least a week of business I'm missing out on."

"I'd say I'm sorry but I'm sure you wouldn't believe me."

"Oh, I believe you. But you're not sorry about me losing my money. You're sorry you got caught." Slim looked over at Bricks. "How much was that house bringing us in a night?"

Rocks went over to the bar and pulled out a notebook and thumbed through it. "Been averaging about $35,000 a night in straight profit."

Slim looked in the air as if he were counting. "So, factor in what you tried to take, the business you cost me and the pain and suffering of the man your boy here shot in the leg and I'd say the two of you owe me about a hundred grand... *each*." Slim leaned forward and held his hand out. "I accept all major credit cards and cash. Can't fuck with checks and shit."

Bricks laughed as if he'd just heard the funniest joke in the world. Slim joined in. Jamal just stared at the two of them. There was nothing for him to say.

"No? Can't cover that?" Slim asked. Jamal shook his head. He understood exactly where this conversation was heading. "Well, I have an idea on a payment plan. The two of you will work for me until that debt is paid off."

"Slanging drugs isn't going to put us anywhere close to paying you off," Jamal said. "We may as well rob a bank. We'll be on a fucking corner until we die."

"First, you may want to consider the fact that the two of you are still breathing. I'd worry a little less about paying off that debt and more about doing what you need to do to stay alive right now. Feel me, little homie?"

Jamal nodded his head. Romeo was quiet the whole time with his head hanging but Jamal knew he was listening.

"And robbing a bank might not be a bad idea," Slim said, laughing. He held his hands in the air as he calmed down. "Seriously though. I got a job for the two of you and it aint slinging dope. So consider this your interview." Slim sipped his drink. "So, tell me how you guys fucked up."

Jamal held Slim's gaze for a moment, looked over at Bricks and then back at Slim. "We got caught."

"True, but how did you get caught?"

Jamal motioned towards Bricks. "Your man was at the

door when we tried to roll out."

"That's it? That's the only thing you can think of that you little niggas did wrong?"

Jamal looked at Slim blankly. He had no idea what else to say; what else Slim wanted to hear. Slim shook his head disapprovingly.

"Motherfucker, do you know how lucky you are that you're alive? Had that trap house belonged to those niggas ya'll be dead. Niggas be on they game when shit is theirs. Hell, I thought you were the smart one. Maybe your little bitch over here can give me some better answers."

Romeo slowly looked up at Slim. His eyes narrowed just as he spoke. "I aint nobody's bitch."

It was little more than a whisper but everyone heard him. An eerie silence hung over the room. The looks on Tasha and Bricks face gave Jamal pause. Slim looked at Romeo for a moment.

"No, you're a dumb bitch. First this nigga cops your kicks and you don't do shit. He makes you hot wire a car and then he drives the motherfucker. And you follow this nigga in a house you know has drug dealers in it. You do that without knowing how many cats is up in there or if they got guns. Shit, you don't even know if the house is being watched by the police. But you still go in behind his ass. Why? Because you his bitch, young nigga. His dumb, little bitch."

Slim watched Romeo, daring him with his eyes to say another word. Jamal just shook his head. Only now did he realize all the things he did wrong. Slim waved Tasha over from the bar.

"Take care of daddy, baby. These little niggas pissing me the fuck off."

"Of course, daddy."

Tasha walked over to Bricks and turned around. He helped her pull off her shirt. Then he pulled her pants down to her ankles. Tasha step out of her clothes and walked over towards Slim, naked. She went to her knees between his legs and pulled at his pants. Slim looked over at Jamal and Romeo.

"Cut him loose," Slim ordered. Bricks walked over and freed Jamal from the chair. The beast of a man pulled out his gun and stepped back. "Ya'll go ahead and strip."

The two of them frowned, looking at each other in disbelief. Slim motioned towards Bricks. The large man stepped behind the two of them and cocked his gun. Jamal and Romeo began to strip.

Jamal was naked first. His dick was on lump. He was pretty sure Slim was hard, getting his dick sucked. Each time Tasha bobbed up and down on the man's meat, her pussy winked back at him and Romeo. Jamal looked over at Romeo from the corner of his eyes.

Romeo's long, skinny dick was brick hard. His eyes were locked on Tasha's ass. Jamal quickly averted his eyes. He'd seen his friend naked before but never aroused. Jamal looked down at his own meat. His dick was thickening with each passing second.

Slim placed his hand on Tasha head, forcing her down until she sounded like she was choking on his dick.

"Ya'll little niggas need a lesson in the chain of command. On top is the nigga in charge. And then his bitches." Slim took another sip of his drink and pointed at Romeo. "You play the role of a bitch but don't know your place. See, Tasha is my bitch. She don't need to be told what to do, she trained."

Slim took Tasha's head with both his hands and thrust upwards, piston fucking the woman's face. Tasha kept sucking despite the oral assault. After a few minutes he sat back and let Tasha work him over again. He looked over at Jamal and Romeo.

"A bitch knows their place. Now, if the two of you want to walk out of here alive, you need to show me you know your place."

Slim motioned towards Bricks. His henchman grabbed Romeo by the neck and led him to one of the pool tables. He bent Romeo over and pressed his face onto the green top. Slim got up and took his clothes off. He walked over to Jamal, butt naked, dick jutting from his skinny frame.

"Come on little nigga. I can tell you want his virgin ass. I can see it in your eyes."

Jamal looked up at Slim. Something raged deep inside him. Anger at Slim. Lust for Romeo. How he wanted Romeo scared and excited him. The moment of reflection was short lived. Slim flicked his knife open again. Jamal stood up, took a deep breath and went over to the pool table with Slim.

Tasha bent over the pool table next to Romeo. She took the boy's hand in hers. Slim wasted no time. He was stroking out Tasha's back as soon as he touched her. He handed Jamal a bottle of lube and a Magnum wrapper as he fucked her.

Jamal looked down at Romeo's smooth, firm yellow ass. He wanted to caress it. Jamal even had the urge to kiss it. Those urges made Jamal uncomfortable. He didn't know where they were coming from and he wasn't about to explore them.

Not here, he thought. Not now.

Jamal put a generous amount of lube on his dick. He was brick hard looking down at Romeo's ass. Jamal looked over at Slim. The man had been watching Jamal the whole time. He motioned for Jamal to start.

Jamal took his meat in his hand and lined the head up with Romeo's hole. He pressed forward until the head popped in. He felt Romeo's body go rigid. Jamal held steady for a moment. But the hot, tight warmth of Romeo's ass felt amazing. Jamal slowly pressed forward. Romeo winced in pain, clawing at the felt top of the pool table.

Taking his time was something Jamal had gotten used to when having sex. His dick got thicker from the tip to the base. He knew from fucking females that it wasn't easy taking him.

Jamal took hold of Romeo's waist and forced him to arch his back. Jamal slowly moved back and forth until all eight inches of his thick dick was buried deep inside Romeo. Jamal rubbed Romeo's back as he made his dick jump inside the boy's ass, loosening him up.

Jamal fucked Romeo's tight virgin ass in earnest, pulling his dick out until only the head was in and driving the length of his pole in to the hilt over and over again. With how tight Romeo was and how horny Jamal was it didn't take long for Jamal to bust. He pounded Romeo's ass ten good times, pulled out and nutted all over his back. Jamal was relieved and disappointed that the experience was over so quickly.

Slim stopped fucking Tasha and patted Jamal on the back. Jamal figured he busted too, despite still being hard. Tasha took Romeo to the back room.

"Good job, youngin." Slim tapped Jamal on his ass. Jamal frowned. "Now bend that ass over."

Jamal looked from Slim to Bricks. He knew he didn't have a choice. But he wasn't going to be a bitch and cry. He was going to take the shit like a man. The single thought in Jamal's mind was the day he'd make this nigga, Slim, his bitch.

Chapter 4

Romeo grinned mischievously as he climbed up and straddled Jamal's lean, muscular thighs. With every ounce of strength he could find, Jamal struggled to keep his body under control. He soon realized it was a losing battle. Every inch of Jamal's flesh that pressed against Romeo's skin felt as if it were set ablaze. The overwhelming sensation kept Jamal teetering on the fine line between sublime pleasure and pure ecstasy.

A savage, lustful hunger burned bright in Jamal's eyes as he looked up at his best friend. Jamal watched, mesmerized, as Romeo's chest heaved back and forth with each labored breath. Jamal reached up, placing one hand on Romeo's hip and the other behind his friend's neck, gripping Romeo firmly in his grasp. Jamal stared up into Romeo's unassuming soft, brown eyes. Jamal felt as if he were somehow lost but found all at the same time.

Romeo ran his fingers over Jamal's chest as he smiled down at his childhood friend. Jamal couldn't control himself. He pulled Romeo down onto him until he felt heat radiating from Romeo's slim, toned body on his own skin. Jamal's manhood stiffened and pressed sharply into Romeo's inner thigh. Jamal shuddered as Romeo grinded his body into Jamal's.

Romeo slowly leaned in until their faces were less than an inch apart. Then he opened his mouth. Romeo slipped his tongue out and dragged it over Jamal's thick, moist lips until they were thoroughly wet. Jamal clenched his eyes shut as Romeo pressed forward and drove his tongue inside of Jamal's mouth, exploring every inch.

The closeness, the heat, the taste of Romeo's flesh; it was all so intoxicating. Jamal reached back and grabbed each of Romeo's firm ass checks in his large hands and spread them apart. Jamal thrust his hips upwards, grinding his hard dick over Romeo's tight, smooth hole. A moan deep in Jamal's throat vibrated through his body. Romeo shifted his weight and whispered in Jamal's ear.

"Damn daddy, I want you so bad. I want you to make love to me. I need you inside me. I want to feel you, Jamal. All of you."

"Fuck. You got my dick spitting and shit. That's all I ever wanted, little nigga."

Romeo smiled as he reached back and pulled at Jamal's brick hard pole, bringing his precum to the head. Jamal's body went rigid with excitement. Romeo gripped Jamal's manhood. He rubbed the head of Jamal's dick over his hole until it was wet with sweat and natural sex juices.

Romeo arched his back and bit his bottom lip as he

pressed down onto Jamal's stiff pole. The head of Jamal's dick pushed at the tight sphincter. Romeo clenched his hole each time Jamal's dick slipped a little further in and jumped up. Jamal's dick stiffened each time he felt the warm lips of Romeo's hole grip the tip of his manhood.

Jamal spit in his hand and stroked his meat until it was dripping wet. He lined the head up with Romeo's wanting hole. Romeo bit his bottom lip and eased down until the length of Jamal was buried inside him. Romeo leaned in and held Jamal's face in his hands.

"I love you, Jamal," Romeo said in little more than a whisper. He leaned in to kiss Jamal.

BANG! BANG! BANG!

"Jamal! Get your ass up out that bed, boy!"

Jamal jumped at the pounding at his bedroom door and the sound of his mother yelling.

"Boy, it's almost one in the afternoon. I done told you; either you get a job or get in school. I aint going to have no grown ass man laid up in my house eating all my damn food and not doing nothing. I aint raise no bum and you aint bout to be no damn rolling stone."

Jamal rubbed the sleep from his eyes and threw the heavy comforter from his body. A frown twisted on his face. Something on his thigh felt sticky and wet. Jamal looked down. His boxers were soaked and clung to his leg and semi-erect manhood like spandex. He shook his head in disbelief. It had been years since Jamal had a wet dream. He had one night the last three days.

Jamal sat up at the edge of the bed and buried his face in his hands. It had been three long days since he last saw Romeo; since the two of them had their run in with Slim.

Jamal had spent every waking hour of those three days thinking about two things: Romeo and killing Slim.

Jamal was under no illusion about how Romeo likely felt about the incident. He saw the tears in his friend's eyes as he walked to the back with Slim's bitch, Tasha, to get cleaned up. But Jamal knew they weren't just tears of pain. Jamal took his time, went easy and finished as quickly as he could. Romeo was ashamed. He was angry and likely felt betrayed.

Jamal would have felt bad but after the brutal sexual encounter with Slim, he had little room to sympathize with anyone. Slim was longer; much longer than Jamal. He fucked longer and kept going after he busted. Jamal's ass was sore all the next day from all the smacking.

No, Jamal went easy on Romeo; he did his boy a favor. But Slim had made it a point to make Jamal feel like a bitch. And Jamal would make it a point to get even.

Jamal went over to the shopping bags and pulled out an outfit and pair of shoes he'd gotten from the mall the day before. He laid the outfit out on the bed and made sure it looked right. He smiled at his good taste and went to the dresser to get some underwear and socks from the top drawer. Jamal checked the wad of cash Slim had given him after the incident. He still had about $1500 left.

After Slim finished with Jamal, he gave the two of them two grand a piece, saying he takes care of his bitches until they can take care of themselves. The comment made Jamal's blood boil. But he wasn't a fool. He wasn't about to turn down money when his pockets were already hurting. Especially not two stacks.

When it was all over, Bricks, Slim's right-hand man, took them home. Romeo didn't say a word or look up. He huddled close to the door in a fetal position. It had been a long ride home that night. Jamal couldn't get that image of Romeo from his mind.

The thought to go see and check on Romeo was a constant one since the incident. Jamal just didn't know what he could say to him. It took Jamal a few days to get his own mind right. And the shopping spree yesterday helped. Sooner or later he had to check on his boy. Jamal figured why not sooner. As soon as he was dressed, Jamal was out the door headed for Romeo's place.

The closer he got to Romeo's apartment, the more anxious Jamal became. He even stopped to smoke a second blunt to ease his nerves. But he had the good sense to make sure he had at least one more in case Romeo was in the mood to smoke. It may have ended up being the peace offering necessary for them to move on and focus on getting Slim back.

Jamal walked up the stairs to the door. He raised his hand to knock but just stood there. His mind went blank and his body numb. For the first time that day, he was unsure about seeing Romeo. The thought to leave jumped in his mind like a rabid dog. But then the door opened.

Romeo stood there with a blank look on his face. He looked tired; his face haggard. Romeo looked at Jamal like he was a stranger. They stood there looking at one another for an uncomfortably long moment. Without a word, Romeo turned and went back inside, leaving the door open. Baffled, Jamal followed behind Romeo to the back.

Jamal looked around Romeo's bedroom. Clothes were all over the floor. Plates of untouched food, some covered in mold, were scattered throughout the room. Jamal shook his head. Romeo obsessed about being clean. Jamal knew that what Romeo was going through was fucking with him on a whole different level.

Romeo walked over to his bed and got under the covers with his back turned to Jamal. Jamal caught a whiff of the sheets and could tell Romeo hadn't bathed in a few days. Soap and water probably hadn't touched his skin since before they tried to rob the trap house.

Jamal sat there for what seemed like forever in complete silence. He didn't know what to say so he just said the first thing that came to mind.

"I went and got me some new kicks and clothes. Won't be roughing you for shit no more."

Jamal let out a weak laugh. Romeo didn't say anything. He didn't even move. Jamal sunk his face in his hands. He needed them to get past this phase. He needed Romeo to be himself again. He needed his best friend back.

"Romeo, I honestly don't know what to say my dude. What happened was fucked up. I don't even want to tell you what that nigga did to me after you left. I'm just sorry he made me do that to you. You my boy and the last thing I wanted to do was hurt you."

Jamal reached out and placed his hand on Romeo's shoulder. Romeo jumped up and cowered into the corner. Romeo's face was wet with tears. He shook like he was having a seizure but his eyes were wide open and focused on Jamal.

Guilt and anger filled Jamal's heart. Jamal tried to comfort and console his friend but Romeo only snapped when Jamal tried to touch him. Jamal cursed aloud. He felt responsible for what Romeo was going through. But Slim was the one that was going to pay. Jamal just needed a plan to get his ass.

Making sure not to touch him, Jamal placed a blanket over Romeo's shoulders. He ran to the living room and grabbed the house phone. He called Romeo's mother. Jamal didn't want to hear her mouth, the two of them had never gotten along, but Jamal wasn't going to leave Romeo alone in his current state. Romeo's mother was there in less than fifteen minutes, bombarding Jamal with questions as soon as she stepped in the apartment.

"Did he say anything?"

"No. I tried to talk to him but he didn't say anything back. I'm not even sure if he was listening to me."

"But he did get up and answer the door?"

"Yea. He looked at me with this blank stare and just went up to his room and got in the bed."

"Why is he in the corner like that?"

"I reached out and tapped his shoulder to get his attention. He flipped out."

Romeo's mother looked at Jamal with a look of fear and concern only a mother could have. "Jamal, do you know what happened? Why he's like this?"

Jamal quickly shook his head. "No. But I promise you I'll find out."

Jamal was out the door before Romeo's mother could ask another question. He wasn't all that fond of the woman but he didn't want to sit there and lie to her in her face.

Jamal racked his brain on how to get Romeo back to normal. Nothing came to mind. Jamal wanted Romeo back to normal. But he felt guilty. Jamal didn't just want his friend back. As selfish as it sounded, he wanted to see if there was more between them. And that wasn't possible if Romeo lost his mind.

Jamal's options were limited. The only thing he could think of doing was to go see Slim. At least he could buy Romeo some time by trying to convince Slim to let Jamal take Romeo's debt.

Jamal made his way to the Marta station. He was determined to make sure his boy was okay and wouldn't be put in harm's way while he dealt with his issues.

Chapter 5

Jamal saw the contempt in Slim's eyes as soon as he stepped inside the pool hall. Bricks had escorted him in and set him down in one of the bar stools once they were inside. Jamal fumed in the seat. Anger and disgust struck him like a runaway train as he sat there waiting and watching Slim play a game of pool alone. The drug dealer and would-be pimp took his time finishing up his game.

Until that very moment, sitting there and looking at Slim, Jamal hadn't thought of the words he would say. His stomach twisted as he realized he was about to beg. Beg the same man that violated him. Not once in his young life had Jamal ever even asked another man for anything. His pride would never allow it.

Jamal subscribed to the belief that a real man took what he wanted. Asking or begging was never given a thought. But all things considered, taking wasn't an option at the moment. Not yet. The only solace Jamal had was that he was begging for his best friend's life. He could live with that. For now.

Twenty minutes had passed since Jamal had walked in the door and Slim had finally gotten down to the eight ball. Just as he lined the stick up with the white cue ball he glanced up at Jamal and back down to the table. The glare was belittling. Slim's eyes made Jamal feel small and insignificant, like some strung out bitch on the corner.

The look was purposeful. Jamal knew that much. He struggled to regain his composure. He hated that Slim had that much control over him. Jamal hated to admit it, but he felt exactly how Slim had wanted him to feel; like a bitch.

Flashbacks of the day Slim made him choose between raping his best friend and death crept in his mind. Jamal had been plagued by the thoughts for the last 72 hours. The only thing that angered him more than Slim's action was the fact that thinking about what had happened on that pool table a few days ago had him brick hard. Jamal wasn't sure how to deal with how he felt. But something in his gut told him he'd feel better once he got rid of Slim.

"What the fuck you want, little nigga?" Slim asked after he knocked the eight ball in the corner pocket. "Aint I tell you to come back next week. It aint but Friday. Didn't I toss your ass enough money to stay busy for a week?"

"I don't want shit," Jamal blurted out. Slim stood straight up and looked at Jamal like a pimp ready to slap his hoe. Jamal clenched his jaw shut and took a deep breath. Anger poured from his body like a waterfall and filled the room. He needed to get a grip and quick. "I'm sorry," Jamal said, holding his hands up. "I need to talk to you."

"Look, you little fucker, I'm busy. Now tell me why you down here bothering me before I break this stick over your fucking head."

"My boy Romeo," Jamal explained, "something's wrong with him. What you did to him has him fucked up in the head. He acting all crazy and shit."

Slim shook his head as he placed his pool stick across the table. He walked over to where Jamal was sitting and just looked at him, as if searching for some sign that Jamal was lying. Finally, he pointed at Jamal as he spoke.

"I aint do shit to that boy. You did. Or don't you remember?"

Jamal buried his face in his hands. It was the only thing he could to look upset and not pound Slim's face in then and there.

"What you mean he acting crazy?" Slim asked, with what sounded like a hint of concern in his voice. Jamal doubted it was genuine.

"He aint the same. He's not eating or bathing. My boy got an appetite and he stayed fresh trying to get females. It aint like him to sleep in his own filth, balled up in a blanket all day."

"So what the fuck you want me to do? I aint no shrink and that little nigga still owes me money."

"That's what I want to talk to you about. Try and work something out."

"Work something out?! Motherfucker, you two are lucky to still be breathing. Naw, fuck that," Slim said angrily. "That nigga got a debt to pay and he better be able to work by next week. Work that out."

Slim turned and began to walk away. Jamal's mind raced as

he struggled to come up with a way to save his friend.

"I'll take on his debt," Jamal offered. "At least until he's back to normal."

Slim looked back at Jamal, narrowing his eyes. He studied the young hustler as he considered his word. Slim's own hustler instinct told him he was being worked over. He sucked his teeth and walked back over to Jamal. Suspicion covered his face.

"Why you trying to carry that nigga load? You got more than enough on your shoulders. He's a man. He stepped in my trap house carrying heat like a man. Let him carry his own, like a man."

"He's my boy and he aint right in the head right now. I can't let shit happen to him."

Again, Slim stood there looking at Jamal, searching. Then a grin spread on the man's face. He wagged a boney finger in the air and pointed it at Jamal.

"You feel guilty, don't you?"

"Guilty?" Jamal retorted as he defiantly crossed his arms over his chest. He cocked his head to the side. "Why would I feel guilty when you made me do the shit? You the one that should feel guilty, sick motherfucker."

Jamal watched at the surprise on Slim's face transformed first to anger and then indignation. The tension in the room needed only a spark. Jamal's adrenaline kicked in. His blood pumped hard and fast in his veins. The overwhelming urge to bust Slim's nose wide open tingled at Jamal's finger tips. He knew he could get in a few good licks before Bricks was on him. Jamal knew he'd probably get his ass whipped but it would be worth it.

Before Jamal could give momentary revenge a second

thought, Slim had the sharp tip of his switchblade pressed against his throat. He was so quick. Jamal only saw a blur and didn't even hear the blade snap open. A drop of blood trickled down Jamal's neck.

"I don't know who the fuck you think you talking to youngin, but we going to get this shit straight right now."

Jamal looked at Slim, wide eyed and nodded slightly to show his understanding without cutting himself more. He held the pimp's gaze. He knew to be careful with his words. The last time someone said something off the cuff they got fucked. Jamal didn't want to set a new standard and get cut.

"Why the fuck I feel like you trying to run game, little nigga?" Slim asked through gritted teeth. He looked over at Bricks. "Why the fuck would someone take another man's debt of a hundred stacks?"

Bricks shrugged, feigning ignorance to the whole situation. The question wasn't meant to be answered. Bricks knew that and so did Jamal. Slim looked back at Jamal. First he frowned and then his left brow rose as if he'd just discovered a scientific breakthrough.

"You sweet for that little nigga, aint you?"

"Romeo is my best friend," Jamal said plainly. "He's a loyal dude. We been in some shit over the years and if it weren't for him I wouldn't be alive today. He wouldn't have gone in that trap house if it wasn't for me. I owe him. That's my brother."

Slim studied Jamal's face and stepped back. He nodded as the tension in his face eased. A wave of relief went through Jamal. He took a deep breath as he watched Slim walk back to the pool table and rack the balls for a new game.

"You know what, I can respect that. You're a natural born

leader. A leader is willing to shoulder responsibility and take care of his own. That's just as important as instilling a good amount of fear and respect in those under you."

Jamal frowned. He was following Slim's every word until the last sentence. Slim looked over at Bricks and motioned for the bald headed gladiator to go into the next room. Panic surged through Jamal's body.

"Now, in a stickup crew there can only be one leader. One that makes the life deciding calls. That would be you."

Jamal shifted in his seat. He didn't know where Slim was going with his little speech but Jamal was certain he wasn't going to like it.

Within seconds of Slim's last word, Bricks came barreling through the door with a tall, slim Hispanic boy. Jamal didn't see an ounce of fear in the boy's eyes; just a familiar anger. Jamal looked over the tats on the boy's neck and forearm. They reminded Jamal of the one's some of the Spanish gang bangers wore. Bricks took the boy over to the pool table and restrained him with his large hands. Slim pointed his switchblade at Jamal.

"You can save this little Spanish bitch's life, Jamal," Slim said. He looked toward the Hispanic boy, reached up and grabbed him by the face. "Diego, tell my friend Jamal why you're here."

"Fuck you, Puta," the Spanish kid yelled.

He pulled his face away and spit at Slim's feet. Jamal shook his head. The back of Slim's hand went across Diego's face as quick as lightning. The boy staggered back into Bricks, struggling to absorb the impact.

"This might be a good time for you to learn your place."

Jamal groaned on the inside. He wasn't in the mood to

watch Slim rape anyone else. But he had little choice but to stand where he was and wait until Slim dismissed him.

Slim gave Diego the same bitch speech he had given Jamal and Romeo just a few days ago. And of course Diego respond like Romeo. Jamal knew what was coming next.

"Take your clothes off."

Diego frowned, his forehead wrinkled and his eyes narrowed sharp enough to cut through steel. He crossed his arms and looked Slim up and down, posturing. Jamal watched as Bricks pulled out his gun and pressed it firmly against the back of Diego's head. He pulled the hammer back without pause.

Diego's skin went ash white, the blood quickly draining from his face. Reluctantly, Diego stripped down to his boxers. Slim motioned for those to come off too.

Jamal was caught up in a daze. Watching Diego strip was titillating. He was very attractive. His body was slim and toned and his dick was thick and uncut. Jamal wondered how his ass looked.

"Put his Mexican ass over the table."

Bricks grabbed Diego by the back of the neck and forced the Latin thug face down on the pool table. His round, yellow ass fully exposed. Diego fought but Bricks punched him in the side over and over again with harder hits until the fight in the boy was gone.

Slim pulled out a bottle of lube and a condom wrapper from his pocket and tossed them to Jamal. Jamal frowned even though his dick jumped in his pants as he realized what was about to happen.

"Go on. The little fucker is going to be part of your stick up crew. Break his ass in." Slim tilted his head and grinned.

"Or let him die."

Jamal slowly stripped naked and walked over to where Bricks and Diego were. Once again, Jamal was given little choice but to rape someone. At this point, Slim might not kill him, the drug dealer had plans for him, but Jamal didn't want to know what would happen if he defied the man.

Jamal didn't see himself as a rapist. The idea of forcing someone to have sex disgusted him. But staring down at Diego's smooth ass made him hard as a rock. Coming to terms with what he was doing and what he was feeling was overwhelming. Thinking about it wasn't helping. So Jamal let his body and lust take over.

He smeared a healthy amount of lube on his dick and Diego's ass. He pressed against the Spanish thug's ass until the head broke pass his tight sphincter. Jamal took his time, not wanting to leave the boy with the damage Slim had left him with a few days ago.

Just as Jamal got into a rhythm he noticed Diego was doing something with his ass; tightening and loosening his hole with each stroke. Diego didn't move; he didn't throw his ass back or grind his hip. His body was stiff and looked like he was very uncomfortable.

But the sex felt good to Jamal and something told him Diego was enjoying it too. Jamal moved his left hand from Diego's hip to the boy's groin. He was brick hard.

Luckily Slim was largely ignoring the two of them, finishing up another pool game and Bricks' only interest was keeping Diego pinned down.

It didn't take long for Jamal to climax. He pulled out and nutted all over Diego's back. Bricks went to grab some towels. Immediately, Diego went to the floor and threw up.

Jamal wasn't sure if the boy was faking to hide his arousal or was really throwing up because he just got fucked. Bricks hurried back with towels and covered the mess. He took Diego to the back to get cleaned up. Jamal noted that Diego's hard-on was gone. Jamal got dressed.

"I'm not raping anymore dudes for you."

Slim kept playing pool. He spoke without looking up.

"I'd have thought that by now you would have realized that you're not raping them. You're making them submit," Slim said. He looked down at Jamal's hard, slick dick and back up. "Now, if you are getting pleasure from the encounter, those are your demons to deal with."

Jamal shook his head. Slim didn't really respond to what he had said and Jamal wasn't about to press the issue. He had something more important to resolve.

"Are you going to let me carry my boy's debt or not?"

"Yea. I just hope you can shoulder it, young blood. You got heart and fire in your belly but you going to press yourself to the limits. I just hope you don't fuck up."

"I won't." Jamal turned and headed for the door.

"Where you going?"

"Home. I thought we were done."

"Naw, since you here, you're training begins today."

Chapter 6

Jamal slouched in the backseat of Bricks' black Cadillac with his arms folded tightly over his chest. He fought the urge to relax and get comfortable but it wasn't easy. The cream colored leather seats were soft. The smell of pastries and vanilla lingered in the car cabin. But Jamal knew he couldn't let his guard down. Not around his current company.

Even though Jamal faced the window he made sure to keep an eye on Bricks, Slim's bullnecked henchman, and the Spanish thug sitting on the other end of the back seat. He didn't trust either one of them. Bricks was little more than Slim's pawn and Diego had just been the victim of Slim's twisted sense of control and domination. And Jamal was the tool used to force Diego's submission.

Diego had been eye-balling Jamal as soon as they got in the car. Whether or not the tattooed gangster was planning revenge wasn't clear. Jamal saw the look on Diego's face. He couldn't tell if Diego was angry, upset or ambivalent about the whole situation. Jamal had a hard time reading the kid. The uncertainty kept Jamal on edge. Either way he was ready if anything popped off.

Jamal blamed Slim for what he had done to Romeo a few days ago and what he had done to Diego a few hours ago. But Diego, like Romeo, may not have seen it that way. That uncertainty kept Jamal on guard around the Spanish boy. Until he was sure where Diego stood, Jamal decided that he couldn't be trusted and he wouldn't turn his back on him.

Bricks made a sharp turn down a narrow street. The abrupt motion dragged Jamal from his troubled thoughts. He shifted his gaze from Diego to the window. The street they rode down looked familiar. Jamal quickly realized that they were a few blocks from the trap house he had attempted to rob earlier that week.

"Never park in front of the house you about to rob," Bricks barked towards the backseat as he parked a few houses from the trap house. He turned around and eyed Jamal as he spoke. "Always have a driver ready to break out. Leaving the car with no one in it and running is dumb as shit and will probably get your ass killed or leave you without a ride to come back to at the very least."

Jamal nodded slightly before looking out the window, breaking his gaze from the man. Jamal didn't fear Bricks and he refused to be submissive towards the man. He may have been big but he was just like any other nigga to Jamal. A bullet to the temple would put his ass to sleep just as easy as the next.

Bricks sucked his teeth. He shook his head dismissively as

he turned off the car and stepped out. Jamal and Diego followed. The bull of a man pointed towards the house.

"You little niggas make sure you listening cause I aint going to repeat myself," Bricks warned. He didn't wait for a response. "Before you hit a spot you need to do some recall. Find out where the fences are; where the dogs at; look for places where you can run to if shit pops off and goes south."

Bricks headed for a house not too far from the original trap house. Jamal stopped in his tracks. He wondered if the same dudes he had tried to rob were in the house. Bricks looked back as he stood at the stoop of the stairs in front of the house.

"Come on little nigga. Aint shit going down. I got this."

Jamal clenched his teeth. The last thing he wanted to show Bricks or Diego was that he was scared. But he was. He wasn't strapped. He didn't even have a switch blade to protect himself. Jamal was about to roll up in a lion's den. And he knew the niggas wanted blood. He would.

Reluctantly, Jamal followed behind Bricks and Diego into the rundown house. His fists were balled and his adrenaline pumped. Despite Bricks' assurances, Jamal was ready if anyone wanted to try him. Going out like a bitch wasn't an option.

The room came to a standstill as soon as Jamal stepped between Bricks and Diego in the middle of the room. The same guys that were tricking off the two crack heads the last time Jamal saw them looked focused on checking the windows of the house. Absent was the laughter and the lingering odor of weed. Things had changed. Slim obviously had made sure of that.

"That's Big Tony and his brother, Little Mike," Bricks

said, introducing the brothers.

The hate in the men's eyes was palpable. The guns they brandished to guard the new trap house didn't make Jamal feel any safer. They're attention was now solely focused on Jamal. If given the chance, Jamal was sure they'd shoot him on the spot.

"That's Smurf. You should remember him."

Bricks pointed at the weed head that had gone for a sawed off shot gun the last time Jamal saw him. Jamal was surprised that he wasn't wearing a cast. He figured the bullet Romeo put in the man's leg had to have went right through and left only a flesh wound. His face was almost healed from the beating Jamal had put on him.

The dark skinned man looked up from the table of scales and crack rocks and narrowed his gaze on Jamal. Jamal wondered if he hadn't beaten the man's face in enough for reaching for the gun in the couch. Bricks motioned his head towards the last man in the room.

"That's Eddy."

Jamal looked at the young, smooth faced teenager. A large open cut still ran the length of the bridge of his nose. He was the unlucky soul Jamal had tried to get to talk. Eddy watched Jamal, rubbing his finger. The same finger Jamal was going to cut off with the cigar cutter.

Bricks turned and faced Jamal and Diego. He didn't speak until he was sure he had both of their undivided attention. "You never run up in a trap house without knowing how many motherfuckers you got up in the bitch at any given moment."

Jamal nodded his understanding. There was no doubt what Bricks was preaching would save his life. But he felt eyes on him. Eyes that would love to see him dead on the ground from a bullet straight to the chest.

Bricks walked the boys through the house, showing where folks could hide their stash and where lookouts could be posted. Bricks was thorough. And as promised, he only said what he had to say once. And he didn't answer questions. Either you got it or you didn't.

Bricks even had Jamal and Diego run through some scenarios on sticking up a trap house. The role playing had Jamal on edge because the four guys running the trap house were helping and all he needed was for one of the cats to accidently shoot him. Three hours went by before Jamal and Diego had completed the tasks the way Bricks wanted. He was intent on getting them ready.

"Alright," Bricks looked outside the window. "It's getting dark. We can hit up the range tomorrow. Come on, got to get you two home."

Diego shook his head. "Naw, I'll walk."

Jamal felt a tap at his side. It was Diego. Jamal shot a sidelong look at the boy. Still, Diego was hard to read. Diego returned the gaze and squinted his eyes. Jamal rolled his eyes and looked up at Bricks.

"Yea, I'm good. I don't want my moms or people in the neighborhood seeing me in the car with a drug dealer."

Bricks looked from Diego to Jamal and back. The beast of a man shook his head as he looked at Jamal and Diego before turning to leave. Jamal was sure he saw a small grin on Bricks face. It was the first time the man's expression had changed all day.

"Fine," Bricks called over his shoulder. "Just be back here by noon tomorrow. Best not be late. Slim will have ya'll asses, literally."

Jamal and Diego stood at the bottom of the stairs in front of the trap house and watched as Bricks pulled off and sped down the street. Jamal shot a quick glance at Diego before heading home.

"Hey son," Diego called. "Where you going?"

"Home."

"Naw, come this way."

Jamal searched the boy's eyes, staring at him for a moment. He wondered if Diego was trying to set him up, to get revenge for what happened at the pool hall. But something pulled at Jamal. He wanted to go with Diego even though he didn't trust the cute Latin boy.

"Nigga, come on," Diego pleaded. "It's getting dark and I don't want no shit with the cats that are from here. *Vámonos*"

Reluctantly, Jamal turned and walked next to Diego. He didn't know where they were going but something inside Jamal said it would be okay. At least he hoped it would be. Jamal could feel Diego looking at him again as they walked in silence. It was killing Jamal. So he struck up a conversation.

"How did you get caught up with Slim?"

Diego exhaled loudly and clasped his hands. A tight grin creased his face. "I didn't. My dad did. He has a gambling problem and racked up a huge debt with dude."

"Hell, what that shit gotta do with you?"

"Slim and Bricks came to my house this morning saying my pops had skipped out on a payment. They were about to break his legs right there in front of my *abuela* and my little brothers and sisters."

"So you stopped them?"

"I said I'd pay them back. Slim asked for the cash and I said I'd work to pay it off. At first he wasn't feeling it then it looked like an idea went off in his head. Guess he thought of you." Diego looked at Jamal with that same look. The boy's grin pushed through Jamal's uncertainty. "How did you get caught up with him? And why did Bricks say you should know dude at that trap house?"

"Me and my boy Romeo tried to rob them niggas. Bricks caught us. Slim said we had a debt to pay. So now we supposed to be his stickup boys."

"Damn," Diego said with a hint of understand. Then he frowned. "Where yo boy Romeo at?"

"He going through some shit right now."

"What you mean?"

Jamal wasn't sure how to answer the question. He knew that the truth would eventually come out if Diego was going to be working for Slim. The simple truth seemed the easiest route.

"Slim made me do to Romeo what he made me do to you."

"You fucked your boy?" Diego asked. Jamal heard the judgment in the boy's voice. "Damn, that's fucked up."

Jamal stopped. His face contorted in anger. "That nigga made me do it. Said he'd kill me if I didn't. Then he fucked me."

Diego only nodded. Jamal noticed the change in his eyes. It wasn't forgiveness or empathy but understanding. They kept walking. After the awkward tension had passed, Jamal started talking again.

"So you in some Mexican gang or something?"

Diego smiled. Jamal's heart felt like it skipped a beat when he saw how bright his face got and how his deep dimples sunk into his cheeks. Diego was a pretty Spanish nigga. And Jamal was definitely feeling him, at least on a physical level.

"Nah, I'm from El Salvador."

Jamal pointed at Romeo's arms. "Wassup with the tats then?"

"My brother had me get them before he got locked up for murder a few months back. I'm the oldest one now. Got to look out for *mi familia*."

Jamal nodded. He asked the question that had been on his mind since they started walking. "So, where we going?"

"My place."

"How far is it?"

"About a mile, it aint far."

Jamal walked with Diego up to a rundown looking apartment building. There were only four buildings and it couldn't be called a complex as all the buildings were adjacent to the street and lacked any sign or fence or courtyard.

Diego trotted up the shaky metal stairwell to an apartment and walked in. Jamal followed behind. Jamal counted four kids, all under six, running around shouting and playing. Diego said something in Spanish and the noise instantly stopped. The three boys went to the bathroom. Jamal heard the shower going.

An older woman, who Jamal assumed was Diego's grandmother, came out from the back with a baby in her hand. She embraced and kissed Diego over and over again. She obviously had been concerned about him.

Diego said something in Spanish, pointing to Jamal. The grandmother's face lit up as she embraced and kissed Jamal. Jamal shot a sidelong glance at Diego.

"What did you tell her?"

"That you were going to help me get my pop's debt squared off."

Jamal only nodded as the old woman spoke to him in Spanish. He watched as Diego walked into the living room and put some money in a purse next to the couch. It was probably the money Slim had given him; just like the money he had given Jamal and Romeo after he raped them.

It wasn't long before the three boys were coming out the bathroom wrapped in towels. Diego's grandmother barked something at the boys and they headed for a pile of folded clothes on the couch and got dressed. The oldest one took out an air mattress from the closet and started pumping it up as the others waited anxiously to jump on it.

The grandmother said something to Diego and then led the little girl to the bathroom. Diego led Jamal to one of the bedrooms.

"Welcome to *mi casa*."

"You got a lot to take care of," Jamal said, motioning back to the living room.

"Yea, no one else is going to look out for my *abuela* and my little brothers and sisters. My pops is an ass. He steals from my *abuela* knowing she can't always feed the kids. His kids."

Jamal nodded as he looked around the room. The walls were barren. One queen sized bed was squeezed into the corner, leaving little room for any other furniture besides the floor lamp and a side dresser. But there were lots of clothes in the closet.

Diego motioned towards the bed. "Go ahead and sit down."

"I don't mind hanging but it is getting late. My moms don't like me being out and she not knowing where I am."

"How old are you?"

Jamal frowned. "Nineteen."

"Still have to check in with moms?"

"Naw, but I aint trying to hear no shit for nothing, feel me?"

Diego nodded his understanding. The two of them stood there, awkwardly, staring at one another. Jamal shifted his weight uncomfortably as his new Spanish friend looked him up and down. Jamal wasn't sure if he should leave or wait for something to happen. He wasn't even sure what he was waiting for. His body was tense with unbridled anticipation.

Then it happened. Diego moved towards Jamal, slowly stepping closer and closer until their faces were only inches away. Jamal could feel the heat of Diego's breath on his lips.

"I feel you," Diego said, licking his full, red lips. He placed his hand on Jamal's waist and tilted his head to the side. "But do you feel me?"

Jamal felt like he was about to jump out of his skin. His heart raced. His chest heaved forward as his breath quickened. Diego's touch sent jolts through Jamal's young body. Jamal searched for the words but could only nod that he understood. He looked like a deer caught in head lights and there was nowhere to run.

"Relax. I got you," Diego whispered. He ran the tips of his fingers over Jamal's taut biceps. "You're in good hands. Trust me."

The Latin thug erased the space between them and pressed his soft, moist lips against Jamal's. A soft, guttural moan of pleasure vibrated from deep within Jamal's body.

Jamal felt like his body went limp. Diego wrapped his arms around Jamal to steady him. Diego pulled back and looked at Jamal with a small smile on his soft face.

"Damn, you taste good."

Diego pressed forward and buried his face in Jamal's neck, kissing and sucking his way down to Jamal's collar bone. Jamal flinched. He giggled at the feeling of Diego's adventurous tongue gliding over his collar bone. Diego watched the smile on Jamal's face and bit down on his bottom lip. Hurriedly, he reached down and pulled off Jamal's shirt and then his own.

Jamal looked down at Diego's chiseled abs and small, but well developed chest. He ran his fingers over the lion tattoo running up and down Diego's side. He looked up at Diego. Jamal recognized the lust in the young Latin's eyes. But there was more. He was sure Diego saw the same in his eyes. The two of them smiled nervously and then looked away quickly.

The emotions bombarding Jamal would have had him on the ground if Diego hadn't steadied him. He'd fucked a man before. Two thanks to Slim. But he'd never been *with* a man. Jamal had never been intimate. He'd never been taken. Until now.

Jamal looked at Diego longingly as the Spanish boy bit his bottom lip and eased down to his knees. Diego pulled Jamal's pants and underwear down to his ankles. Jamal's manhood sprang to attention. Diego took the swollen member in his hand and went to work.

Jamal watched in amazement as the length of his dick disappeared in Diego's hot, wet mouth over and over again. Jamal tried to hold back but his orgasm came rushing like a flood. His balls tightened and ropes of cum exploded down

Diego's throat. Diego didn't flinch. He swallowed every drop, licking his lips when he was finished.

Spent, Jamal fell back onto the bed. Diego pressed forward and pushed Jamal's legs in the air. The surprise and panic Jamal felt were quickly replaced by a wave of pleasure. The warm wetness of Diego's tongue exploring and pressing against Jamal's tight, brown hole made Jamal twist and turn in ecstasy. It was the most tender and intimate feeling he'd ever felt.

Diego's tongue darted into Jamal's insides quicker and quicker. Jamal's moans got loud. Too loud. Diego looked up with a devilish grin and put his finger over his lips, nodding towards the door. Jamal understood. Before he could think, Diego was flipping him over on his stomach.

Diego climbed on top of Jamal, pressing his hot, tight body against Jamal's back. The feeling of Diego's flesh pressed against his was intoxicating. Diego slowly but firmly grinded against Jamal's round ass. Instinctively, Jamal arched his back and met each stroke of Diego's hips. Jamal's hole flinched each time Diego's long, uncut meat brushed against his virgin rosebud.

Jamal felt the head of Diego's latex sheathed dick press against his ass. Instead of tensing up he just let go and relaxed. Pain shot through his body as the tip of Diego's dick broke through his tight ring.

It didn't take much for the pain to turn to pleasure and for Diego to bottom out in Jamal's ass. Diego leaned down until the length of his body was pressed against Jamal's. Diego whispered in Jamal's ear.

"Damn, I feel you," he said, giggling. "Do you feel me, nigga?"

Jamal could only moan his approval as Diego took him to a place of pleasure he had never known.

Chapter 7

Diego smiled down at Jamal's motionless body as he straddled the stickup boy's hips. The soft snoring that vibrated from Jamal's mouth made Diego grin. Diego leaned down, dragging the tips of his fingers over Jamal's bare abs up to his bulbous chest. He moved to the side of Jamal's face and gently nibbled on Jamal's ear.

Jamal gently turned away and giggled. He opened his eyes sleepily and looked up at Diego. Jamal couldn't help but smile at the cute Latin thug. He gripped Diego by the waist and pressed his morning wood up against Diego's ass. The thought of driving his swollen shaft in the boy's ass made Jamal's heart race.

"Morning, papi," Diego said shaking his head. He placed his hand on Jamal's chest and raised his right brow. "We have to get up. There's a lot of shit we need to get done."

"Hmm, I know," Jamal groaned, pouting. "But do we have time for a little fun? All I need is five minutes. Trust me."

Diego narrowed his gaze and exhaled loudly as if he were annoyed. Jamal looked up at him. His eyes shifted down to his groin and back up to Diego. Jamal moved his hands down and squeezed Diego's ass. Diego bit his bottom lip and shook his head. He was fighting his sexual desires but the look on his face showed it was a losing battle.

Diego brought his hand to his mouth and spit in his palm. He reached back and stroked Jamal's exposed hardness. Jamal flinched at the firm tenderness of Diego's grip. His hand was like velvet caressing every inch of Jamal's engorged manhood.

Jamal could feel his orgasm build at the base of his meat. But this wasn't how he wanted to cum. He reached up and grabbed Diego by the wrist.

"No, not like this. I want to feel you."

Diego nodded. He held Jamal's stiff pole in his hand, slipped a condom on and lined the tip up with his hole. Diego rocked back and forth, his head tossing from side to side, until the broad head of Jamal's dick pressed pass the tight entrance. A hearty moan flowed over Diego's lips as the length of Jamal's dick filled his insides, rubbing against his walls with every pulsating inch.

A knock at the door made Diego freeze mid-ride.

"Diego," the voice of a young girl called through the door. "Wake up, Diego."

Diego jumped up like the apartment was on fire. He tossed a pillow and blanket on the floor. He snatched his underwear and shorts from the bottom of the bed and put them on. Finally, he turned to Jamal and motioned for him to put on his clothes and move to the floor where the blanket and pillow were. Confused and somewhat angry, Jamal obliged.

Diego went to the door, his dick still hard, and opened it. A gorgeous Hispanic girl with long brown hair stood at the entrance in form fitting jeans and a red halter top. Diego pressed against her body and started kissing her. The two were going at it like a pair of sex starved sex addicts. The girl groped Diego's hardness without any shame or pretense.

Jamal frowned. First he was angry and then jealous. Why he felt how he felt made him even angrier. The thought of being jealous over some chick Diego was kissing and dry humping made Jamal more than uncomfortable. How he felt confused the Hell out of him.

Sure, they'd shared a night. Jamal and Diego had sex over and over again until neither of them could move. But the best part for Jamal was waking up in the middle of the night with Diego holding him from behind. Jamal had slept like a baby until the sun came up and birthed a new day.

Jamal wasn't sure what last night meant or if it meant anything at all. He couldn't escape the fact that he'd just met the boy less than twenty-four hours ago and not under the best of circumstances. Now he was looking at Diego touching and kissing all over some female while he sat there on the floor with a hard dick covered in spit and ass juices.

Five minutes went by. Jamal couldn't take anymore. He cleared his throat loudly. Diego pulled away from the tongue wrestling and looked over at Jamal.

"Isabella, this is my boy, Jamal."

"Nice to meet you Jamal," she said, smiling. Her hand was still palming Diego's dick.

"Likewise," Jamal said dryly.

"Uh, Jamal is going to help me pay off Poppo's debt."

Isabella's face twisted. She rolled her eyes and pressed her finger against the middle of Diego's chest. Isabella was saying something in Spanish. Jamal couldn't make out what she said but he did recognize a couple of the curse words. Isabella pushed Diego into the door and she stormed out the room. Diego turned to Jamal.

"Go ahead and get dressed. I'm going to deal with her and we'll be out."

Jamal pulled his shirt over his head and slipped on his pants and shoes. He was out the door in under a minute. He wasn't going to wait. Jamal didn't like drama, especially other people's drama. And he had to get some things done before he met up with Bricks back at the trap house. Diego was fun but he wasn't worth the trouble.

The walk to his house took about an hour. Jamal's mom was still asleep. The last thing he wanted was to wake her up and listen to her fuss about where he'd been all night. Quietly, Jamal jumped in the shower, washed up, got dressed and was back out the door. He made sure to pocket a stack before he stepped out.

Jamal tried to focus on the things he wanted to get done but all he could think about was Diego. Jamal didn't even try to deny that he was attracted to the boy. His body was on point, he had a cute face with a nice smile and the sex was crazy. Thinking about the things they did the night before had Jamal on brick all over again.

But for Jamal, the best part about the night was laying in Diego's arms. It didn't make him feel weak or like he was someone's bitch. It made him feel wanted, desired. Jamal had never felt that way. Not with another man or with anyone for that matter. And it felt good as shit.

Jamal rounded the corner and headed down the street of Romeo's house. He hadn't planned on visiting but he wanted to check on his best friend. He just hoped that his boy was a little less crazy than the day before.

Romeo's mother's old beat up car was still in the apartment parking lot. Jamal checked his watch. Usually, she was at work by now. Concern swept over Jamal's body. The only times he could remember Romeo's mother not going to work was when Romeo was really sick and needed to go to the hospital. Jamal hoped Romeo hadn't gotten worse.

Jamal trotted up the stone stairs and knocked on the door. Romeo's mother opened the door. Her disheveled hair, blood shot eyes and heavy lines under her eyes made Jamal instinctively step back.

"Mrs. Williams, are you alright?"

"Jamal, please tell me you've seen Romeo."

Jamal shook his head. Mrs. Williams looked as if she were about to cry as she ran her fingers through her unruly hair. She looked a mess.

"The last time I saw him was yesterday, when you were here. I was just stopping by to check on him."

"Romeo left the house before I went back to work yesterday. I figured he was feeling better and wanted some air. I went to work and came back to the house to check on him."

"And he was still gone?"

"Yea. I went back to work. I called your mom and she said she hadn't seen you all day. I figured he was out with you and would be back by now."

"I haven't seen him, Mrs. Williams. Did you call the police?"

"They said it was too soon to issue a missing person's report. And that he was an adult and has every right to up and leave if he wanted."

"I can check around," Jamal said, not knowing what else to say.

Pain covered her face. "Thank you baby, just tell him to call me or something. I just hope nothing happened to him. It's not like him to not come home."

Jamal nodded and stepped away from the door. He could hear Mrs. Williams crying through the door as he walked away. Checking out their normal spots was the only thing Jamal could think of doing. But none of them were places where Romeo could squat at for a whole night. And Romeo wasn't all that sociable with anyone besides Jamal. Jamal was his only friend and he didn't have any females he could just stay the night with.

Jamal stopped by all the stores, the arcade and the skating rink and asked about Romeo. Everyone said the same thing: they hadn't seen him. Jamal even went by the abandoned warehouses they used to tag when they were in middle school. Nothing.

It was almost noon and Jamal wasn't getting anywhere with his search. He figured he'd pick up where he left off after he was done with Bricks. He hopped on the bus and headed for the trap house, where Bricks had told him and Diego to meet him.

Jamal only had to make two transfers to get to the house. Bricks car wasn't there yet. Jamal had beat him to the house. He sat on the curb and waited. The last thing he was going to do was wait in the house with the guys he'd tried to stick up just a week ago. That beef wasn't going anywhere anytime soon. The brothers would love nothing more than to put a few bullets in Jamal's scull.

Sitting there, Jamal couldn't help but worry more and more about Romeo. There were only so many places in the city he could go. And the boy wasn't all that cut out for the streets. Jamal just hoped he didn't run across anyone that tried to punk him. No telling what Romeo would do the way he'd been acting lately.

"Hey nigga!"

Jamal turned to the sound of the voice. It was Diego coming down the street. Jamal nodded, his gaze focused ahead of him.

"Sup man."

"Shit, nothing. Wondering why you couldn't wait for me."

"Had shit to do," Jamal said plainly.

Diego frowned. "Yea, I know. And I said I would go with you."

Jamal looked up at Diego. "You seemed busy."

A grin spread on Diego's face. "You not jealous are you?"

"Jealous of what?" Jamal retorted. He shifted his feet. The annoyance he felt was written all over his body language. "Aint shit to be jealous about. Feel me?"

"Alright. I aint gonna press it."

Diego sat down next to Jamal and didn't say a word. It frustrated the hell out of Jamal. He wanted Diego to press the issue. Jamal wanted to know what Diego thought about him. If he even saw what they had done as anything besides a fuck. But Jamal wasn't going to press the issue either. At the end of the day, Diego had a girl. And even though Jamal liked

Diego, he wasn't even entirely sure what that meant.

Diego nudged Jamal in the side. Jamal was annoyed. But he liked being touched by the boy.

"Did you put down money for that car?" Diego asked.

"Didn't have a chance to stop by the place. Some shit came up."

"What—"

Bricks pulled up just as Diego was about to start questioning Jamal about what he'd been doing all day. For the first time, Jamal was relieved to see Bricks. He waved Jamal and Diego over to the car as he walked back to the open trunk.

Bricks looked at Jamal. "What's a gun?"

Jamal frowned at the question. He wondered if it was a trick question but answered anyway. Jamal shrugged his shoulders and gave the best answer he could think of.

"A weapon," Jamal offered. "Something used to kill people?"

Bricks shifted his gaze towards Diego. Diego shrugged his shoulders and looked down at the ground. He didn't have an answer to offer.

"A gun is a tool. It's a hunk of metal that can be replaced."

Bricks opened the silver brief case in the trunk. Two .9mm guns lay inside.

"These guns are stolen. Your name is not on them. If you ever fire the gun, you get rid of it. Even if the bullet ends up in a wall and not someone's chest. You got me?" Both the young scribes nodded. "Alright, let's go. The two of you need some time at the gun range."

They all hopped in the car. Jamal could feel Diego's eyes on him the whole ride. He ignored him. Jamal had more important things to worry about, like where his best friend was. Jamal looked out the window and noticed that they weren't heading to any gun range he knew of. He leaned forward towards the front seat.

"Thought we was going to the gun range, Bricks?"

"We are. Slim just texted me and said swing by the pool hall first."

Jamal nodded and sat back. He hated going to the pool hall. He knew there was going to be some shit with Slim. There always was.

The sound of sex met Jamal's ears before he even made it to the door of the pool hall. The moaning and screaming sounded like Tasha, one of Slim's girls.

The first thing they saw when they went into the pool hall was Tasha bent over one of the pool table and Slim hitting her from the back. He looked up at the three of them as they walked to the bar. Slim pulled out and smacked Tasha on the ass.

"Go bring the boys."

Slim grabbed the towel draped over one the chairs and started patting the sweat from his body. His long, hard dick swayed in the air as he walked over towards Brick, Jamal and Diego.

"Got here sooner than I thought, Bricks."

Bricks grinned approvingly and shook his head. "Naw, you just long winded, partner."

Slim chuckled as he looked over at Jamal and Diego. Jamal averted his eyes. He knew he'd get hard looking at Slim. Even though he hated the man with all his heart his body did its own thing and Slim wasn't all that bad on the eyes.

"Sorry for cutting into your training time but I just had to introduce you to the rest of the team."

Jamal and Diego frowned as the side door opened. Smurf, the weed head Romeo shot in the leg came in the room.

"You guys already know Smurf, he's your new driver." Slim looked towards Bricks. "Make sure you get him ready."

Jamal shook his head. There was no way he could trust this dude to be his driver. Jamal figured Smurf would leave him to get killed for payback. The door opened again.

It was Romeo.

"And you already know Romeo. He and I had a nice little chat," Slim said looking at Jamal. "So you won't need to cover his debt."

Jamal's mind raced. He wondered if Romeo had been there at the pool hall all day and night. Jamal searched Romeo's face. He looked okay, but different. Scary different.

"Good, now that everyone knows everyone, ya'll need to get ready," Slim said. "You all heading up to DC tonight for your first job. Good luck."

Chapter 8

Jamal couldn't take his eyes off Romeo. Just the other day the boy was an emotional wreck bordering on bat shit crazy. Now, Romeo was standing next to Bricks with a 9mm Beretta in his hands getting instructions on how to properly hold, aim and shoot a gun. He was attentive and wholly focused on what Bricks was saying. He seemed normal again but different. Jamal couldn't explain it. His boy had definitely gone through a transformation.

The look in Romeo's eyes at the pool hall had sent cold chills through Jamal's body. It was the same look he had now shooting at the targets they'd set up. He looked distant. Like a blank slate. As if he was there but not *really* there. It scared Jamal; almost as much as him acting like he'd lost his mind just a few days ago.

Jamal wondered what had triggered the sudden change in

Romeo. He suspected Slim had some part in the whole thing. Jamal just couldn't imagine Romeo seeking out Slim in the condition he was in the time last he saw his childhood friend. No, Slim came after Romeo. Jamal was sure about that. What Slim did to bring Romeo from the brink was what worried Jamal.

Romeo wasn't the same person and it wasn't just the look in his eyes. The way he stood and walked was different. The way he spoke and interacted with people seemed calculated and cold. Everything about Romeo seemed cold. Romeo had changed and Jamal knew it wasn't for the better.

Despite it all, Jamal resolved to speak with his childhood friend before the night was over. He was anxious to resolve what had happened between them. There was a lot to discuss. If nothing else, Jamal was going to make sure Romeo gave his mother a call if he hadn't already.

Jamal raised his gun to eye level with his right hand and held the butt of the Berretta with his left, just like Bricks showed him. He cleared his clip, taking out all the cans and bottles lined up on the haystacks about thirty yards away. He even took out some of the cans Diego had missed.

"Fucking show off," Diego mumbled. He pointed towards the haystack. "I was going to hit those."

"Shit, not the way you was shooting," Jamal teased. "We be here all night waiting for your ass to knock those cans over. You need to work on that shit."

Diego sucked his teeth and walked over to Jamal as he reloaded his gun. Jamal watched Diego as he cocked his gun and swayed towards him. The way he walked made Jamal's wood stiffen in his pants. There was something sexy and erotic about Diego. Jamal was having an increasingly difficult time controlling how his body responded around the Latin heartthrob.

Diego stood next to Jamal and leaned against him, nudging his side playfully. Initially, Jamal smiled at the flirtation but quickly shifted his weight away from Diego. His eyes darted over to Romeo. Diego frowned as he followed Jamal's gaze.

"Sorry *papi*, didn't mean to be so obvious in front of your boyfriend."

Jamal gave Diego a sidelong glance and sucked his teeth. "He aint my boyfriend. He's my boy. Known his ass since grade school. That little nigga like my little brother."

"Hmm. If you say so. The way you looking at him looks like you want to be more than his brother. Unless you into that incest shit."

"Naw. It aint even like that," Jamal said. He knew it was a lie as soon as the words left his lips. "I'm just worried about him. Lots has happened these past few days. Not sure how he's dealing with the shit."

Diego scrunched his face. He looked from Jamal to Romeo and back and began to nod. "Yea, your boy does seem off, though." Diego cocked his gun. "I aint trying to be rude or nothing but your boy slow or something?"

"No. He's not slow," Jamal said. He exhaled loudly. "He just aint take Slim's sick ass initiation all that well."

"That nigga Slim is one fucked up dude," Diego said. "He must get off on that shit. Watching young cats fuck that aint bout that shit."

Jamal shifted his weight from one foot to the other and nodded. It was the only response he could offer. The shame and guilt of what he was forced to do was still raw in his mind. Diego shook his head as if he understood the demons Jamal was wrestling with.

Jamal turned and looked at Diego. He was right about Slim but Jamal had a hard time believing Diego wasn't at all interested in messing with dudes. The way he moaned the night before as he and Jamal took turns fucking each other said otherwise.

"Maybe, I'm not sure. After I did Romeo, Slim fucked me. And he wasn't nice with it. He didn't even nutt. Just kept on going like he was making a point or something. It's about power with his ass."

"Yea? So that's why he got you fucking everyone in this stick up crew bullshit?"

"Not everyone," Jamal said as he looked over Diego's shoulder and motioned towards Smurf. "Not everyone."

The weed head walked towards them with a smug grin on his face. For the first time Jamal took a good long look at the boy. He was actually attractive in a trap boy sort of way. He was tall and brown-skinned with an arm full of tattoos. He looked like a low level drug dealer to Jamal, whatever that meant. The gold grill in his mouth shone brightly before he spoke.

"What you two motherfuckers over here scheming?" Smurf asked with a half serious tone.

Diego turned around reeling on his heels. "By the time you find out, it'll be too late, *vato*."

Smurf stopped mid step. He licked his lips and tilted his head to the side as he looked Diego up and down. Smurf planted his feet squarely and cracked his knuckles. He raised his hands and motioned for Diego to step to him.

Diego set his gun on the rusty barrel in front of him and

balled his fists. Things were escalating so fast that it took Jamal a moment to realize that the two of them were about to throw down right there in front of him. He was mainly surprised at how Diego was acting. Jamal was sure Diego liked him but he never expected the boy to fight his battles or create them with guys Jamal wasn't fond of. Jamal placed a hand on Diego's shoulder and looked at Smurf.

"What you want Smurf? Really aint got time for your shit."

"Damn, it's like that? Can't even be social and shit with the niggas I'm supposed to be trusting my life with?" Smurf moved closer and pointed at Jamal as he looked him up and down. "The same niggas that's going to be depending on me to get they ass to safety?"

"You threatening me, nigga?" Jamal asked.

He narrowed his gaze and tilted his head. The calm in Jamal's voice gave Smurf pause. Aside from the fact that he was taller than Jamal and about the same build, Jamal's bravado was hard to case. Smurf couldn't tell if the boy was flexing or had the hands to back up his posturing. Smurf put on a tight lipped smile and threw his hands, palms open, in the air.

"Threat? Naw, I don't do threats. The last thing I want to do is threatened the head man. Feel me? You got it, money."

Smurf grinned. He turned to Diego and sucked his teeth before he turned around and walked over to where Bricks and Romeo were standing. Jamal watched him say something to Bricks. The two of them looked over at Jamal and Diego. Diego got fidgety. He shook his head and ran his fingers through his jet black hair.

"What the fuck is that about?" Diego asked. "He snitching or some shit?"

"Relax, dude. We aint in high school no more. Aint no more running to the teacher to tell shit. Besides, aint shit for him to say except that he just got punked. Naw, he aint going to say a damn thing. He going to wait til he has an opening and come for me. Shit aint going to be pretty either."

Bricks came towering over with Romeo and Smurf flanking him on both sides. Jamal looked up at him, his face soft and unassuming. He looked like an angel. Bricks frowned at the feigned innocence.

"Alright, I'm going to take Smurf over there to the parking lot." Bricks pointed towards the abandoned factory about a quarter mile away. "There's enough ammo for you all to keep on practicing." He looked over at Diego. "And you need it."

"Aww, come on now Bricks, I aint that bad." Diego tapped on the inside of his forearm. "All this El Salvadorian blood running through my veins. I know I got some Conquistador ancestry up in here."

"I hope so, cause you can't shoot for shit." Bricks motioned towards Jamal. "Take care of your crew. Make sure you guys reset the targets together. We don't need any accidents."

Jamal nodded. He turned and led the way across the field to large hay blocks. The hay stacks were only a few dozen yards away but it felt like a mile. No one spoke. Jamal stole glances at Romeo as they all set the cans and bottles back atop the hay stacks. Romeo seemed so distant and oblivious to the world around him. Or at least oblivious to Jamal.

As the trio headed back Jamal slowed down and tugged at Romeo's arm. The two of them stopped. Diego realized his steps were the only ones he heard and looked back. Jamal motioned for him to keep walking. Diego shook his head and reluctantly kept walking.

"Where have you been all day?" Jamal asked.

"Nowhere," Romeo answered plainly. "Why?"

"Your moms is going crazy worrying about you."

"I'll call her." Romeo shifted his weight. "Anything else?"

Jamal searched his friends face for some sign of emotion. He felt like he was looking at a stranger. Jamal took in a deep breath and tried to summon enough courage to say what needed to be said.

"Look, the last time I saw you, you were screaming and climbing up the wall. Now you're out here shooting guns like nothing happened."

"Well, I guess it's safe to assume that I'm okay."

Romeo turned to walk away. Jamal grabbed him by his arm. Romeo looked down at Jamal's hand and slowly pulled his arm away. He looked up at Jamal, death lingering in his eyes.

"Don't touch me like that again...ever."

Jamal watched as Romeo walked away. He had so many questions for Romeo. Jamal wondered if Romeo blamed him for what happened or if Romeo had a festering hatred for Slim like he did. He wanted to know if they were okay; if they were still friends. And Jamal longed to know if, despite the circumstances, there was anything Romeo felt for him.

Guilt surged through Jamal's body at the thought. He wondered how he could be so selfish. How he could wonder if his raping Romeo could have awakened some deep, hidden attraction. But that's what had happened to him. He wasn't on the receiving end but something in him came to life after the incident. The whole thing made him feel conflicted. But one thing was clear; he wanted Romeo to be more than a friend.

Jamal rejoined Romeo and Diego at the rusted barrels. The trio quietly let off round after round until Diego's shooting had slightly improved. The sun was setting by the time Bricks and Smurf got back.

"Alright gentlemen," Bricks called from the car. "Time for us to hit the road."

"I need to stop by the house to get some clothes," Diego said.

Jamal shook his head. "Naw, we'll get some on the way up to DC."

No one argued. The three of them made it to the backseat of the car without incident. Jamal could see the grin on Bricks face in the rearview mirror. Romeo turned his back to Jamal and the rest of the guys in the car and looked out the window. They rode in silence until they hit I-285.

"What about the shit we need for the stickup?" Diego asked.

"We'll get everything we need on the way up; dark clothes, gloves, ski masks, all that," Jamal explained. "Besides, we don't want to be seen buying all that shit here and have someone we know clock us."

"So where we staying when we get up there?" Smurf asked.

Jamal looked towards Bricks. "I'm guessing we going to find a motel that takes cash, nothing fancy."

Smurf looked back at Jamal from the front seat. "Shit, why can't we at least stay somewhere decent, like a Holiday Inn or something? Trying to sleep and relax in an alright spot."

"This aint a holiday, nigga," Jamal barked. "Besides, we deal in cash and avoid places with cameras. No one knows we leaving Atlanta and no one sees us in DC or Bmore. Got me?"

Smurf smacked his teeth and sulked back in his seat. Bricks turned up the music signaling the end of the need for conversation and further explanation.

Jamal couldn't help but think the ride up to DC was the calm before the storm. Smurf was a liability that would put him and the crew in danger. He had to take care of him first. Jamal knew Diego had his back if even to save his father. He was just a horrible shot and therefore unreliable if shit turned into a shoot out. And then there was Romeo.

Before the botched stick up of Slim's trap house Jamal had never seen Romeo fire a gun. And today, he shot just as well as Jamal did. But Jamal felt like something was off about Romeo and he couldn't shake that feeling. If nothing else, Romeo was unpredictable and definitely dangerous.

At the end of the day Jamal knew that no one was going to make sure he came out on top still breathing but himself. It was his crew but he wasn't fool enough to think any of them would go the extra mile to save him or each other. They were all there because they had to be there not because they wanted to and Jamal would not forget that.

Jamal leaned against the window of his door as he played the what-if game in his mind. Thoughts of saving Romeo and Diego flooded his mind if things went wrong. Ideas of taking out Smurf and making it look like an accident gripped and teased his mind. Despite his active imagination, it wasn't long before he dozed off.

The weight of Diego on his shoulder gently pulled Jamal from his sleep. Jamal looked down at Diego peacefully asleep leaning on him. He felt pressure on his thigh. Jamal looked down. It was Diego's hand.

Jamal looked over at Romeo to see if he was sleep. He wasn't. Romeo's eyes caught Jamal's. They shifted down to where Diego's hand was and back to Jamal's eyes.

For a moment, Jamal thought he saw a hint of anger or jealousy in his friend's eyes. But then they reverted to that cold, blank stare again before he turned and looked out his window again.

Jamal shook his head and let out a deep sigh. He pressed his head against the seat and closed his eyes. He needed his rest to get ready for tomorrow. He'd deal with the rift between him and Romeo later.

Chapter 9

Jamal snapped awake as Bricks brought the car to a jerking stop. It was still dark. Jamal had no idea how long he had been sleep or how far Bricks had driven. He brought his hands to his face and rubbed the sleep from his eyes and looked out the car window. They were parked in the far corner of a Walmart parking lot. Jamal tried to stretch out but something heavy held his legs down. He looked down.

Diego was sprawled out over Jamal's lap. He was knocked out, sleep. Jamal could hear Diego's soft snores. Gently, he reached down and ran his fingers through Diego's long black hair. A wave of calm flowed through Jamal's body. For a moment he was envious. He wished he could have someone make him feel safe enough to be as peaceful and relaxed as Diego was at that moment.

Jamal shook the alluring fantasy from his mind and looked

around the car. Romeo was curled up in a fetal position nestled against the back passenger door. Smurf was snoring erratically with his mouth wide open and drool dripping down to his chin. Bricks was in the front going through a folder looking for something. Jamal was the only one that was yanked from his sleep.

It didn't surprise Jamal that he woke up when the car came to a stop. He always used to wake up on road trips with his parents. His mother would be knocked out and his dad would pull into a rest stop or a fast food place to grab some food and Jamal would spring right up.

His father never made him go back to sleep. He always told Jamal that it was a good that he woke up. It showed that his body was programmed to notice the small things and that a man that noticed the small things was a man that lived another day. That sage advice was the last thing Jamal remembered his father telling him for the umpteenth time right before he saw his father gunned down so many years ago.

Jamal tilted his head back and rubbed his forehead. Thinking about his father always made him feel helpless. He was only eleven when it happened. At the time he didn't know that the road trips were actually drug runs. A deal went bad and his father got caught in the crossfire in what was supposed to be a simple drop-off. Luckily, his father had left Jamal and his mother a nice safety net. Since Jamal's father died his mother never looked at another man and pounded it in Jamal's head that he needed to make an honest living. She'd kill him if she knew what he was doing, if only to beat the streets from taking his life.

The sound of someone smacking their teeth gripped Jamal

and pulled him from his thoughts. His eyes locked on Smurfs as soon as he sat up. Smurf's eyes shifted down to Diego and back up to Jamal. Smurf twisted his face. Jamal recognized the look. It was disgust. Jamal was about to say something but he felt Diego move under him. He was waking up.

"Yo, we there yet?" Diego asked as he sat up, stretching and yawning.

Bricks looked in the rearview mirror and made eye contact with Diego. He shook his head.

"Not yet youngin. We're a little more than thirty minutes out from DC. We need to stop and get all the shit you all are going to need to take care of this business."

Jamal frowned. "Why are we just now getting what we need?" He didn't attempt to mask how annoyed he was that they had gotten so far and were just now stopping. "We should have stopped somewhere before we hit Richmond. That's what we discussed. What the fuck?"

"When I drive, I decide when we stop. Got me?" Bricks didn't even look back or in the rearview mirror when he spoke. "Besides, I didn't want to wake you little fuckers. Might be the last time you all get a good night's sleep."

Jamal clenched his teeth and looked the bald henchman up and down. Most times Bricks was easy to deal but the asshole in him came out every so often. Jamal was getting used to it. He watched the man pull out a piece of paper from the folder and laugh a small laugh of victory. Bricks turned and faced the boys.

"Smurf and Diego, you two go inside and get everything we need," Bricks ordered, handing Smurf a wad of cash. "And hurry up, we need to get back on the road as soon as we can. We aint got time for no bullshit."

Diego didn't move. He stared at Jamal, confused. They were thinking the same thing. Jamal leaned up in the seat.

"Shouldn't I go in and help get all the stuff?"

"Naw, you're good. Smurf knows exactly what ya'll need. We went over the list while you were sleep." Bricks tilted his to the side dismissively. He met Jamal's gaze in the rearview mirror. "That work for you?"

Jamal shook his head slightly and sat back. He was irritated and tired of arguing with Bricks. Diego climbed over him and joined Smurf outside the car. Jamal watched the two head towards the Walmart entrance. Bricks opened his door.

"Going to smoke me a cigarette," Bricks said mostly to himself. He looked back at Jamal and then Romeo, who was now awake. Jamal didn't like the look. Bricks stepped out the car and walked towards a group of people smoking, huddled near an outdoor ashtray.

The quiet in the car was deafening. From the moment he saw Romeo at the pool hall, Jamal had wanted nothing more than to have a chance to talk to Romeo. Now, he didn't know what to say or where to begin.

Romeo sat with his back to Jamal, acting like he was going back to sleep, nestled into the car door. Jamal saw the slight reflection of Romeo's face in the window. He was wide awake. Jamal didn't want to wait to find the right words to say. At that moment, alone with Romeo, he felt like he couldn't go another minute and let what was between them to not be addressed. He blurted out the first words that came to mind.

"I'm sorry, Romeo. I am so fucking sorry. I don't even know what to say, homie."

Jamal waited anxiously for a response. Romeo just sat

there, motionless. Jamal knew he heard him. He could still see Romeo's face reflected in the window. He saw how sad and hurt Romeo looked. Jamal wanted to reach out and comfort Romeo. But the fear of how he might respond destroyed that thought. Romeo was holding him at arms' length and Jamal wasn't sure if there was anything he could say to him. But he tried anyways.

"I didn't want to hurt you. That's the last thing in the world I would want to do." Jamal rubbed his face and put on the most apologetic expression he could. "I didn't have a choice. You know that."

Romeo turned around slowly. An eerie look settled on his young face as he locked eyes with Jamal. The tension made Jamal shrink back.

"You didn't have a choice?" Romeo asked. His voice rose as he spoke. "Are you fucking serious? You didn't have a choice?!" Guilt surged through Jamal as he recoiled in fear. "Nigga, you raped me. Do you understand what the fuck that means? Do you have any idea how that fucked me up? For a motherfucker I thought was my best friend to do that?"

"What was I supposed to do?"

The question came out as little more than a whisper. Jamal felt his face get hot. His eyes were moist with tears of regret and anger. He hung his head. He hated what he had done to Romeo but it was Slim's fault. At least Jamal had convinced himself it was. He couldn't understand why Romeo didn't see that.

"What the fuck do you mean 'what were you supposed to do'? How about not rape me, nigga. Cause that's what it was…rape." Romeo raised his hand in anger as he spoke. "I don't remember any one pointing a gun at your head."

"What do you think he would have done if I didn't do what he said?"

Romeo threw his hands in the air. "Fuck if I know. Pretty sure we'll never know now. You didn't even wait for him to threaten you. Almost like you wanted to fuck me."

"He would have killed me if I didn't do what he said. He had that knife."

"Whatever man, you didn't even try to refuse. I would have at least taken a bullet in the arm or leg before I fucked someone I called my boy." Romeo shook his head. "Naw, you enjoyed that shit. You been wanting to fuck me. Just admit it. You wanted to fuck me."

Jamal's blood boiled. Anger and regret surged through his veins. "I made sure that it didn't last longer than it needed to," he said through gritted teeth.

Romeo shook his head. "You saying you did me a favor? Seriously, is that what you saying to me? That's some bullshit. Your faggot ass was so turned on that you just busted quick. Ol' scab ass nigga."

Jamal looked up at Romeo with tears in his eyes. "Do you know what he did to me after you were gone? You have any idea how much pain I was in?"

Romeo tilted his head to the side. A look of indifference covered his face.

"The same thing he did to me." Romeo opened his door. "You dead to me. Nigga, you raped me. And I don't want no part of the faggot shit you got going on, feel me? Keep that shit to yourself and your little Mexican butt chaser. Just kick rocks, slim. I'm fucking done."

Romeo left the car without another word. Jamal was speechless. But Romeo was right. He did want to fuck him.

For a long time. It was a truth that he'd ignored for years. And he did next to nothing to spare his boy the assault Slim forced upon Romeo.

Jamal punched the back of the driver seat over and over again until he was out of breath. His eyes were wet but the tears stopped flowing. Anger had dried that well. Forging any type of relationship with Romeo was impossible now. Jamal knew he had to accept that. He had no choice. Things could never be the same between them. The only ties that bound them now were that of being stickup boys and that was at the will of Slim.

Jamal struggled to catch his breath. The only recourse now was to make money and come up with a way to kill Slim. That goal and that goal alone was the only thing that gave Jamal any relief. Even if Romeo didn't see it now, Slim would pay for what he did to the two of them.

At this point Romeo couldn't be depended on to fulfill that goal. Diego came to mind. The boy was fiercely protective of Jamal and shared Jamal's hatred for Slim. Jamal had to find a way to bring the idea up to Diego without giving away too much. They were fucking but Jamal didn't know where the boy's loyalties lay.

Jamal still needed a plan to deal with Bricks and Smurf down the line when everything was ready. He didn't want to kill them but he knew that if it was them or him the answer was simple.

Bricks opened his door and hopped back in the car. Smurf and Diego were right behind him. Romeo got back in the car last and this time he sat in the front.

Jamal tried to hide his face and look out the window. The tears had dried but he knew his eyes were red. Diego looked quizzically from Romeo to Jamal and back. He knew something was wrong. Jamal felt Diego tug at his arm. Jamal kept looking at the window. Diego leaned in close enough to whisper in Jamal's ear.

"I don't know what this motherfucker said to you but don't worry, I got you."

Jamal took a deep breath. He didn't have the strength to consider Diego's words. Maybe he meant he would be there for Jamal. Maybe he meant he was going to get payback on Romeo. At that moment, Jamal didn't care. He was lost in his fury. And he planned on channeling it into their first stickup. A small part of Jamal actually felt sorry for the cats in D.C. A storm was coming and Jamal would leave nothing in his path of destruction.

Chapter 10

Jamal angrily crossed his arms over his chest and slouched in the backseat sitting next to Smurf. He couldn't believe that after an hour of driving around parking lots, Bricks and Romeo decided to hi-jack a silver Lincoln Navigator. Jamal only shook his head to show his disapproval. Saying something seemed trivial at that point.

It seemed like Bricks had done the exact opposite of everything Jamal and him discussed with Slim to make their trip look as inconspicuous as possible. First they get thirty miles from DC and then purchased supplies. Jamal thought they should have taken care of that when they were in North Carolina or at least before they had hit Richmond, Virginia. And now they were taking a luxury vehicle. The shit was crazy.

Jamal wondered if Bricks was trying to set them up so

they'd get caught. The man didn't even let them relax for a minute when they checked into the motel just outside of Southeast, DC. Bricks had them back on the streets before they could even sit down on the dingy double size beds. Jamal had hoped for at least a quick shower after the nine hour drive. He didn't even let them get what little luggage they had from the trunk.

According to Bricks, the only reason they even stopped at the motel was so Smurf would know where to go when they were done scouting the trap houses. Jamal was tempted to jump in the shower despite what Bricks had said when they got in the room. But Jamal knew that crossing Slim's right hand man wasn't a good move no matter how he tried to justify the act. Not this soon anyways.

Jamal wasn't afraid of the beastly man but he knew that testing Brick's loyalties down the road would be smarter than alienating him so early in the game. Bricks might be an asset at some point. Jamal wanted to sow the seeds of trust and respect. At least until Bricks was no longer useful. Then his fate would be sealed like everyone else who had crossed him.

Jamal sat up and watched Romeo run over to the Lincoln Navigator he and Bricks decided would be their getaway vehicle. Every inch of Jamal's body screamed for him to speak out about taking the car and suggest an older, more practical car. But he shook the thought and just let Bricks run the show. He had done so thus far.

Bricks grabbed a bag from near his feet and passed it back to Smurf. "Here, go ahead and switch up the plates."

Smurf nodded and was out the door in a heartbeat. Romeo was already in the car and working on hot wiring it. Bricks took out his phone and gave someone the description of the car and the old plate number. Jamal remembered Brick saying he'd take care of the plates so they'd have more time with the car before they had to ditch it.

Damn this nigga flexing, Jamal thought. Doing all this unnecessary shit.

He knew they couldn't pull all what Bricks was doing if he wasn't there. He was showing off. If they got an old ass car and just changed the plates they wouldn't be going through all this. Jamal would make sure that they'd boost a car from a used car lot next time. He wasn't going to be taking any chances. Next time it would be his show and he didn't care what Bricks had to say.

Bricks ended his call and looked over his shoulder at Jamal. "Alright, you ready?"

Jamal gave a slight nod. He jumped out the car and headed for the Navigator. He yanked open the driver side door. Romeo sat up and looked Jamal in the eyes. There was so much hate in those eyes that if Jamal were a weaker man he'd have shriveled up and backed away.

Romeo jumped out the car and squeezed past Jamal. He moved to join Bricks back at the car but Jamal placed his hand on Romeo's chest to stop him. Romeo looked at the hand until it moved.

"Jamal, I already told you not to touch me." Romeo looked up. "Next time I won't do much talking. Believe that."

Jamal narrowed his eyes. Granted Romeo had been through a lot and had changed, but Jamal wasn't a punk. There was only so much shit he was willing to take from Romeo. And he'd just about had his fill. Jamal ignored the comment.

"Did you disconnect the GPS or any Lowjack they might

have?"

A wry grin spread on Romeo's face as he pushed Jamal's hand off him. "Of course. Wouldn't want you getting caught up and snatched up by the police. Besides I don't think you would look good in prison orange. It's not your color. Plus, I wouldn't want a nigga to drop the soap around your ass. Wouldn't be right to let you get locked up."

Jamal watched Romeo walk back to the car with Bricks. He wondered if Romeo would actually set him up. It would be the perfect time to do it.

"Hey, shouldn't I be the one driving?" Smurf asked.

Jamal looked at Smurf, wishing he had killed him the first time he had a chance back at the trap house. Jamal nodded and walked over to the passenger side. Bricks had said Smurf knew the area and where all the spots they were going to hit were located. It actually did make more sense for him to drive even though Jamal hated the idea of him behind the wheel.

As soon as they left the parking lot and were out of eye shot of Bricks, Smurf pulled out a blunt and lighter. Jamal snatched it from his mouth before he could spark up.

"You can do that shit when we done on your own fucking time." Jamal cut his eyes at the weed head. "I'm not going to get caught up because your ass stays high."

Smurf waved him off. "Whatever nigga. Aint shit but a fucking buzz. I got this."

"Naw, not with me. That dumb shit will get niggas killed cause they aint sharp. Just do what the fuck I say and maybe you'll live to buy as much weed and whatever else you pollute your body with to zone the fuck out."

Smurf sucked his teeth but didn't argue. Jamal looked out the window and watched as rundown warehouses gave way to rundown houses and ghetto looking apartment complexes. From the looks of it, Jamal figured they were in Southeast DC. He'd never been to the city but he heard how hood it looked.

Smurf turned into an apartment complex and backed into a parking spot. He pointed at one of the apartments on the first floor. "That's one of the spots we hitting tonight."

Jamal frowned. "Wait, that shit's an apartment."

"We not in the south anymore man. This is how these cats operate."

Jamal shook his head and just started watching. It didn't take long for the traffic to pick up. Jamal wrote down the number of people going in and out the spot. He made note of which one's looked like they'd be posted there and selling that night. Jamal also wrote down how many duffle bags came in and out the apartment.

Two hours went by before Jamal had what he needed. He drew a small map and noted a couple of places to come in at the apartment before he tapped Smurf. The boy had fallen asleep.

"Nigga, I hope you taking note of how the fuck we can get out this bitch if shit gets real."

"I got this," Smurf said as he pulled out the apartment complex.

Jamal wasn't convinced. Smurf kept looking over at Jamal as he drove. It got to the point where Jamal noticed it and got annoyed, quick.

"What the fuck you keep looking at?" Jamal demanded, irritation laced in his voice. "You got a fucking staring problem, nigga?"

Smurf bit his bottom lip and looked over at Jamal for a

long moment as if weighing whether or not he was going to say what he wanted to say. He blurted the words out. "How long you been fucking that Mexican?"

Jamal's fists balled. Anger twisted his face. Had Smurf not been driving Jamal would have let loose a fury of fists to the boy's face. "Nigga, what did you just say to me?"

"Aww, don't act like you don't know what I'm talking about. I know you was forced to do it the first time by Slim but ya'll still fucking. I can tell by how ya'll look at each other. That Spanish bitch be up under like a female and shit."

Jamal's first thought was, 'how did Smurf know what Slim had made him do'. If Smurf knew about Diego then he probably knew about Romeo too. Knowing Slim, he probably fucked Smurf too.

"I don't know what you talking about nigga. Just drive. All this conversation aint even necessary."

"Damn, Slim got you fucked up that bad, hunh? Fucked the Mexican and fucked your best friend. Now the Mexican love that black dick and your boy don't want shit to do with you." Smurf looked over at Jamal. "You in love with Slim or do you hate him? Cause I know he tore that ass up."

"You sound like you speaking from experience, motherfucker. You and Slim have a go?"

Smurf chuckled. "Yea. And that shit felt good as fuck. Nigga got mad and stopped when he saw my dick was hard. I guess it fucked up his power trip."

Jamal frowned. He couldn't believe what he was hearing. For a second he thought Smurf was flat out lying but for what? Information? He already knew everything. Then understanding washed over him. Jamal knew what he was doing. He was trying to get a rise out of him. To see what buttons he could push.

"Why you telling me this shit? What you want, Smurf?"

"I'm just making conversation. Showing we not all that different from each other. That I understand what you going through."

"Oh, you think you understand? How's that?"

"I'm saying. I got me a girl back home that I dick down good, trust. But every so often I like to get a pretty little piece to fuck around with." Smurf pulled at his goatee. "Hell, your boy Romeo the type I go after too."

Jamal shifted in his seat. He was getting angry again. Now he understood. Smurf was going to try to get at Romeo to fuck with him. Jamal's mind raced. Smurf had to go and soon.

"Romeo don't get into all that faggot shit you talking."

"That's what you think."

Jamal frowned. "What you talking about?"

"Nothing man." Smurf turned down a narrow street and parked. "I'm just making sure you don't mind me getting at Romeo since you got the Mexican."

"You niggas grown," Jamal blurted out. "I don't give a fuck what ya'll do long as you don't jeopardize what we doing."

"Cool." Smurf said and then pointed at a small house on the corner. "That's the house right there."

Smurf curled up against his window and closed his eyes. Jamal fumed. He wished he could take out his pocket knife and end that niggas life right there. But he knew he couldn't. When he did take Smurf out it would have to look like an accident. He didn't need any added attention from Bricks or Slim.

Jamal tried to focus on watching the house but his mind was flooded by thoughts of Romeo and Diego. The idea of Smurf and Romeo turned Jamal's stomach. Jamal and Romeo had history and a part of Jamal prayed that they could salvage what they had even though Romeo seemed to want nothing to do with him.

Then there was Diego. He was Jamal's 'something new'. Even though the Latin prick had a girlfriend there were feelings there. Deep feelings. Considering the possibilities actually put a smile on Jamal's face. He hurriedly straightened his expression. Jamal looked back over at Smurf.

The nigga was trying to manipulate him. Jamal was hip to what he was doing. But it wasn't going to work. Jamal was going to take Smurf out. He just prayed he could do it before Smurf brushed up on Romeo. Seeing his boy with another nigga would be too devastating to deal with, whether he was fucking Diego or not.

Chapter 11

Jamal was so tired and drained that he missed the lock and dropped the key card to the motel room on the floor. He scooped it up and tried a second time. His arms were heavy. His body was weak. Jamal hadn't slept in over twenty-four hours.

The light above the lock finally turned green after Jamal patiently slid the card back and forth. There was no point in getting mad. It was a rat motel used mostly by hookers and Johns. Jamal let out a sigh of relief and pushed the door open.

Romeo walked out the bathroom just as Jamal and Smurf stepped inside the room. He only had on a pair of boxers. Jamal ached at the sight of his boy almost naked. He remembered how muscular but soft his ass was. He longed to touch those yellow cheeks again.

Without pause, Romeo glanced over at Jamal and Smurf and quickly averted his eyes dismissively. He went to the bed on the far side of the room and put on some lotion and a black tank top.

"Damn, slim got a little phatty," Smurf said, only loud enough for Jamal to hear. "Nigga probably got some bomb ass, too."

He nudged Jamal like a guy would another dude looking at a female with a fat ass. Jamal looked at Smurf with a sidelong glance. He wondered how long he could put up with Smurf without knocking him on his ass. Jamal pushed the thought from his mind. Last thing he needed to do was lose his temper and ruin any chance of getting rid of Smurf, permanently.

Jamal looked over at Bricks. The bald headed giant was going through his duffle bag on the cot next to the window. Map in hand, he headed towards Jamal and Smurf.

"Here, add anything you think will help to the map." Bricks looked down at his watch. "You have five hours. I'm going to run an errand. I'll be back in like thirty."

Bricks pulled the cigarette from his ear and fished for his lighter in his pocket as he reached for the door. Jamal grabbed him by the arm before he could get out the door. Bricks looked at him ambivalently.

"What's up youngin?"

"Where did you guys put our stuff?"

"Over there in the closet across from the bathroom." Bricks said, motioning in that direction. Then he looked towards Diego; sleep and sprawled out on the bed. Bricks looked at Jamal with a grin. "Try to get some sleep, boy."

Jamal nodded and walked towards his duffle bag. He made

a mental note of how Bricks responded to his grabbing him by the arm. He wasn't distant or hostile anymore. Bricks apparently was in a better mood than earlier. Making the man more comfortable was now a top priority.

Jamal snatched up his bag. He stood there looking from Romeo getting dressed to Diego sleep on the bed. Jamal struggled to understand the emotions burning through his body and the thoughts running through his head. Whatever was going on inside him made him feel torn beyond comprehension.

Smurf squeezed past Jamal and got his bag. He looked at Jamal and grinned. Jamal didn't face him but he could feel Smurf staring at him. For a moment Jamal entertained the fantasy that Smurf was a loud, buzzing house fly and Jamal had the swatter. A mischievous grin spread on Jamal's face.

"Let me make this easy for you," Smurf said.

He tossed his bag on the end of the bed where Romeo was. He walked over and flopped down on the bed. He dapped up Romeo and started up a conversation. Smurf shot a quick glance at Jamal over his shoulder and smiled. Jamal got the message.

That nigga gonna die, Jamal thought. He walked over to Diego's bed and set down his bag. He sat down and took off his shoes. Jamal laid back and took a deep breath. It had been a long day. He laced his fingers behind his head and turned towards Diego.

Diego looked so peaceful and beautiful laying there asleep. It almost looked like he was smiling in his slumber. All the anger Smurf had stirred up in Jamal faded away like a forgotten memory. Looking down at Diego calmed Jamal. He wanted nothing more than to lean in and kiss Diego or to wrap his arms around him and hold him close. But Jamal wasn't going to do that. At least not in front of Romeo.

Jamal saw the frown on Diego's face come first. Then his body twisted as he turned his head up and started smelling the air. Diego's eyes opened and locked with Jamal's. Jamal smiled. The frown stayed on Diego's face.

"You stink."

Jamal chuckled softly. "Nice to see you too, man."

Diego sat up on his elbows. "Naw, I'm so serious. You smell like shit, papi." Diego nudged Jamal in the side. "You need to take a shower before you get in this bed."

A look of defeat covered Jamal's face. "Look, I'm tired as shit. Can't you just face the other way? Hell, I won't even get under the covers."

"Maybe I want you under the covers." Diego said.

He bit his bottom lip and tilted his head to the side. Jamal shook his head and smiled. There was no point in arguing. Diego was laying it on thick and he wasn't going to budge. Jamal pulled himself out the bed. He looked over his shoulder at Diego, feigning anger as he walked to the bathroom with a towel draped over his shoulder.

Jamal jumped out of his clothes. He smelled the pits of his shirt and recoiled in disgust. Diego was right, he was foul. Jamal turned on the shower. The water was still warm from Romeo using it. Jamal got in and put his head under the hot water.

Jamal wished all the stress and problems would wash away along with the dirt and grime from his body. But he knew that wasn't going to happen. Wishing and hoping was for fools. He grew up believing that things got done when a man decided to get something done and did it. And Jamal was dedicated to working his situation to take out Slim and fatten his pockets while doing it.

"Got room for me, papi?"

Jamal turned around and got a full view of Diego, naked, stepping in the shower with him. Jamal wasn't surprised that Diego had joined him. Part of him wondered what had taken the El Salvadorian so long. He left the door unlocked for a reason.

"Wherever I am there is always room for you."

Jamal saw the seriousness cross Diego's face after hearing Jamal's response. The words had flowed freely and honestly. And Jamal meant it. Diego moved in close and laced his fingers around the nape of Jamal's neck. He looked into Jamal's eyes, searching. Jamal tried to say what he felt with his eyes. To express what he felt for his Latin lover.

Diego broke off his stare and closed his eyes. He leaned in and pressed his lips onto Jamal's. Diego was gentle but firm. His tongue slipped through Jamal's lips and explored every inch of Jamal's mouth, slowly. Jamal closed his eyes and allowed Diego to take control. He wanted to feel good, like the last time. With Diego he could let go. And that's all he wanted at that moment. Just to let go and not be afraid.

The tips of Diego's fingers ran down to the small of Jamal's back. Jolts of pleasure teased Jamal everywhere Diego touched him. The heat between their bodies and the hot water on his back put Jamal in a place that tortured the senses with rapturous bliss. Jamal was on cloud nine.

Diego moved to Jamal's neck kissing and sucking. He bit at Jamal's collar bone. A small, forced moan slipped from Jamal's mouth. He tilted his head back in ecstasy.

"Damn Diego," Jamal said in a low, throaty voice, "the

shit you do with your mouth."

"I got you, papi. Just relax and let me make you feel good."

Jamal gripped at the walls of the shower as Diego reached down and wrapped his hands around his hard dick. He stroked Jamal's pole in rhythm with the kisses he planted on Jamal's chest and abs.

Relief and tension intermingled through Jamal's body. Diego was already dragging his wet tongue pass Jamal's belly button. The foreplay was amazing but Jamal was on edge sexually. He wasn't sure how long he could take what Diego was doing to him.

Diego cupped Jamal's heavy hanging balls and took the length of him in his mouth. Jamal's legs buckled. The blood engorged head of his dick poked at the back of Diego's tight, wet mouth. The back of Diego's mouth tickled every sensitive nerve ending on Jamal's dick.

Jamal reached down and grabbed a handful of Diego's hair. Jamal pulled him off his dick and looked down. The head of Jamal's dick sat on Diego's bottom lip.

"You keep on and I'm going to bust," Jamal warned. "That shit is feeling too good."

Diego smiled. He opened his mouth, slid his tongue out and ran it around the tip of Jamal's straining dick. The teasing sensation made Jamal's body shuddered. He pulled Diego's head forward until the length of his meat ran down Diego's throat. The teasing was over.

Jamal could feel his orgasm build. His balls tightened and his shaft hardened almost to the point of pain. Jamal took hold of Diego's head. He slid his dick in and out of Diego's mouth, faster and faster until he was piston fucking his face.

A guttural groan rumbled from deep down in Jamal. He pulled Diego's head down on his dick until his pubes brushed against Diego's nose. Shot after shot of nutt erupted from Jamal's body down Diego's throat. Diego just swallowed. Shivers ran up and down Jamal's spine from the added sensation of Diego's throat contracting around his dick.

Jamal pulled his softening dick from Diego's mouth and leaned back against the shower wall, spent. He watched Diego wipe the corner of his mouth and stand up. Diego kissed Jamal and smiled.

"You taste good as shit, papi."

Jamal put his hands on Diego's waist and cocked his head to the side. "Damn, you a little freak, hunh?"

Diego pressed up on Jamal, his hard dick wedged between Jamal's body and his. He grabbed Jamal's ass and pulled his cheeks apart. He ran a finger over Jamal's hole. The stickup boy gasped.

"Shit, I'm just getting started, you aint seen freaky yet. Let me play in that chocolate ass, nigga."

Jamal ached to feel Diego inside of him again. But he needed a moment to recuperate. And it was a good time to see where Diego's head was. He pressed his hands against Diego's chest. Diego looked up confused.

"Hold up. I need to ask you something."

Disappointment clouded Diego's face. "Alright, go ahead."

"What do you think about Smurf?"

"Shit, I don't know," Diego said frowning. "He's our driver. He used to work out a trap house and he's trying to push up on Romeo. Not much to really base an opinion on."

Jamal nodded. The last part of Diego's summary got

Jamal's attention. He wondered how obvious Smurf's intentions with Romeo were. He had no idea until the pot head said something in the car earlier. Maybe he wasn't paying enough attention. Or paying too much to Romeo and not what was going on around him.

"Alright, what about Bricks?"

"Bricks is cool." The lines in Diego's forehead got deeper. "Why you asking all these questions about them? What you not telling me?"

"Do you really think Slim is going to let you pay your dad's debt back?" Jamal saw Diego's eyes glaze over. Diego hadn't even considered the idea that Slim wouldn't let the debt be cleared. But the thought had took hold. Jamal cupped Diego's face in his hands. "Baby boy, I need to know you there for me when shit goes down." Jamal searched Diego's face. "You understand what I'm saying?"

Diego nodded. "You sure you want to go after Slim?" Diego asked. He reached up and clasped his hands around Jamal's wrists. "You do know how connected he is, right?"

Jamal's first instinct was to say yes, but he didn't want to lie to Diego. He needed Diego to trust him. Jamal hung his head low.

"He runs drugs up and down the East Coast," Diego explained. "He just set up shop down in Jacksonville."

"I understand that but that nigga got the shit coming."

Diego shook his head. "You're bout as good as Romeo at holding on to that shit."

"Seriously? You're okay with what that nigga did?"

"No, I'm not. But damn, what was the alternative? And now we bout to make money."

"Look, we gonna make money and that nigga going to

keep finding ways to keep us giving him a piece. He got to go." Jamal moved closer, his eyes piercing. "I just need to know you down with me to the end."

Jamal saw the fear and uncertainty in Diego's eyes. But he still nodded.

"I got you, papi. To the end." Diego brought his hand to the back of Jamal's neck and pulled him into a kiss. Diego pulled back and looked at Jamal again. His face was awash with emotion.

"I think I'm falling for you, Jamal. And hard, papi."

Chapter 12

BANG, BANG, BANG!

Jamal and Diego both jumped at the sound of someone banging against the bathroom door like they were the police. Nervous grins spread on their faces as they realized how shook they were from the knocking. For a moment Jamal even thought that they had been caught. Bricks had changed so many plans and let Romeo get that truck, it all had Jamal on edge.

"Hey, get out the fucking shower," Smurf said, barking his orders through the cheap motel door. "Ya'll using up all the goddamned hot water!"

Jamal pulled Diego in tight as the lukewarm water cascaded over their bodies. Jamal wasn't sure how to take Diego's declaration of love. It both startled and warmed him. He'd never had anyone say that they loved him. But Jamal was skeptical. Diego had a girlfriend.

Even though Jamal wasn't marching in any parades he was sure that he didn't want to be involved with a DL dude who had a public girlfriend and only fucked with him behind closed doors or road trips. Besides, Jamal knew he still had very strong and very real feelings for Romeo. Not knowing what else to do, Jamal just held Diego and looked in his eyes.

BANG, BANG, BANG!

"I swear to God I'll kick this bitch down!" Smurf yelled.

"Motherfucker, I wish you would," Jamal called back. He shook his head and looked back at Diego. "Come on, the water's getting cold anyways. I want to catch a nap before we head out tonight."

Diego simply nodded. He reached to turn off the water but Jamal took him by the wrist and stopped him.

"Naw, leave it on. Shit will be ice cold by the time that nigga gets in here."

Jamal smiled. Diego offered only a slight grin, avoiding eye contact. He got out the shower without a word and quickly dried off. Diego was out the door before Jamal was finished patting his legs down.

"Damn nigga," Smurf said, peeking inside the bathroom. "I aint know you was packing like that." Smurf's eyes lingered on Jamal's manhood. He licked his lips and watched Jamal, lust flaring in his eyes. "Balls big as shit."

Jamal snatched up his towel and pulled it around his waist. He shot Smurf a hard stare as he pushed past him. Smurf laughed loudly as he squeezed into the bathroom and shut the door behind him.

Jamal went to his duffle bag on the dresser and ruffled through his clothes looking for something to wear. His eyes darted up and over to Romeo. He was sleep on his stomach and lying on top of the covers. He still was only wearing a pair of boxers and a tank top. His somewhat exposed body was in full view.

Jamal's eyes moved from Romeo's toned thighs and small waist to his small but plump ass. Jamal could feel his meat thicken under the towel as his mind played with thoughts of all the things he would do to Romeo if given the chance. More than anything, Jamal wanted a chance.

With a deep breath, Jamal shifted his gaze off his ex-best friend. He looked over to Diego. Their eyes locked. Jealousy and pain twisted the boy's face. Jamal watched Diego's eyes move from the tent of Jamal's towel to Romeo's ass and back. Diego didn't say anything. His face said enough. He threw the covers back and got into the bed, turning his back to Jamal and covering his head.

Jamal exhaled heavily. He knew what Diego had wanted to hear in the shower but Jamal couldn't reciprocate the feelings when he still wanted Romeo. Jamal put on some clothes and sat down. His thoughts were chaotic. Jamal buried his face in his hands. There was so much going on.

Tonight the four of them would hit up the trap houses Jamal and Smurf had scouted earlier. Jamal had little choice but to rely on Romeo and Diego to have his back when they raided the houses and depend on Smurf when they got in the car to get away.

Jamal was worried about how Romeo and Diego would do. Romeo was still just a hop and a skip from being a nut case and Diego needed more time to improve on his gun skills. He couldn't hit the side of barn. But in the end, despite it all, Jamal knew he could depend on them to try their hardest to make sure they all came through the night still breathing. He was more worried about Smurf.

Smurf had no allegiance to any of them. Slim had made him the crew's driver. Jamal knew nothing about the boy, aside from what he said Slim did to him and Jamal wasn't even sure he was telling the truth about that. Something in Jamal's gut told him that Slim had put Smurf there to be his eyes and ears. Jamal would love to do nothing more than to take out Smurf and blind and deafen Slim in the process.

"You might want to catch a couple hours of sleep, little nigga," Bricks said, looking over his shoulder. "It's going to be a long night and you need to be sharp."

Bricks didn't wait for a response. He turned back around, looked down at the map and continued to take notes. Jamal got up and got in the bed. He got under the covers and inched towards Diego until his body was pressed against Diego's back and ass. Diego tried to pull away but Jamal hooked his arm around him and pulled Diego in tight.

"Calm that shit down," Jamal said, whispering in Diego's ear. "Look, I got feelings for you too but how you expect me to say what you said when you still got a girl? All this shit is new to me but I still need loyalty. I'm selfish. I don't like sharing."

Diego tried to turn around and face Jamal but Jamal didn't let him. He tightened his grip on Diego's waist and kept talking.

"We aint got to argue, baby boy. You just deal with that and I got you. We can talk about everything later. We need to worry about what needs to go down tonight. Everything else can be figured out when we get back to Atlanta."

Jamal felt Diego's body relax in his arms. Diego pushed

his ass back into Jamal's groin. It didn't take much for Jamal's body to respond. Jamal reached down and tucked his dick between his thighs. He leaned in and kissed the back of Diego's neck.

"Stop before you start something. We need to get some sleep before tonight. Afterwards, I promise you I'll give that ass what you want."

Diego moaned his agreement and held the hand Jamal had on his stomach in his own. It wasn't long until Jamal heard the same soft snoring he heard in the car ride up to DC coming from Diego.

Jamal closed his eyes. He felt bad for lying and leading Diego on. Even if he wanted to be with Diego he still had to deal with all the feelings he had for Romeo. The baggage between Jamal and Romeo went back years. They had a history. Moving on to someone else wouldn't be easy even if he wanted to.

But until he crossed that bridge, Jamal needed Diego to be on his side, unconditionally. And if that meant promising his love, so be it. Jamal fought the guilt tormenting his mind and willed himself to sleep.

It seemed like as soon as Jamal closed his eyes, Bricks was nudging him in the side to get up. He sat up and looked over at the old radio clock on the dresser. It was midnight. He'd gotten a solid three hours of rest. Jamal looked over Romeo and Smurf. He clenched his teeth and shook his head.

Smurf spooned Romeo on top of the covers. He had his arm wrapped around Romeo's waist and his groin was pressed against Romeo's ass. Jamal got angrier by the second. He reached back for a pillow but Diego grabbed him by the wrist.

"Stop. Don't throw a pillow at them. Bricks will wake them up. Just get dressed."

"Alright. You right," Jamal said, dropping the pillow to the bed. "But I wasn't going to throw it. I was going smother the little motherfucker."

Diego grinned and shook his head. He got up and grabbed a duffle bag from the dresser in the front of the room. He pulled out some clothes and tossed them over to Jamal.

"That's the clothes we picked out from the Walmart. All black. Make sure you don't lose the gloves or the mask. No fingerprints and no visual identifications."

Jamal nodded that he understood and put on the clothes. He watched Bricks wake Romeo and Smurf up as he got dressed on the corner of his and Diego's bed. Jamal expected Romeo to pull away from Smurf as he woke up. He didn't. Romeo got up like nothing happened. He even ignored the hard-on in Smurf's pants that was obviously poking him when they were lying down.

Jamal slid on his black boots and dreamt about putting his gun in Smurf's mouth. Thinking about taking him out made Jamal's dick hard. He grinned at the thought of Smurf dead.

"What you over there grinning about?" Diego asked.

"Nothing," Jamal said. "Just looking forward to counting all that money when we get done tonight."

"Shit, me too. Ready to get this shit over with."

"I feel you. Just make sure you be careful. I don't trust these niggas. We alone out there, feel me?"

Diego's expression turned somber as he nodded.

"Alright," Bricks called out. "Ya'll little niggas get over here. We need to go over this map."

Everyone moved over to the table where Bricks sat, more

or less dressed. Jamal shot Smurf a hard stare, daring him to put a hand on Romeo. Smurf grinned but didn't touch Romeo.

"This is a map of Southeast D.C. and parts of PG County," Bricks explain. "I've made some notes on the three spots you all will be hitting tonight. I went out while you all were sleep and did some reconnaissance myself. Next time that'll be you alls job."

"What are those stick figures?" Jamal asked. "And why you got them in different colors?"

"A lot of the cats up here got trap houses and work corners. The corners they work usually aren't too far from the trap house. The trap house might serve as the re-up or the supply to heavy hitters looking for more weight than the typical addict."

"You didn't answer my question," Jamal said coolly.

"Calm down, young hustler. I'm trying to school you." Bricks pointed on the map. "These red stick figures work these two corners. The number of cats on the corner will vary over the course of the night but usually aint no more than six of them that got heat on 'em."

Bricks looked up and made sure he had everyone's attention. He had a captive audience. Bricks moved his stubby finger over the map.

"The house with the red dot is their re-up spot. Jamal and Smurf already got the info on the trap houses. I got pictures of the dudes working the corners and the one's that run to get the re-up."

"So we got to wait for the re-ups to hit the house before we move on it," Jamal said.

"Exactly youngin,' exactly. I see why Slim made you the

point man."

Jamal ignored the compliment and looked over the map at the green and yellow dots and stick figures. He didn't need praise from anyone, let alone the fat fuck that caught him trying to steal from Slim.

"But won't we be losing money by waiting for the re-up?" Smurf asked.

"Naw stupid," Jamal said. "The runner drops off the money from the corner when he picks up the re-up. They aint going to let the cash and dope be stuck on the corner."

Smurf sucked his teeth and sat back. Bricks smiled. He looked at Jamal like a proud father would look at a son headed off to college.

"Now, it looks like we're going to have to be careful here," Jamal said, pointing at the green stick figures on the map. "They work four corners encircling the trap house. Each one is no more than a half mile away."

Bricks sat back and let Jamal take over the meeting. He handed him the folder of pictures he had taken of the corner boys and listened as Jamal came up with a strategy. After about twenty minutes the plan was set.

"Alright, let's go make some motherfucking money," Jamal said, leading the crew out the door.

Chapter 13

"We been waiting out here for like an hour," Smurf said. "When the fuck we going to move? I'm tired of sitting in this bitch."

Jamal rolled his eyes and exhaled loudly. Smurf had been getting on his nerves from the moment they got in the car. He was worse than a three year old on a road trip.

"Motherfucker, you got somewhere you got to be?" Jamal asked. He cocked his head to the side as he looked at his appointed driver. "You aint even the one going inside. What the fuck is wrong with you? We the one's running up in this bitch and we aint going in until I say we ready so calm the fuck down."

Smurf huffed and folded his arms over his chest. He turned his back to Jamal and slouched in his seat as if he were sleeping.

Fucking childish ass nigga, Jamal thought. Trying to get a motherfucker killed and shit.

Diego reached up from the back seat and tapped Jamal on the shoulder. "Papi, you see what I see?" He asked as he leaned forward.

Diego pointed towards the corner, three houses down from the trap house. Jamal followed his finger. A large smile spread on the crew leader's face as he shook his head. *Finally*.

"These niggas can't help but get they dick wet," Jamal said. His eyes shot over to Smurf. "That's why a nigga can't never come up. Always trying fuck and make money at the same time."

Jamal, Diego and Romeo all watched as the tall, skinny dark skinned runner from the second corner stumbled towards the house with two females in tow. He had his arms hooked around both their waists. A large duffle bag was strapped over his shoulder. Every five steps or so the girls would stop him and feel up on his thin frame, kiss on his neck and grab for his groin. Jamal could tell from the way the dude walked that he was hard.

"Déjà vu," Romeo mumbled.

"Yea," Jamal said agreeing as he looked over his shoulder at Romeo. "Only this time there aint going to be no big nigga like Bricks stopping us. And if a nigga do show up we just going to have to put his ass to sleep for good."

Romeo didn't say anything or even acknowledge what Jamal said. His eyes simply shifted back to the trio walking outside. Jamal pulled his eyes from Romeo. He didn't have the luxury of being upset about not even getting his friend's acknowledgement.

Jamal looked through his binoculars again and scanned the

street. It was pretty much deserted. A couple of homeless guys squatting in an abandoned house were about six houses down but weren't paying the runner any attention. The coast was clear.

"Alright, it's that time," Jamal announced. He looked back at Romeo. "You go ahead and walk up to the corner. Cross the street there and then double back. Cut into the backyard of the second house so you can come up behind the trap house and flank this nigga from the side. But don't move until you see me and Diego."

"Alright," Romeo said plainly. He cocked his gun and slid it down the front of his pants.

"And if you get a chance to peek in one of the windows, get a quick head count. It might help."

Romeo nodded and reached for the car door.

"And Romeo," Jamal said. He waited for Romeo to look back. "Please be careful."

Romeo rolled his eyes dismissively and got out the car. Smurf, who was acting sleep up until that moment, looked over his shoulder at Jamal with a judgmental gaze and shook his head. A teasing smirk spread on his face. Jamal felt the urge to back hand the driver but fought the feeling. He looked back through his binoculars. He didn't even want to look and see the expression on Diego's face.

Jamal followed his best friend with his eyes. Less than a minute passed when Romeo finally disappeared behind the house. Jamal looked back at Diego.

"I'm ready when you ready, Papi," Diego said with a lusty smile.

Jamal felt his manhood awaken in his pants. Diego always found a way to make Jamal horny as hell but he knew he had to focus. He forced himself to look through the binoculars again, this time at the trap house runner. The runner and the two females were about twenty feet from the house.

"Alright let's move," Jamal ordered.

Jamal and Diego quickly got out the truck and crossed the street with swift but quiet steps. They headed straight for the trap house. Jamal knew the dark skinned guy or one of the females would notice them but he hoped it would be too late for them see anything afoul about the pair before they could reach them.

"You ready?" Jamal asked.

Diego nodded and pulled his ski mask over his face. Jamal did the same. They both reached to the small of their backs and grabbed their guns. Jamal broke out into a full out sprint. Diego stayed right on his heels. They were on the trio just as the runner and the girls made it to the patio of the house.

The brown skinned girl in the tight purple dress with weave down to the middle of her back saw them first. Her eyes went wide with fear when she saw the guns. She looked like she had never seen one before. Before she could scream or warn the other two, Diego leveled his gun at her forehead. He brought his pointer finger to his lips and motioned for her to be quiet.

The guy must have felt the girl's body tighten in his arms. He spun around quickly, reaching for the gun in his pants but it was too late. Jamal had his gun pressed against the man's chest before he could blink. Jamal cocked his head to the side as he looked the guy up and down. He snatched the gun from the boy's pants, brushing against the dude's manhood in the process.

A calm rage covered the runner's face. Jamal recognized

the look. He had worn it himself many times before. Jamal could tell the kid was no dummy. He knew he just got caught with his pants down. Jamal smiled on the inside. *At least I don't have kill this little nigga*, he thought.

"Give me the bag," Jamal ordered.

The runner clenched his teeth and shook his head as he reluctantly pulled the strap to the bag with all the cash the corner he ran for just made over his head.

"Just put it on the ground," Jamal said, motioning to the ground with his gun. "And don't do anything stupid. It's just money. Try to live another day so you can make more."

The runner sighed and tossed the bag on the ground at Jamal's feet. Jamal felt giddy on the inside. The bag hit the ground with a heavy *THUMP* and it was all cash. He fought to contain his own excitement. Jamal knew Diego had heard it too and was probably just as ready to grab the loot.

"Good. Now let me quickly explain how all this is going to go down," Jamal said. "You're going to act like –"

The sound of a gun cocking stopped Jamal midsentence. His eyes shifted to the origin of the sound. It was Romeo. He had his gun pressed against the temple of the other girl; the light skinned one with the short cropped hair and black shirt. Jamal got a good look at her. She looked very calm compared to the other girl. Too calm.

"Move your hand," Romeo ordered, "or I'll put a bullet right through your head."

Jamal was speechless. The cold calm in his childhood friend's voice sent arctic shivers up his spine. He could only imagine how the girl with the gun to her head had felt. Romeo moved behind the three of them and pulled out a second gun from the runner's back pocket. Jamal shook his head. She was reaching for her dude's gun.

"Sweetheart, its only money. If you want to die over some cash and dope, that's fine. We can take you out and be one our way," Jamal licked his lips and gritted his teeth. "Bitch, don't be stupid and try to be one of those ride or die chicks you read in those busted ass hood books. I will shoot your ass and walk the fuck away like aint shit happened, feel me?"

Jamal waited for the girl to respond. She simply nodded.

"Good. Now this is what's going to happen," Jamal started and pointed at the runner. "You're going to knock on the door and act like aint shit wrong. Just follow instructions and you'll live through the night. Fuck up and try some shit and I'll let my boy here use his piece."

The trio all looked to Romeo. His gun was still on them. The three of them nodded in unison.

"Happy you all understand. Now turn around and knock."

The three of them turned around and faced the door. Romeo stayed where he was and kept his gun on the girl. Jamal and Diego shifted to the other side, out of view of anyone looking out the door, and kept their guns pointed at the other two.

The runner knocked on the door three times.

Chapter 14

"Aww shit, Black done brought back some breezys," a chubby brown skinned man announced as he flung open the door.

Jamal and Diego charged forward and pushed the runner and his two females over the threshold. One of the girls fell to the ground with a cry. Jamal locked his eyes on the man who had opened the door. The giddy smile morphed into an expression of shock. Just as he was about to yell, Jamal held up his gun and pointed it directly between the man's eyes.

"Say something and I swear I'll blow your fucking head off," Jamal said in a low, even tone.

The teddy bear of a man snapped his mouth shut. Jamal motioned for Diego to restrain the four of them. Jamal and Romeo watched the hallway as Diego quickly fastened zip ties to all of their hands and feet. Finally he put a generous amount of duct tape over their mouths, wrapping it all the way around their heads twice over. When he was done, he looked at Jamal to give him the green light.

"They all probably in the kitchen," Jamal whispered to Romeo. "You get that side and get over there." He looked back at Diego. "Watch our backs and keep an eye on them."

Diego nodded that he understood and leveled his gun on the four tied up and gagged on the hallway floor. He kept his eyes on them while he stepped backwards with one hand on Jamal's hip. Jamal stepped cautiously, leading with his ear. The closer he got to the kitchen, the louder the voices got. Jamal held up his hand for them to stop as he listened.

"Man, I got this one bitch up in Suitland that can suck a mean dick, Moe," one voice said.

"Yea?" another asked. "Shit, you need to put your boy on, nigga."

"Man, you going to fuck around and catch some shit fucking with that nigga over there," a third voice said.

"It don't even matter my dude. I never fuck these nasty bitches raw dog."

Laughter erupted from the kitchen and echoed through the house.

Jamal stood there, listening, until he was satisfied that the three of them were the only ones left in the house. He looked at Romeo, narrowed his gaze, and nodded. He mouthed the words: *three, two, one...*

Jamal and Romeo stormed into the kitchen. Diego still had his sights on the four on the floor in the hallway but stepped halfway down the hall so he could see what was going on in the kitchen. Jamal pointed his gun at the two guys at the counter, bagging up vials of crack. The third guy was at the stove.

"Put your motherfucking hands up," Jamal ordered.

The two men looking at Jamal shot their hands in the air. The third man fell to the ground. Jamal was sure he heard a firecracker pop. Like a bottle rocket. He looked over at Romeo.

The boy didn't flinch. "Look at his hands," Romeo said.

Jamal's eyes shot down to the man bleeding out on the ground. His eyes were shut. There was no doubt in his mind that the man was dead. His chest was red with blood. Jamal looked over his body. His eyes narrowed where the man's hand reached in the front of his jeans. He was packing.

Romeo kept his gun on the two at the kitchen counter as he walked over to the body and pulled the gun from the man's waist. Jamal watched as Romeo looked down at the body, without emotion or remorse, kicked it in the stomach and looked away at the two left alive.

Damn, Jamal thought. Nigga is just vicious as shit.

"Get ya'll asses up," Diego yelled. "Get in the kitchen and sit down."

Jamal and Romeo kept their guns on the six of them as Diego tied up and gagged the last two. Once they were secure and bunched up on the floor. Diego went upstairs to check the rest of the house. Jamal reached down and pulled the tape off the face of one of the guys.

"Where is the money?" Jamal asked, holding his gun at the guy's temple.

He didn't say anything but his eyes went straight to the cabinet above the fridge. The man's friends shook their heads and frowned as Jamal went straight for the cash. There were three more bags just like the one the runner had up there.

Jamal dropped them on the ground.

"Damn," Jamal said. "You niggas making that guap. Don't worry, I'm sure you all will tighten up after this shit."

"Who the fuck is you, nigga?" A voice from behind them demanded. Jamal began to turn around. "Don't fucking move or this Spanish bitch going to die."

Jamal froze in place. He looked over at Romeo. He still had his gun pointed at the folks on the floor. Contempt covered his face. Romeo was facing the man talking. There wasn't a hint of concern or fear on Romeo's face. Jamal felt his adrenaline rush as panic surged through his body.

"Put your guns down," the voice ordered. "Now!"

Jamal set his gun down on the counter, held his hands above his head and slowly turned around. His eyes locked with Diego's. The fear Jamal saw dancing in his eyes made his heart race. Hopelessness ravished his body. Jamal wondered how he was still standing he felt so powerless.

The large brown skinned man had one arm hooked over Diego's shoulder, clenching the boy's neck between his huge forearm and flexed bicep. Jamal could tell he was taller than Diego the way he had him propped up. His feet barely touched the ground. Diego's hands gripped at the man's arm, trying to breath. The large gun pressed firmly against Diego's left temple is what Jamal stared at.

"Nigga," the man barked, "you aint hear what the fuck I said?!?"

Panic hit Jamal's chest. Confusion was all over his face. His gun was on the counter. His hands were in the air. The way he tightened his grip on Diego and pressed the gun in his skull harder made Jamal wince.

Diego's eyes were locked on Jamal's. The tears ran down

his cheeks but his face was stone hard. Words weren't said but the two of them had a conversation. Jamal felt the resolve radiating from Diego. It scared him. He didn't want to lose Diego. Then, suddenly, Diego's eyes shifted. They were on Romeo. Jamal looked over at his ex-best friend.

"Motherfucker is you deaf or you just don't give a fuck about this Mexican bitch?"

Romeo shrugged nonchalantly. "That nigga shouldn't have gotten caught."

Jamal balked at the total lack of concern in his voice. Romeo still had his gun pointed at the hostages on the floor. That explained why none of them had gotten up and went for his gun on the counter.

"I don't know what the fuck kind of game you're playing," the man started, "but you better put that shit down or I'm going to shoot him."

Romeo looked unbothered by the threat. Jamal's mind raced. Romeo was going to get Diego and maybe the two of them killed acting all crazy.

Fuck, nigga probably kill us after Romeo puts his gun down anyways, Jamal thought. I got to do something.

Sweat ran down the man's face. "Nigga, I'm going to count to three. Put that gun down or I'm going to put a bullet through his head."

Romeo didn't flinch. He cocked his head to the side, looking at the man funny. Jamal looked from the corner of his eyes at his gun on the counter. A heavy frown formed on the man's forehead. He began to count.

"One…"

CRACK! CRACK!

Jamal jumped to the counter and grabbed his gun. He

swiveled around as quickly as his body would allow, pointed and let three rounds go off in the man's chest. He fell to the ground with a heavy thud. Diego stood there, in shock, covered in blood. Jamal snatched off his ski mask and ran to him.

Jamal hooked his arm around Diego's neck and pressed his forehead against Diego's. Their eyes locked. Relief covered both their faces. Neither one of them even noticed the three wounds in the man's chest or how his hand looked like something ripped through it. There was a bullet wound going straight through his forehead.

"Are you okay?" Jamal asked, his breath labored.

Diego nodded. Overcome with emotion, his hands slipped from Jamal's shoulders down to his torso and pulled him in tight. Diego buried his face in Jamal's neck. He squeezed so tight that Jamal couldn't draw a breath. Jamal didn't care. He hugged the boy back and planted a small kiss on his head.

"The fuck," the one with the tape off his mouth said. "These some fucking faggots?"

Jamal's body steeled. He slowly peeled from Diego's grip. He looked over at the guy who had spoken. The man visibly flinched under Jamal's hard glare. Jamal stampeded towards the man like a bull on crack. He came to an abrupt stop as soon as he stood right atop the man. He bent down until he was face to face with him.

"What did you say?" Jamal asked.

His voice was deceptively calm. The man looked up at Jamal with pure hate and disgust in his eyes. They stared each other down for a minute until the man looked away. Jamal clenched his teeth in anger. He was fuming.

"You call me a faggot, bitch nigga?" he asked.

The man shot a hard stare at Jamal before he twisted his head in the other direction. Jamal took out pulled his gun up and put it right on the man's forehead. The contempt and disgust on his face dissolved into fear. Jamal noticed a dark spot spread on his dark cargo pants. He pissed himself. Jamal grinned.

"You wet, nigga? A faggot got you wet?" The man didn't answer. "Open your mouth, bitch?"

The man looked up at Jamal in horror. He didn't move. Jamal backhanded the man so swiftly the man didn't fall to the ground for a split second, not until the pain hit him like a ton of bricks.

"Get your ass up and open your mouth."

Jamal nudged at the man with his foot when he didn't move. Then he kicked the man with bottom of his shoe. Slowly, the man got up on his knees, coughing. He opened his mouth, slightly. Jamal watched him as his eyes shot side to side, looking at his crew and then back at Jamal.

Jamal placed the nozzle of the gun at his lips. "Suck it."

The man looked at Jamal, the hate returning to his eyes, and closed his mouth. Jamal laughed, loudly. He backhanded the man again. Blood ooze from the guys face. His mouth was bloody.

Jamal started to unbuckle his pants. "I'm going to give you something to suck on and we going to see who the fucking faggot is, bitch!"

Before Jamal could pull down the zipper a hand pressed down on his shoulder. Jamal recoiled, sidestepped and turned. His gun was level at Romeo. Romeo was just as quick. He had his gun pointed right at Jamal's head.

"We don't have time for this...*Slim*," Romeo said,

emphasizing the last word. "Get your mask. Get one of the bags. Lets go."

Jamal stood there in disbelief. What Romeo said to him left him in shock. He hated Slim with all his heart and Romeo just called him by that man's name. In his heart, Jamal knew he wasn't wrong. A bad taste filled his mouth. Jamal's head hung and his gun fell to his side.

Diego walked up, avoiding eye contact and handed Jamal his mask and one of the bags. "Come on baby boy, let's go," Diego said. "We got more money to make and the night is still young."

Jamal took a deep breath and pushed the self loathing from his mind. He laced his thumb around the bag strap and pulled it tight to his back. He followed behind Romeo and Diego back to the truck. They jumped in and Smurf sped off. Once they were back on the highway, Smurf spoke.

"What the fuck happened?" he asked, yelling. "That shouldn't have taken more than five minutes. Seven tops. You niggas was in there for like fifteen."

No one answered. Smurf looked from one to the next, searching for a response. Diego looked down at his palms. Romeo looked forward, towards the road. The map was in his lap. He still looked unfazed. Jamal looked out the window.

"No one is going to say anything?" Smurf asked incredulously.

"Relax," Romeo said. "Focus on the road. We have two more spots to hit."

Smurf looked at Romeo. His eyes darted over to Jamal. He was met with a evil glare from the crew leader. Reluctantly, Smurf put his eyes back on the road.

"Baby," Diego whispered. "Are you alright?"

"Yea, I'm good," he answered, just loud enough for Diego to hear. "That shit was just too fucking close."

"I know. It was my fault. I got caught."

Jamal reached over and placed his hand on Diego's leg. "Naw. We went in there half cocked. You shouldn't have been roaming in that bitch alone. We might need another person to join the crew."

"You think Slim will let you do that?"

"I don't give a fuck." Romeo turned from the front seat, his ear facing the pair in the back. Jamal noticed. "We have to do what works for us. We the ones running up in trap houses."

"Even if it means we'll be splitting the money five ways instead of four?"

"Dead men don't spend paper, baby. We got to breathe to eat, feel me?"

Diego nodded. He brought Jamal's hand to his lips and kissed the back of his hand. Jamal reached over and cupped Diego's neck. He pulled him in to a kiss, his lips pressing against his Latin lover hard.

"I love you," Jamal said as soon as he pulled back from the lip lock. Diego smiled.

Jamal sat back and looked towards the road. He saw Romeo looking at him from the corner of his eyes. He looked like he was giving Smurf directions but Jamal knew he was looking at him and Diego. Jamal knew Romeo saw the kiss. But for the first time, he didn't give a damn what he or anyone else thought. And that scared him.

Chapter 15

The door swung open before Jamal could put the card key in the door. The face he saw wasn't Bricks'. Without a second thought, Jamal dropped the bags in his hands to the ground and pulled out his gun. He leveled the pistol at the unfamiliar woman standing in the doorway. Romeo and Diego quickly did the same.

"Bitch, who the fuck are you?" Jamal demanded.

She was speechless but there wasn't a tinge of fear in her expression. The calm on her face sent a cold shiver through Jamal. His eyes narrowed as he clenched the handle. Before he could press the strange woman with another question, Bricks walked up behind her and placed one of his large hands on her shoulder. A subtle grin pursed her full lips.

"Ya'll put ya'll guns down," he said in a low, measured tone. "Now."

Jamal didn't move. He could feel his heart pound relentlessly against his ribcage. His gun stayed on the woman, his arms taut as a steel cable. His eyes moved from her to Bricks and back. A wave of reassurance cascaded over him. Jamal could still see two guns in his peripheral pointed at Bricks and the mystery woman. It was *his* crew. They took *his* orders.

"Why the fuck you got a bitch up in the spot, Bricks?" Jamal asked.

Bricks frowned. "What little nigga?"

The bull of a man started to push the woman aside to get to Jamal but stopped in his tracks when one of the guns moved and pointed down at his groin. His gaze locked on something behind Jamal. Jamal glanced over his shoulder. It was Diego. The slight shaking of the El Salvadorian's head furthered the intent of warning he sent with the gesture of his gun at Bricks' manhood.

Bricks nodded his head and looked to each one of them. His eyes stayed on Jamal. The tension in his rounded face eased, smoothing the wrinkles of anger of frustration fairly quickly. It looked as phony as a three dollar bill. He began to speak.

"This is my ex-wife, Shonda." He looked at her. "She was just leaving."

Bricks took the woman by the hand and placed his hand over her shoulder as he slowly walked her past the throng of young thugs. Reluctantly, Jamal backed away and lowered his gun. The rest of them followed suit. Bricks walked her down the hall and spoke with her. Jamal and the crew watched.

"You sure you want to be beefing with Bricks, nigga?" Smurf asked.

Jamal sucked his teeth. "Why the fuck is you talking? You the driver. Don't think, motherfucker, just drive."

"Jamal," Diego began, "he got a point. The last thing we need is to have his ass acting all loco on some bullshit. He was probably just getting some pussy, man; we are back a little early."

Jamal shook his head. He ignored the words of Smurf and Diego. Bricks headed back towards them, a grimace on his face. Jamal kept the same stoic expression up until Bricks was just a foot away, towering over him. Jamal put his gun back in his pants and looked up at Bricks, daring the gladiator to do something with his eyes.

The tension between the two was palpable. No one moved. Only Romeo had a maniacal grin on his face. It stood in stark contrast to the somber expressions on everyone else's face. Finally, Bricks broke the en passé and spoke.

"Ya'll come inside and count the money so we can call Slim and let him know how much he made."

Jamal clenched his jaw at the sound of that name for the second time that night. He held his cool. He didn't want Bricks or anyone else to see him fazed. Jamal motioned for Bricks to go back inside first. The big man obliged with a mischievous grin. Jamal scooped up the bags he'd dropped moments ago and followed Bricks inside. The rest of them were close in tow, still silent.

"Put the bags on the bed," Jamal said as he began peeling off layers of clothes. "Romeo, get the bill counters and scales we got from Walmart. Diego, start separating the dope from the cash. Put it all at the top of the bed."

Romeo and Diego moved with purpose. Bricks walked over to his rollout bed and flopped down, eyeing the young men warily as he grabbed a bottle of gin and turned it up in his mouth two times. Smurf stood near Jamal, like a pet dog, awaiting instructions.

"Sit down," Jamal said.

Smurf opened his mouth to protest just enough for his gold grill to shine in the dimly lit motel room. Jamal held up his hand before the boy could speak. He pointed towards the second bed and motioned for Smurf to sit down.

"Man," Smurf huffed as he dragged his feet to the bed. "I can help too, dog."

"Nigga," Jamal began. "Didn't I tell you what you can do? Drive. That's it. You aint go inside those fucking houses with us, nigga. Calm the fuck down and smoke or some shit. We done working. Get high and zone the fuck out cause I'm tired of hearing your fucking mouth."

"I can help, nigga," Smurf grumbled under his breath.

Jamal stepped towards Smurf's direction, his fists clenched and his face scrunched up in anger. By the time he took a second step, Diego caught Jamal's balled hand in his own. All the anger drained from Jamal's body. He looked back at Diego's welcoming face. He smiled.

"We got everything you asked for," Diego said, rubbing his thumb over the back of Jamal's hand. "You want to count the money with Romeo while I weigh the drugs?"

Jamal nodded and went over to the little work area Romeo and Diego set up. Jamal looked over his shoulder and cussed Smurf with his eyes. The stare and sentiment was returned in kind.

"Come on baby," Diego said, his voice soothing. "You been through enough tonight."

For the first time, Jamal didn't feel an ounce of shame

from the pet name. It felt appropriate. It felt right. Even the raised brow Romeo gave him didn't fluster how he felt at that moment. After everything that had went down that night, Jamal didn't give a damn about what Romeo, Smurf or anyone else thought about him and Diego. It felt good. It felt right.

Jamal, Diego and Romeo worked in silence. Diego sat at the top of the bed, undoing the packaged dope and weighing it. He kept a count on a tablet he found on the nightstand in the room. Jamal and Romeo separated the money by denomination.

There were a few moments where Romeo and Jamal's hand brushed against the other. Each time, Jamal felt like a strong current of electricity ran through his body. The first time it happened he ignored it. Then it kept happening. It got to the point where Jamal wondered if Romeo was doing it on purpose to just fuck with him.

Jamal tried to focus on Diego's foot rubbing against his leg but he couldn't knock the feeling of guilt that seemed to creep up his arm like a spider. Each time he looked at Diego and smiled. Luckily, Diego was oblivious. It made Jamal feel all that more guilty. As much as Jamal wanted to just focus his affection on Diego, he knew there was something between him and Romeo even if his former best friend hated him.

"I'm done," Diego announced.

Jamal simply nodded as he finished up putting stacks of cash in the machines. He was meticulous about the count, noting the raw number amount and the bill denomination before tallying up the amount. He had Romeo keep a running count along with him.

A huge grin spread on Jamal's face. "We made $107,285. Straight cash."

Diego jumped up and hugged Jamal and planted kisses all over his face. He fell on top of Jamal, grinding his hips into the crew leader's. Smurf sounded like he would cough up a lung when he heard the figure. He even dropped his blunt on his chest. Romeo sat there, smiling coolly. The only one that didn't celebrate was Bricks.

Jamal hugged Diego, reached around and grabbed his plump, Latin ass. "Your man made some cash tonight." He bit his bottom lip. "You going to give me some of that ass?"

Diego pushed up on Jamal's chest and smirked. "Papi, we both made some dough." His left brow rose. "So what does that mean?"

Jamal bit his bottom lip, rolled over and pressed his firm body against Diego's. "Shit, you tell me."

"Aye," Romeo said, interrupting the two love birds. "Before ya'll start doing whatever it is that ya'll are doing. How much money will all that dope bring us?"

Diego shrugged. He looked from Romeo to Jamal. "It all depends?"

Smurf sat up and cleared his throat. "On what?"

"On whether we sell the shit or give it to some street dealer who will want it at a discount."

"How much if we sold it?" Jamal asked.

"Street value?" Diego asked, his eyes protesting the idea of being a dope dealer. Everyone looked at him, awaiting an answer. "Maybe twenty-five, thirty thousand."

Jamal nodded. He calculated everything in his mind. His eyes were glued on Bricks as he thought. The room was quiet once again. All eyes were on Jamal. Each of them took in the thoughtful look on his face. After what seemed like an eternity, he began to move.

Jamal motioned for Diego and Romeo to move from the bed. Reluctantly, they both obliged, but their eyes were glued on the dope and the cash spread out on the bed.

Duffle bag in hand, Jamal packed up all the dope and the jewelry they had stolen from the men. He doubted it was worth more than a thousand dollars. Then Jamal reached for a couple of the stacks of cash and wrapped them in rubber bands. He threw them in the bag too. Jamal zipped up the bag. He counted off two more, much smaller wads of cash. He tossed the larger of the two rolls of money at Bricks.

"That's $2,000," Jamal said. "Thank you for your help." Jamal tossed him the duffle bag and the smaller wad of cash. "That's Slim's cut; $20,000, the dope and the shit we stole from them nigga's bodies. The two hundred should cover all the shit we got from Walmart."

Bricks stuffed the cash in his pockets. He sucked at his teeth as he looked down in the bag thoughtfully. After a long moment, he looked up at Jamal and nodded. He picked up his stuff, grabbed his keys and headed for the door. Jamal cut Bricks off before he made it to the door.

"Don't fuck with me, Bricks," Jamal said. His voice was low and level but still carried the intended threatening tone. "Make sure that nigga gets everything in that bag."

Bricks grinned nonchalantly. "I got you little nigga," he said. Bricks looked over his shoulder at the others and back at Jamal. "Try to relax. Enjoy yourselves for a few days before you all head back for the next assignment."

Jamal shook his head and stepped aside. Bricks began to whistle, *A Change is Gonna Come*, as he walked out the room.

Jamal gritted his teeth. He knew the song well. It was his father's favorite song. Jamal's old man played it every Sunday night. He wondered why the brute had chosen that moment to whistle that song.

No one in the room moved. Jamal just stood there, staring at the closed door as if he were looking right through it. The look on his face paralleled the expression Romeo wore on his face after the first night with Slim.

"Yo, can I get my cut now?" Smurf asked.

His shaky voice cut through the thickness in the room. Jamal snapped from his daze, wheeled on his heels and turned towards the weed head. Everyone could see the insults and curses on the tip of Jamal's tongue. Surprisingly, he didn't say anything. Jamal grabbed five thick rolls of cash, each totaling $5,000 and handed them to Romeo. He did the same for Diego. Jamal kept six rolls for himself and tossed one roll to Smurf.

Smurf was about to have a fit. Diego tossed him a roll before he could complain. Romeo didn't hesitate to do the same. The three of them looked at Jamal. Jamal rolled his eyes and sucked his teeth before he relented and tossed one of his rolls to Smurf. Diego stood up and patted Jamal on the shoulder.

"We're a team," he said. "Everyone has an important role to play."

Jamal nodded. He didn't agree but he didn't want to argue. Especially when Romeo obviously agreed even though he didn't say anything. Smurf was just a driver who didn't do a damn thing but bitch and moan in Jamal's mind.

It don't matter, Jamal thought. That nigga won't be around long.

Jamal stared at Smurf with a menacing glare. Smurf didn't back down. He put his money in his small suitcase and got under the covers of the bed. His gaze went to Romeo for a second. He licked his lips and looked back at Jamal, teasingly.

"Don't get too comfortable," Jamal said, loud enough for everyone in the room. "We not staying here."

"Wait, why not?" Diego asked.

"Why you think?" Jamal retorted. "That shit with Bricks. No way that bitch with him was his ex-wife. I don't give a fuck what he said. I don't trust that nigga and we definitely aint staying here after he done left."

"So where we going?" Smurf asked.

Jamal looked at him suspiciously. "Nigga, you'll see when we get there. But first we going to get another ride. I don't want to be riding in that bus of an SUV no more. It was stupid as fuck to get it in the first place."

No one argued. Everyone moved to pack their belongings. Even Romeo moved with purpose. Once they got in the SUV, with Jamal driving, Diego leaned over and whispered.

"Where we going, baby?"

Jamal smiled. He reached down and took the Latin thug's hand in his own. "We going to get another car. Something practical. And get a new room somewhere so we can rest and get ready for tomorrow."

"Get ready?" Diego asked. "We not heading back to Atlanta?"

Jamal shook his head. "Naw, Bricks said we had a couple days to relax."

"Shit," Diego began. "I aint known your black ass that long but I don't see you ever relaxing."

"You right," Jamal confirmed with a soft chuckle. "We

going up to Baltimore as soon as everyone is rested."

"What's in Baltimore?"

"Shit, what else? More money."

Chapter 16

Jamal felt the warmth of the sun tumbling between the open blinds onto his skin. He turned on his side and pulled the covers up to his chin. He was awake but he didn't feel like getting up. It was almost six in the morning when he finally collapsed onto the queen sized bed in the slightly cleaner motel Smurf had found after Romeo hotwired a new car; one that wouldn't raise as much suspicion with four young men of color riding in it.

After passing up three motels that Jamal said no to, they found one that took cash and didn't require ID. Smurf and Romeo went inside to get the room and came back with two keys. They had got two rooms that connected to each other. Any other time Jamal would have been irritated but he was too tired to complain and the idea of finally having some time alone with Diego made the situation easier to swallow. He didn't even let the idea of Smurf and Romeo being alone bother him that much.

I aint got no claim to that nigga, he had thought. Fuck it.

Jamal took in a deep breath and let the air flow gently from his lungs. He laid there and enjoyed the silence. There was little doubt in his mind that the peace and quiet would be gone soon enough. For now, he wanted to just enjoy the calm before the storm. And he knew a storm was coming.

As much as he tried, Jamal couldn't shake the feeling that something bad was going to happen. He never trusted Slim or Bricks for that matter. Jamal always had a critical eye on them niggas. He was still plotting on how he was going to eventually take Slim's ass out and put him six feet under. But something he couldn't put his finger on nagged at him. It was like a feeling that seemed to taunt him from the back of his mind and he just couldn't reach it.

So many things had went down that put Jamal on edge. First, Bricks waited until they were close as shit to D.C. to stop and get all the shit they needed. And then they boosted a truck that cost as much as some houses in Atlanta. And to add insult to injury, he brings some chick he says is his ex-wife back to the motel room.

If that nigga was trying to get some pussy he could have went to that bitch, Jamal thought. Something wasn't right about that hoe. She aint even flinch at the sight of a gun in her face.

Jamal reached up and rubbed the sleep from his eyes. He looked at the alarm clock on the dresser. It was a little past noon. He looked over at the two duffle bags holding his and Diego's cut from the stick ups from the night before. The smile that spread on his face from thinking about that cash slowly faded as a series of question exploded in his mind. They were so obvious that it scared him that he didn't think of them before.

Why did Bricks pick those specific trap houses to rob, Jamal thought. Did them niggas know Slim? Were they beefing?

More and more questions flooded Jamal's mind. Paranoia gripped him as he turned his head towards the door. He slid his hand under his pillow and gripped his Glock, finding reassurance in its presence. It took a while before he could shake the feeling that someone was after him and the crew and right on their asses.

It aint paranoia if someone really is following your ass, he thought.

Movement in the bed drew Jamal's attention away from his troubling thoughts. He looked over his shoulder and saw Diego, his mouth wide open, gently snoring and drooling onto the pillow. Jamal was tired and he knew everyone else was tired. Lying there, looking at the El Salvadorian thug made Jamal feel like he was invincible.

Diego was no super hero but he gave strength to Jamal. His support and love had given Jamal the courage to face all the things that worried him. Just a few weeks ago Jamal had no idea what it meant to be in love. Or that he could ever share something so deep and emotional with another man. But there he was, his Glock in his hand and his nigga in the bed next to him. Despite the shit him and the crew were in, there was nowhere else Jamal wanted to be.

Jamal turned around and faced Diego. He looked at his face, studying it as if he could commit it to memory. The lines of Diego's nose and jaw line were so prominent but soft. His eyebrows, Jamal's favorite part of his face, were thick and bushy and almost connected. The wisp of a mustache above his thin, pick lips was a testament to the fact that he was a man wholly invested in shedding his youth. Many times he had seen Diego brushing the impossibly thin thatch of hair.

Jamal let go of the gun, reached up and ran his fingers through Diego's jet black hair. He was gentle as not to awake him. The feel of the soft, long strands between his finger tips made Jamal smile. Diego made him happy. Happy in a way that no one had ever made him feel.

Yet, despite how the Latin thug softened Jamal's heart, the crew leader knew that the boy wasn't his. He might have professed his love for Jamal but he was still in a relationship with some chick back in Atlanta. It was a fact that Jamal made sure he never forgot.

Jamal got lost in his thoughts of Diego and his hand pressed against his head. Diego shifted and moved onto his stomach. He was still sleep but the snoring and drooling had stopped. Jamal let the tips of his fingers play with the wisps of hair on the nape of Diego's neck. A small moan left Diego's limber body. Jamal's manhood responded to the sound.

Jamal inched closer until his leg pressed against Diego's bare flesh. He didn't remember seeing Diego get in the bed naked or taking off his own clothes for that matter. Jamal bit at his bottom lip, thinking about Diego stripping him as he slept. He wondered if his freaky ass copped a feel or not. He wouldn't have minded either way.

Emboldened, Jamal moved his hands down Diego's neck along the curve of his spine down to the small of his back. He flattened his palm and pressed his hand against the warm flesh. Jamal moved his hand to Diego's ass cheek and gave it a gentle squeeze. Another moan echoed through Diego's body. Jamal's dick was brick hard.

The young hustler's heart raced. His mouth was whet with anticipation. He reached up and pulled the covers back, slowly revealing Diego's smooth, naked flesh. Awestruck, Jamal clenched his jaw and gazed down on his Latin lover's body. His skin seemed to glow like gold the way the sun cascaded over his flesh.

Jamal got up and straddled Diego's thighs. He bent down and planted a kiss on the back of Diego's neck. Slowly, Jamal worked his way down, pressing his moist lips against Diego's hot, tender skin. A heartier moan reverberated from Diego's body. Jamal made it to the small of his back and stuck his tongue out. His wet, fleshy muscle glided all the way down to the crack of Diego's ass. Jamal leaned down and gently bit at Diego's left butt cheek, holding the supple flesh between his teeth as he pulled away and made a sucking sound.

"Good morning to you too," Diego said groggily.

"Morning beautiful," Jamal replied. He gripped both of Diego's ass cheeks in his strong hands.

"Don't start something you can't finish," Diego warned.

"I always finish what I start," Jamal said. "You best believe that."

Jamal parted Diego's ass and exposed his cinnamon brown rose bud. His dick aching at the beckoning hole. Without thought or concern, Jamal bent down and buried his face in his ass. His tongue pressed against the El Salvadorian's tights hole, prying the sphincter open. He darting in and out until he worked the meaty fuck tool inside Diego's body.

Diego arched his ass in the air and steeled his body,

meeting the thrust of Jamal's mouth into his bowels. He clawed at the sheets and buried his face into the pillow to stifle the moans forcing their way out of his young, taut body.

"Damn!" Diego moaned. "That feels so fucking good!"

Jamal ate at his boy's ass hungrily. His finger dug into his ass cheeks as he tried to pull them back further so he could go deeper. Jamal pulled away and sucked in a hard breath. He looked down at the glistening, wet hole he was eating. Blood rushed from his head to his dick. Jamal smacked Diego's plump, firm ass right before he bent back down and pushed his tongue back inside of Diego as far as he could.

Diego pressed his ass back and began to fuck himself on Jamal's tongue. "Damn, papi," he cooed. "Fuck me, nigga. Fuck me!"

Jamal pulled away from Diego's ass and wiped the saliva from his mouth and chin. He reached over onto the nightstand and pulled out the lube and a Magnum. Jamal strapped up and smeared a generous amount of lube on his engorged dick and Diego's hole. He pressed his shaft against the hole, rubbing his dick over Diego's crack. Jamal smacked the boy's cheeks, hard.

"You ready for this dick?" Jamal asked. "Cause I aint holding shit back, boy."

"Yes," Diego said, his breath labored.

"Do you want this dick?" Jamal teased. He held his pole by its thick base and smacked at Diego's wanting hole. "I need you to tell me you want it."

"Yes, papi, please fuck me," Diego begged.

Jamal pressed his left hand on the small of Diego's back as he scooted up and lined the thick tip of his head with Diego's entrance. Sweat from want and desire slickened both of their young bodies as Jamal pushed the head inside Diego's bowels. The Hispanic thug's body shook, like he was going into convulsions, as inch after thick inch burrowed inside him. Once Jamal bottomed out, he collapsed on top of Diego and bit at his ear.

"Do you feel me?" Jamal asked as he rotated his hips, driving his dick deeper inside. "You better answer me."

Diego gripped at the head board. "Fuuuucccckk!"

Jamal bit and sucked at Diego's neck as he fucked him. He reached down between Diego's legs and wrapped his fingers around the boy's hot, thick shaft. Jamal pumped his dick in unison with each stroke.

Moans of pleasure and flesh smacking against flesh echoed in the small room. Diego turned his head and kissed Jamal. They sucked at each other's mouths like starved dogs. Diego came first. His body shuddered and his ass clenched unimaginably tight around Jamal's dick. Jamal felt the cum in his palm as Diego's orgasm tumbled over him like waves. The sensation took Jamal over the precipice. His body steeled. He pressed inside of Diego as deeply as possible as he released his seed.

Spent, Jamal rolled over on his back, sucking in heavy breathes. He felt light headed. His balls tingled, in a good way. A small smile covered his face as he reached down and smacked Diego's sweat laden ass cheek.

"Oh my God," Diego said. "That shit was fucking amazing."

"I know right."

"You might as well turn over," Diego said. "Cause it's my turn, nigga."

BANG! BANG! BANG!

"Ya'll done fucking yet?" Smurf asked from behind the door connecting the two rooms.

Jamal looked over at a disappointed Diego and shrugged.

"It's all good," Diego said. "I'm going to get some of that ass. Just don't be surprised when I try to taste all that chocolate."

Jamal shook his head and threw his legs over the bed. "What the fuck you want, Smurf?"

"Ya'll need to get up," Smurf answered. "We got moves to make."

Jamal went to the restroom, washed up and threw on a pair of shorts. He went to the door between the rooms and opened it. Smurf stood there, fully dressed with a stupid grin on his face. Jamal wanted to smack him so badly.

"What moves you talking about, nigga?" Jamal asked. "Ya'll supposed to be getting some rest before we make these moves tonight."

His eyes darted past the weed head into the room. Jamal caught sight of Romeo ironing his clothes. He only had on a pair of boxers. Jamal quickly scanned the room and saw that one of the beds was made up. Like it was never used. Romeo had a shirt on the disheveled bed. Jamal doubted Smurf would have made his bed up that well if at all. Jamal's mind raced.

"We trying to go to the mall and get an outfit and shit."

Jamal shook his head. "I already told ya'll that we going to Baltimore to scout some spots out to rob later tonight. We aint got time for all that."

Jamal started to close his door but Smurf pressed it back open. "We can't scout until later tonight," Smurf reasoned. "Besides, I want to get some fresh kicks and an outfit for when we go out."

"Go out?" Jamal asked, baffled. "Why the fuck would we go out? We trying to make money, nigga. We aint got time for all that other bullshit."

Smurf stood there like his hopes and dreams had been shattered. Jamal smiled on the inside for being the cause of the boy's depressed mood. Yet it was short lived. Romeo walked up to the door and looked Jamal right in the eye.

"Get dressed," Romeo said in an even tone. "We're going to the mall and enjoy a little bit of the money we risked our lives to get. We're not going to splurge and bring too much attention to ourselves. We'll be careful. After that, we're going to head up to Baltimore, get a room and find out where some of the trap houses are. We'll get some rest before we go rob them and be done by midnight. After that, we're going to the club. Tomorrow we'll head back to Atlanta."

Jamal stood there and stared at Romeo. Part of him screamed to say no to all the shit he'd just said but something cautioned him against crossing Romeo. He was the crew leader but he needed loyalty and if that meant a trip to the mall and some club, so be it. Jamal nodded.

"Alright," Jamal agreed. "Sounds like a plan. But we need to make a stop first."

Romeo shrugged and went back to the ironing board. Smurf frowned. "A stop where," he asked.

"A used car dealership," Jamal said, smiling. "I need to get me a whip cause I'm not going to be cruising at the mall in some stolen shit."

Chapter 17

The chubby, bald headed used car salesman dropped the keys to the jet black Ford F250 truck in Jamal's hands. *This baby is mine*, Jamal thought. He looked at the dealer, salivating over the eight grand in cash he handed to him for the truck. It was an older model but it had less than 100,000 miles and the interior was well taken care of. It was a good first vehicle for any young man. Jamal and Romeo stepped out of the cramp office and went to the truck.

"Did Diego or Smurf hit you up and say where they were?" Jamal asked as he revved up the engine. "I haven't heard from either one of them all day."

"No," Romeo said. He offered no further explanation and just looked out the passenger window.

Jamal exhaled loudly as he backed out of the dealership. Romeo's dismissive and nonchalant attitude was working his last nerve. When Romeo said he was going to the dealership instead of going to eat with Diego and Smurf, it surprised Jamal. It even elicited a suspicious look from Diego. Based on the way he acted the last few days, being around Jamal seemed like the last thing he wanted to do.

"Could you do me a favor and text them and find out so we can get rid of that Escalade and head up to Baltimore?" Jamal asked politely as possible. "We need to take care of that shit as soon as possible. Last thing we need is for them to get caught up and carried off in someone's jail."

He watched his onetime best friend from the corner of his eyes. Romeo pulled out his phone and began texting. He didn't look annoyed or angry. Ambivalence was the only word that seemed to fit his disposition in Jamal's mind. Distant, maybe. That troubled Jamal the most. At least when he went off on Jamal in the Walmart parking lot a few days ago there was some type of emotion.

Jamal pulled into a McDonald's drive thru and ordered some burgers and fries. He didn't ask Romeo what he wanted. He just ordered what he remembered Romeo liked. He knew if he had actually asked he would have gotten a smart ass reply. He just wasn't in the mood.

Jamal went to a gas station next to fill up. He and Romeo sat in the truck, eating in silence. Finally, Romeo's phone went off. Jamal looked at him expectantly. Romeo didn't flinch. He sat there and acted like Jamal wasn't even looking at him. Jamal shook his head, went outside and removed the gas nozzle from the truck. He went back in the car, sat and waited. Finally, he looked over at Romeo.

"Where we going, Romeo?" he asked. Jamal tried not to sound annoyed. "I still don't know where Diego and Smurf are right now."

"They're in Baltimore already," Romeo calmly explained. "They got a room. Some hotel they found downtown."

Jamal exhaled loudly and put the truck in drive. He couldn't blame the two of them for heading to Baltimore and getting a room. It had taken him longer than expected to get the truck. He haggled with the dealer for more than an hour. Jamal got on the highway and merged onto 295. Baltimore was a straight shot.

Jamal turned the radio up and tried to focus on the music but his mind wouldn't let him. For the next thirty minutes he would be alone with Romeo. It was the best opportunity he had to talk to his boy and finally try to squash all the bad blood between them. There had to be a reason for Romeo to invite himself to the dealership with Jamal, knowing they'd be alone together. Jamal just hoped that he was ready to talk things out too.

"Do you think you could ever forgive me for what happened?" Jamal asked, not knowing how else to initiate the conversation.

"You mean for what you did," Romeo countered. There was a distinct edge to his voice that wasn't there just moments ago. "Something didn't just happen. You raped me, nigga."

Jamal clenched the steering wheel. "You're right," Jamal conceded. He figured there was no point in arguing when trying to seek forgiveness. And at the end of the day, he did rape Romeo, even if it was at the threat of death from Slim. "Do you think you could ever forgive me?"

"What the fuck do you want forgiveness for?" Romeo asked. "It aint like we got to be friends to run up in trap houses and get paid. We work together. That's it."

That edge in his voice teetered over to a controlled anger. Jamal sighed and shook his head. Guilt spread through him like blood in water. He sincerely wanted his friend back but his motives were tainted by want and lust. How could Jamal ever tell Romeo that the incident that had put him on the brink of insanity had opened up a new world for Jamal? Jamal loved Romeo and not just as a friend. And that love made him feel guilty every moment of everyday.

"You been my boy since grade school," Jamal explained. "We been through a lot together. You're my best friend, Romeo. I just want to get back to where we were before all this shit with Slim happened."

Silence filled the small space between them. Jamal kept looking over at Romeo, waiting for a reply. Then, Romeo turned and stared directly at Jamal. The look on his face was hard to read.

"Just friends?" Romeo asked.

Before Jamal could say anything he felt Romeo's hand running over his stomach. His body tensed. He was so surprised that he almost swerved into the lane next to him. Jamal looked over at Romeo, baffled. He saw something he had dreamed of seeing since he felt his boy's soft insides; lust and desire. Jamal's dick stirred in his pants.

Romeo eased his hand down to the buckle of Jamal's pants. "I know you want to be more than just friends, nigga. Aint that right?"

Jamal's eyes jumped from the road down to Romeo's hand and back. He searched for a response to Romeo's piercing question but he only stammered and mumbled something unintelligible.

Romeo unfastened Jamal's pants and let down his zipper. He slipped his hand over Jamal's underwear bulge and cupped his heavy balls over the cotton fabric. Romeo leaned over the arm rest, until he was only inches from Jamal's face.

"This is why I can never forgive your faggot ass," Romeo hissed. "Slim may have made you do that shit but you can't tell me that you didn't want to. You've always wanted to fuck me."

Romeo squeezed Jamal's sac, hard, before he could protest. He swerved as he reached down and snatched Romeo's hands from his balls. Tears of pain welled in his eyes as he looked over at Romeo. He fought the urge to back hand his boy right then and there.

"What the fuck is wrong with you?!?"

"What's wrong with me? Naw, what the fuck is wrong with you!?! Here I thought I was the one that almost went crazy. You must be out of your mind if you think I could ever forgive you for what the fuck you did. I don't trust you. You raped me, Jamal!"

Jamal hit the steering wheel. "Fuck! I know!" Tears streamed down his face. "I'm sorry. You have no idea how sorry I am. I wish I could go back and not let that shit happen. I wish I didn't ever come up with that stupid ass idea to run up in that trap house like I knew what the fuck I was doing. I'm sorry."

Again, the tight space in the truck got quiet. The tears had dried on Jamal's face. Romeo slouched in his seat, the expression on his face as blank as it was on the first day Jamal saw him on the edge of being bat shit crazy. The tension between the two of them was palpable. Romeo turned and looked at Jamal.

"I don't believe you," he said. "You might think that you are sorry but I just can't accept that shit."

"Why not?" Jamal asked in a whisper. He felt guilty for even asking.

Romeo's nostrils flared. "I have nightmares of that day. Sometimes I wake up, drenched in sweat and can't close my eyes again. And I don't ask myself why it happened but I do have a lot of questions." He looked out his window blankly. "Was your dick hard when Bricks held me down on the pool table?"

Jamal clenched his jaw shut. He knew the answer to the question and knew Romeo did too. He was just making a point that Jamal was well aware of. Jamal didn't say anything.

"How about when you were fucking me," Romeo started. "What was going through you mind? Did you wish you could have fucked me without Slim and Bricks there? And how about after you nutted. Did you want to fuck me again?"

Jamal just sat there. He didn't have an answer for Romeo. His silence only enraged Romeo even more.

"You don't want to go back to the way things were, nigga. Admit it," Romeo demanded. "In your sick, twisted mind you thought we could work things out and be together is some type of faggot relationship. Is that why you fucking that Spanish nigga while you keep giving me the eye. You trying to make me jealous or some bullshit? Show me what it could be like with you?"

Jamal cupped his mouth and pinched the bridge of his nose with his thumb and finger. His ears burned. The blood in his brain throbbed without mercy. Romeo's barrage of questions was beginning to take its toll. Jamal looked over at Romeo, his eyes blood shot red and full of remorse.

"Fine, I get it," Jamal said. He couldn't take being a punching bag anymore. "So what now? You hate me? Do you want to kill me? Should I be watching my back?"

The anger drained from Romeo's face. He sighed. "No, I don't want to kill you. And I don't know if I hate you. I'm just mad as fuck and I can't really put into words how what you did makes me feel. I just feel violated."

"I know."

"No, you don't. You've been like a brother to me for years. Even though you punked me and wore my shit when I said no you still had my back. I trusted you. I trusted your dumb ass enough to run up in that house with you. I'm not stupid, Jamal. I knew shit could have went south from the jump. But I went anyways."

Jamal frowned. "So what are you saying? Are we boys? You my nigga?"

"Naw," Romeo said, shaking his head. "I don't hate you but I sure as hell don't trust you anymore. I don't know where that puts us. You not my friend. But we do have to work together, for now. And as long as we're running up into trap houses I'm going to do what needs to be done to make sure you, me, Smurf and Diego make it out alive. That's all I can promise right now, man."

Jamal nodded. "I guess I can't ask for much more."

The conversation ended there. Jamal had so many more questions he wanted answered but knew he had no place to ask them. He wanted to know what, if anything, was going on between Romeo and Smurf. And he wanted to know how Romeo went from being crazy to a cold hearted and meticulous stickup boy over night. The questions seared the back of his mind but he dared not ask them. He gotten the most important question answered. Romeo didn't hate him but he didn't trust him. In Jamal's mind there was still hope. There was room to rebuild.

Once they made it to the hotel in Baltimore Jamal cringed. It was nice. Too nice for a group of black and Hispanic kids who were trying to stay out of sight and out of mind. To add insult to injury, Smurf and Diego had a suite that had an in-room kitchen and two bedrooms. Jamal had decided on the elevator that he was going to fuck up Smurf and cuss Diego out as soon as he saw them.

"Baby don't get mad," Diego said as soon as Jamal stepped inside the room. "We didn't pay for the room." Jamal frowned. "Well, we paid for it but not at the desk. We got a guy to pay for the room for us. He thought we were a couple or some shit and thought we were cute. Some old white guy."

Jamal shook his head, too tired to argue. "Whatever, I don't even care anymore. I just want to take a shower and get a quick nap in."

Diego put his hand on Jamal's shoulder, squeezing it. "What's wrong? Did something happen on the ride up here?" His eyes shifted over to the couch where Romeo sat. "Did that nigga say something to make you upset?"

"Yea," Jamal admitted. "But he had every right to. He had some shit he was carrying and he got it off his chest. We're good for now."

Diego only nodded. His eyes still focused on Romeo. Jamal could tell that the boy wanted blood. He reached up and cupped Diego's face and pulled him in close.

"Why don't you hate me," Jamal asked.

Diego frowned, confused. "What? Why would I hate you?"

"Because of what Slim made me do to you."

Diego hung his head for a moment. He looked back up and wrapped his arms around Jamal's waist. "Is that what's bothering you? Romeo is mad because of what Slim made you do to him? Look, I understand that you had no choice. Slim is a vicious dude and no one goes against what that nigga says. No one. And to be honest, I kind of liked it. Besides, despite how fucked up it is, if that shit didn't happen you wouldn't be my nigga now."

Diego leaned in and kissed Jamal on the lips. He pressed his forehead against Jamal's and looked him in the eyes. Jamal felt a calm come over him. Even though he wanted to say something about Diego's girlfriend back home, Jamal just enjoyed the moment.

"Since ya'll kissed and made up," Smurf said, "can we go to the mall now? It's getting late."

"Yea man," Jamal relented. "Ya'll figure out where the mall is?"

"Yup," Diego said. "It's right back down on 295. Called Arundel Mills. Supposed to be big as shit and nice. Even got a theatre and a Dave and Buster's."

"Alright, good, good," Jamal said, thinking up a plan of action. "I'm going to drop you guys off and run some errands. You all might as well eat, catch a movie and hang out for a while."

"What errands you running, papi?" Diego asked. "Want me to come with you?"

"Naw I got it. I'm going to need to come back to Baltimore and get the word on the street on what dealers got the best shit and where they operate. Can't rob niggas we don't know where they deal from. It might take a while and it

BEAST

probably be easier if I was alone looking like I was trying to cop some shit."

"Sounds good to me," Smurf said, "let's go!"

Jamal was the last one out the room. His body ached and his head hurt. He felt a migraine coming. The only thing that helped him keep going was the promise of money to be made. Now, he was actually looking forward to hitting the club after they went through some Baltimore niggas. Some relaxation and celebration was long overdue.

Chapter 18

"How much did we make this time?" Smurf asked.

Jamal looked up at him, annoyed, and shook his head. If Diego and Romeo weren't hovering over him waiting for an answer he would have ignored the inquiry. He started wrapping the cash up in rubber bands.

"$64,820," He said. "Not as much as last night but it aint a small drop in the bucket. And besides, we aint splitting any of this with Slim. This is all ours."

"I'm going to be balling like a motherfucker tonight!" Smurf said. He rubbed his hands together and bit at his bottom lip. A distant, plotting stare darkened his face. "Yea, going to get me some bitches too."

"Isn't it kind of late to be going out to a club?" Jamal asked. "Why don't we just get some rest so that we can head out tomorrow?"

Jamal looked to Diego. He just shrugged. His gaze shifted to Smurf. He looked like he wanted to protest but surprisingly he held his tongue for once. Then Jamal's eyes settled on Romeo.

"It's only midnight," Romeo said. "We can get dressed and be at the club in an hour. Besides, I'm not trying to head back so soon. I don't know about Diego but none of us have been outside of Atlanta. Baltimore is known for its crabs. I want to go to some crab shack tomorrow before we leave. May as well enjoy all that Baltimore has to offer."

Jamal sucked his teeth and shook his head. His eyes again went to Smurf. Jamal wondered how much of what Romeo had said was really what Smurf wanted. And how he knew that Smurf hadn't traveled outside of Atlanta. He doubted it was true since he knew his way around D.C. The weed head was grinning from ear to ear. Jamal gave in.

"Fine, then ya'll need to hurry up and get dressed," he said. "Oh, and were not taking all this money with us. We're going to split that $820 up four ways and that's it for the night. Two hundred dollars should be enough to have a good time at some fucking club."

No one argued. Jamal headed for the bedroom as everyone else was pulling off clothes and pulling out the outfits they'd gotten from the mall. There was so much going on and there was no way Jamal was going to be able to keep control of the group. Smurf was the most vocal, but he knew Romeo and Diego would want to splurge at some point. They all had made $25,000 the night before and $16,000 just a few hours ago. Jamal couldn't blame them. He'd gone out and bought a truck earlier that afternoon.

As much as Jamal hated to admit it, this wasn't his crew.

These weren't his boys. These were just a group of grown ass kids who wanted to make money because they'd never had anything and were guided by a fucked up drug dealer who wanted to be a pimp and drug lord at the same time. Jamal went to his and Diego's room and got in the bed. He laced his fingers behind his head and stared at the ceiling, thinking.

Jamal could see the bonds between the four of them unraveling before his eyes. Diego was the only one who had any type of loyalty. But even that was as fickle as the supposed love they shared. Jamal was still on the fence with that whole thing.

He didn't trust Smurf as far as he could throw his conniving ass. Jamal was still trying to think of a way to kill him. Even though the dude wasn't as annoying as when they first met, Jamal still believed that he would put a knife in his back if given a chance. Naw, Jamal had decided a long time ago to strike first and strike hard. Then there was Romeo.

He had been Jamal's best friend since they were in grade school but with all they'd been through even he couldn't be depended upon. To top it all off, Jamal knew they needed another member to make sure their stickups didn't run into any issues like the first night.

Considering everything that could have possibly went wrong with the rag-tag team, Jamal wondered how they had made it through that first night.

Shit, maybe that was why Slim put us all together, Jamal thought. So that we'd end up dead. But why? He could have killed us all in his pool hall back in Atlanta.

There were no answers, just questions, and it was making Jamal's head hurt. It seemed like the world was crumbling around him and he didn't know what to do. He looked over at the duffle bags full of money. For the first time in his life, he wondered if all the bullshit he was dealing with was worth it. With the crew or alone, Jamal knew that he had the skills and drive to make money. But now he knew it came at a price.

"Hey babe," Diego called from the door. "You alright? Look like you got the weight of the world on your shoulders. Been looking upset all day. "

"Yea, I'll be okay." Jamal's brow wrinkled as he let out a heavy sigh. "Just got a lot on my mind, that's all."

Diego came in and sat down on the edge of the bed. He rested his hand on Jamal's stomach and gently stoked at the crew leader's midsection. Diego gave Jamal a look that meant only one thing; talk or else.

"What are you going to do with your money when you get back to Atlanta?" Jamal asked.

Diego frowned and smiled at the same time. "Um, I don't know. Buy a car," he teased.

Jamal laughed. "I'm being serious."

"Shit, me too, *papi*. I needs me a whip to keep tabs on your ass. Besides I want something that's mine. You know? Never really had my own shit."

"So you going to spend forty-grand on a souped up car? What? You want the candy paint and hydraulics and shit? Be all flashy making niggas jealous."

"Naw, I don't need all that. Just something simple but nice that will get me from point A to point B. Besides, I got my *abuela* and little brothers and sisters to think about. I can't buy a house but I can put them in a nicer apartment with nice furniture and appliances that work."

"That's wassup. They're lucky to have you, Diego. You're

a real special dude."

"I know, *papi*. I know."

"So you going to stay with them or get your own place? I'm sure Isabella wouldn't mind playing house. You know these females bitch and moan about that illegal shit until they got some dough in they hands."

Diego's brow frowned. The slits of his eyes narrowed at he stared Jamal in the face. "Is that what's been bothering you? That why you been acting so distant with me? I was wondering why you was giving me the cold shoulder."

Jamal shrugged. "Maybe. How can I trust you when you say that you love me and you got some chick back home? I mean, I don't know what we are. I'm not saying I'd have it all figured out if you were just with me but it'd be a start."

Diego held his hand up and motioned for Jamal to stop talking. "I called Isabella a couple of nights ago and broke up with her. I'm not in this for a quick nut and I don't play with people's feelings, Jamal. I want to be with you. When I said that I loved you I meant it. It's you and me, you understand?"

Jamal looked down at his palms and simply nodded. He didn't know what to say.

"But I'm not blind," Diego said. "I see how you look at Romeo. And I can't help but wonder if he ever wanted you then you'd drop me in second to be with him."

"Romeo isn't gay," Jamal said bluntly. "Aint shit going on with us."

Diego's face scrunched up. I stood up and circled the bed. "That's not the issue. I need to know that if I give myself to you then you'll be there regardless of anything. I need you to be my rock and Romeo not being gay isn't a good enough answer." Diego ran his fingers through his hair. "And if you don't see what's going on between him and Smurf then you must be blind."

"What? They're fucking?"

Diego cursed in Spanish. "Why do you even care if they're fucking? That's what I'm talking about. You can't have me now only to drop me when your best friend stops being mad at you and helplessly falls in love with you. I can't be your back-up plan. You need to choose. I need to be your first and only choice."

Jamal looked up at Diego and saw the hurt in his eyes. For the first time he knew that the El Salvadorian was being sincere. Diego stood there, vulnerable. Jamal wanted to be his rock, his lover, his everything but he just couldn't cut off how he felt for Romeo. But it didn't matter. He knew that no matter what, the divide between him and Romeo might mend one day but it would never be as strong as the love between him and Diego could be.

Jamal stood up and walked up to Diego. He pressed his forehead against Diego's. They're eyes locked. Jamal reached over and laced his fingers with Diego's.

"You're the only one I want," Jamal said. "You're the only one I need. And when we get back I want us to find a place to get. Just you and me."

Diego grinned from ear to ear. He leaned in and pressed his lips against Jamal's. The kiss was long and purposeful. Jamal wrapped his arms around Diego as the two of them stumbled back onto the bed. Just as Jamal ran his hands up Diego's shirt there was a bang at the door.

"It's 12:30," Smurf said through the door. "Ya'll hurry up so we can ride out."

Diego pressed his hand onto Jamal's chest. "You lucky,

papi. You know you owe me some ass."

"Hold up, I think we need to talk about this sex thing," Jamal said, grinning.

"What you mean?" Diego asked. He stood up from the bed. "We equals. We fuck each other or don't fuck at all."

Jamal opened his mouth but snapped it back shut as he thought about what he was going to say. "You're right," Jamal conceded.

"Good, cause I aint bout to be no nigga's bottom bitch. Fuck that."

"Bottom bitch?"

Diego's face got red. "Never mind."

Jamal was about to press for an explanation but Diego ran over to the bags he'd gotten from the mall. He pulled out two outfits. He handed one to Jamal.

"You trying to dress me now?" Jamal asked.

Diego shrugged. "It's not hard to figure out your style. Besides, if we stepping out my nigga got to look fresh as me, right?"

Jamal nodded. "Yea, you right. You going to plug the iron up?"

"Yea, I got you"

Jamal looked at the clothes and smiled. It wasn't something that he would typically wear but it was fly. The high cut v-neck and the dark cargo jeans along with the necklace and bracelet looked alright. Jamal stripped down to his draws and walked over to the iron with his shirt. Diego eyed Jamal and bit his bottom lip. He walked over to Jamal and cupped his bulge in his hand.

"Can I taste that chocolate, papi?"

"I don't think we have time for all that."

"Just iron," Diego said. "I'll get my fill."

Diego stepped behind Jamal and pulled his underwear down to the middle of his thighs. Jamal looked back, confused. Then it became clear. Diego buried his face in Jamal's ass and flickered his tongue over his hole. He reached around and stroked Jamal's brick hard dick as he ate his ass.

Undulating waves of pleasure slammed into Jamal's body and settled in an insistent tingling in his ass and the tip of his dick. He'd forgotten to iron his shirt. His eyes were tightly shut and he was bracing himself against the creaky ironing board. He was close to climax when there was another bang on the door.

"Let's go guys," Smurf said. "We're ready!"

Diego pulled back and sighed. He pulled Jamal's underwear back up and gently patted him on the ass.

"Tonight," Diego threatened. "I don't want to hear no shit. That ass is mine, *papi*."

Jamal shook his head. "We'll see." He looked at Diego and wondered how much he could trust him with the doubts and suspicions he had. "Have you given any thought to what we talked about a few days ago in the shower, when we first got up here? About Slim."

"Yea," Diego admitted. His voice lowered. "I'm not sure if going after Slim is a good idea. I don't think you really understand how connected that nigga is up and down the east coast."

"It don't matter," Jamal barked. "All I need is a bullet and opportunity."

"You don't think anyone would come back and retaliate?"

"I doubt anyone gives a fuck enough about that nigga to come like that. I'm pretty sure we're not the only one's he's fucked with. I'm pretty sure that if we did enough digging we'd find mad dirt on his ass. He's a grimy dude, that's who he is."

"So why are you so intent on killing him?"

"Why do you think?" Jamal asked as if the answer were obvious.

Diego shrugged. "If we hit off a couple of more drug dealers we'll all have paid our debt by the end of the year. So it can't be that. Maybe because he raped you like he raped me. Or maybe because how he messed up you and Romeo's friendship. I don't know why you want to retaliate so badly. Especially when it'd be easier to hustle, get cash and move on."

"My pride won't let me move on," Jamal admitted. "I'll be honest. I need to kill that nigga for all the reasons you just mentioned. And this robbing niggas aint going to last, not with Romeo and Smurf. Them niggas not loyal like we are to each other."

"I get that. But what can you do? We still need to pay Slim before we can step out on our own."

"Kill that nigga. Shit is simple as day to me."

"Fine. How you going to do it? And when?"

"I don't know yet," Jamal said. The lie slipped through his lips with an ease that scared even him. He'd worked out some details of a plan already. He just needed to know Diego had his back when the time came. "Just tell me that you got my back when I do figure that shit out."

"Don't worry about me. I'm down for whatever you want, *papi*. It's me and you. To the end."

"Cool," Jamal said.

He got dressed. Jamal strapped his gun on the inside of his

thigh when Diego wasn't looking. Taking out Slim wasn't going to happen anytime soon but if the chance to kill Smurf's ass came up tonight he'd sure as hell wanted to be prepared to take it.

Chapter 19

Jamal leaned over the balcony and scanned the massive dance floor for the third time that night. For an hour he'd endured the bullshit house music that made his head pound and let Romeo, Diego and Smurf enjoy themselves. The only reason he didn't turn around and leave when he stepped in the club was because Smurf offered to get a private VIP room where the music wasn't nearly as loud.

Even Jamal had to admit that the room was nice. It was on the second level, had its own security guard, some plush sofas, a complimentary bottle and a huge, heavy curtain that almost silenced the room from the noise below when closed. Based on the crowd and the clean, sleek layout, it was a hot club.

This shit probably cost a grip, Jamal thought. Probably making a grip every night, too.

Jamal was pretty sure Smurf and even Romeo and Diego had brought more than the $200 he told them to take to the club. There was no way Smurf got one of eight of the VIP rooms in a club that had over a thousand folks on just $200. Jamal didn't care. As much as he could, he tried to relax and enjoy himself. Jamal had been in the room the whole time they were there. He wasn't a dancer and he wasn't in the mood to be around a bunch of drunken strangers.

He looked over the crowd again and an especially animated circle of people caught his eye. It was Smurf and the rest of them. They were near the DJ booth surrounded by a group of people laughing and hugging in a drunken melancholy. Diego was doing some Latin moves on a pretty redbone. A hint of jealousy poked at Jamal. The way he laughed and grinded into the girl made Jamal uncomfortable. He wondered if Diego would have snuck the girl into the VIP room to fuck her if he hadn't come.

I could have stayed at the fucking room for this bullshit, he thought. Shouldn't have let these niggas drag me out in first place.

The club was only a mile or so from the hotel and they could have gotten a cab. Jamal had suggested as much when they were in the truck about to ride out. Smurf had had a foot out the door when he suggested it and Diego didn't even protest. It was Romeo that said no and essentially dragged him to the club. Jamal's eyes moved to Romeo.

His boy was chatting it up with a strikingly pretty brown-skinned chick whose hair flowed down to the back of her red polo shirt. She wore cargo shorts and sneakers. Her demeanor and dress evoked a very masculine disposition but her face and smile looked homely and sweet. Jamal frowned, wondering what Romeo and the girl were talking about and why he'd struck up a conversation with a girl that didn't seem like she'd be sexually interested in him or any other man. She was pointing at something. Jamal followed the path. Smurf.

The recluse was surrounded by a bevy of females. Jamal wondered if one or more of them were friends of the girl Romeo was talking to. If they were they definitely were having a good time with Smurf. The inept driver had his shirt off and held what look like a bottle of Grey Goose in his hand. Jamal hated to admit it but the boy's body was looking on point in the barely lit, strobe light flooded dance floor, especially when he raised his bottle and poured its contents down one of the chick's throat.

Jamal rubbed his eyes and cut the thought that Smurf looked good from his mind like it was cancer in the brain. He was sure that he was just tired. That was the only way he could see Smurf as more than the leech that he was. Or it could have been the blunt he rolled and smoked on the balcony a few minutes ago. He hadn't smoked in what seemed like forever. Jamal stood up from the rail and was about to go back into the room when Smurf's head swiveled up in his direction.

They're eyes locked for a moment and Smurf smiled. Jamal recoiled. Smurf handed the half empty bottle in his hand to one of the females and began to wade his way through the crowd. He was headed back up to the VIP room. Jamal groaned and went back inside. He slid the curtains shut behind him and flopped down on the plush sofa. He pulled out the bag of Kush he had and began breaking the buds down. By the time he was sprinkling the weed into the blunt the door to the room swung open. It was Smurf.

His eyes glazed over at the sight of the weed. Smurf smiled, revealing the gaudy gold grill in his mouth, and nodded his head like him and Jamal had been boys for years. He flopped down on the couch and sat uncomfortably close to the crew leader. Jamal looked over at the boy in disgust, shrugged his shoulders dismissively and focused back on his blunt.

As much as Jamal tried to send a clear message of disdain he couldn't help but look over the wanna-be trap boy's smooth, wiry but taut body. The hood tats on his arms glistened with sweat. His small but defined chest and abs flexed with each heavy breath he took. Even the smell of musk, sweat and cologne emanating from Smurf's body aroused something very basic and sexual in Jamal. The crew leader struggled to squelch the unnerving attraction.

"I got some to match, nigga," Smurf said as he reached in his pocket. "Let me put in on this."

Jamal slipped his hand to his hip as he eyed the boy suspiciously. He may have been high but he wasn't slipping. The first thing Jamal did when he was alone in the VIP room was untape the gun from his thigh and put it on his hip. When Smurf produced a bag of weed and a lighter Jamal relaxed, just a little.

"I thought Romeo was lying when he said you smoked," Smurf said. "You be acting so damned uptight and shit, I just didn't see it."

"Yea, well I'm sorry to disappoint you," Jamal said, disinterested in the dialogue.

Smurf wrapped his arm over Jamal's shoulder and laughed. "Romeo said you was a funny dude."

Jamal shrugged the boy's hand off his shoulder and

scowled at him. *I wonder how hard it would be to get rid of the body if I shot his ass right now,* Jamal thought. If there wasn't a guard at the door to the VIP rooms at the bottom of the stairwell Jamal would have seriously considered the idea. He brushed off the thought and finished rolling his blunt. He snatched up Smurf's lighter to spark it up.

"Sounds like you and Romeo having a lot of conversations and shit," Jamal prodded. "Like ya'll all buddy-buddy now. Unless ya'll more than buddies. Something you want to tell me, Smurf?"

Smurf's smile dissolved into a tight lipped grin. He shook his head and shrugged his shoulders. Jamal stared at him disbelievingly as he passed the boy the blunt. Smurf pulled hard on the spliff twice before passed it back to Jamal and spoke.

"I ain't going to lie to you. I was trying to get at him a few days ago but it just aint happen. I don't know if it was me or just that he aint want to mess around with no one."

"So you telling me aint shit going on between the two of you?"

"Naw, we just cool as fuck. We talk, a lot. And he listens. You're boy is mad cool."

"Yea?" Jamal asked reaching for the blunt Smurf was nursing. "What exactly do the two of you have to talk about?"

Smurf shrugged. "I don't know, stuff."

"So you guys just sat down one day and started talking? Just like that. Now my best friend trusts you with all his deep dark secrets."

"I'm pretty sure he doesn't consider you his best friend," Smurf said matter-of-factly. "Not anymore at least. He don't like you."

Jamal pulled the blunt from his lips and gawked at the boy. The comment was blunt as hell. Jamal hated the idea that Romeo would say something like that about him to Smurf of all people.

"So he said that?" Jamal asked, trying to keep his cool. "Or is that the conclusion you came to all on your own?"

"Both really," Smurf said simply.

"You lying nigga," Jamal countered. "My boy wouldn't say some shit like that to you. He don't even know you."

"Maybe. But that night when he was crying in his sleep having nightmares I was the one there to hold him all through the night."

Jamal stared at him a blankly. He didn't believe a word he said.

"And he let you hold him?"

"Yea," he answered like it wasn't a big deal. "I mean, we laid there until I calmed him down and then we talked for a while. It took a while for him to fall asleep but he did. Right in my arms."

"Yea, okay. So ya'll fucking?"

Smurf shook his head. "Nope, just friends, like I said. He's cool people but just not my type. He's kind of soft, you know. I can fuck me a female if I want soft. When I deal with a nigga I want a man, feel me?"

Smurf inched closer to Jamal and bit his bottom lip. Jamal looked at him and shook his head dismissively. He passed the boy the blunt and leaned forward, pressing his elbows into his knees. Jamal buried his face in his hands. Smurf was turning him on somehow and he felt bad all over again about Romeo. The shit was blowing his high.

"So what was all that shit about trying to get at Romeo?

When you was asking about him on the first stakeout? You was bullshitting me?"

"I was trying to get your attention, nigga," Smurf scoffed. "I wanted to make you jealous. It wasn't until I said all that shit that you actually looked up from the crack of that Mexican nigga's ass and looked at me."

Jamal snickered. "You think I be looking at you?"

"Yea, nigga. The same way you was looking at me when I came in the room. You aint got to fake, nigga, it's just you and me."

"Just you and me, hunh? And I'm supposed to trust you now? You might go blabbing to Romeo and shit since ya'll so cool now."

"Oh naw, come on now," Smurf pleaded. He reached over and stroked Jamal's stomach. "I wouldn't say shit to him or your little Spanish boyfriend. What happens between me and you stays between me and you. Shit, I aint trying to do anything but play with that dick anyways."

"Nigga, I don't even know why Slim added your ass to the crew."

"I fucked up in the trap house that you robbed and he said I owed him."

"Is that right?"

"Yea," Smurf said. He ran his head under Jamal's shirt and pulled at his nipple. "That's right."

Jamal gripped the boy's hand and looked him in the eye. "And he fucked you like he did the rest of us?"

"I already told you that. The only reason he stopped was because my dick was hard when he was doing it. Now let's stop talking. I want to taste that dick."

Smurf slid his hand down the front of Jamal's pants. He

was hard but the urge to choke Smurf tingled in his finger tips. The only reason he was even playing this game of cat and mouse was to get information. He was going to ask the druggie why Slim didn't make him take his dick like he did Romeo and Diego to be part of the crew but he was sure Smurf would have an answer for that. And there wasn't any point in asking him how he was given the job of being the driver, the one spot on the crew that had the lowest risk of getting caught up and killed. Jamal was convinced that Smurf was a mole for Slim and that he had no debt to pay the man.

"How much money you owe Slim?"

Smurf shrugged. "I don't know," he said. He was obviously more interested in the hard dick he had his fingers wrapped around. "Not like that nigga gonna ever let me pay it off."

Jamal frowned. "What you mean? We just sent that nigga a grip of money. We all paid down some of our debt."

Smurf laughed gently as he scooted up and nuzzle his face in Jamal's neck. "You think that nigga gonna let you go with you feeding him all that money and drugs? He's going to find a way to keep you on his leash. First it will be some shit about interest. And then he'll come up with some other shit. Once you're in debt to Slim you're his for life. You aint know that?"

The words sunk like an anchor. They were the only words Smurf had said that Jamal had actually believed. He was so distracted that he didn't even feel Smurf pulling his dick from his pants. It wasn't until the boy had his thick lips wrapped around his pole that he noticed that he was getting head.

Jamal looked down and saw his dick disappear in Smurf's mouth over and over again. He felt the wet warmth engulf every inch of his meat. The tip of his dick pressed at the back of his throat and the boy didn't even gag. Smurf's head game was vicious.

Jamal fought the urge to reach down and fuck his face. He placed his hands on Smurf's shoulders and tried to push him off. But the more he pushed the harder Smurf sucked.

"Stop," Jamal said, barely loud as a whisper.

He said it again, but louder. Smurf just kept slurping and bopping up and down. Jamal reached for his dick and tried to pull it from the dude's mouth. Just as he pried his manhood from Smurf's vacuum of a mouth the door to the VIP room swung open.

"Hey, I have—"

Diego's mouth snapped shut and the bottle of Hennessy fell from his hand. His face twisted in anger as he took in the sight of Smurf wiping spit from his lips and Jamal trying to pull his pants back up. That anger quickly morphed into pain. Jamal saw the emotions pouring from his dude's body.

"Baby," Jamal began. "I tried to get him off me, I swear."

Diego shook his head. He turned and left without a word. Jamal jumped up, shot Smurf an evil glare and chased behind Diego. He brushed past Romeo and the chick he was talking to on the dance floor. Jamal avoided eye contact and made his way to the stairs.

When he got to the dance floor he searched through the thick crowd but couldn't find Diego. He looked and looked but couldn't find him. He was about to give up when his eyes caught movement. Three guys barreled through the crowd quickly, knocking over everyone in their path. Jamal narrowed his gaze and focused on their faces. He recognized them.

The guys plowing through the crowd were the same one's

Jamal and the crew stuck up the night before in D.C. He looked to where they were rushing to. Jamal's heart sunk. Diego was at the bar and they were headed straight for him. Jamal pulled his Glock from his hip and bolted for the men. He was too late. Jamal saw the glint of the gun in the man's hand right before he heard the shots ring off.

Chapter 20

Chaos consumed the club. Folks were screaming and running for the exits. Jamal panicked. He still had his eyes set on the guy that had fired the shot but he was sure he saw Diego slump down on the bar from the corner of his eye. Jamal thought he could probably hit the guy from where he stood but he didn't want to risk shooting one of the bystanders running across the dance floor. He had to decide: chase after the gunman and get a clean shot or go to Diego.

The lights went out. More screams filled the quickly emptying club. Darkness covered the dance floor. Unbothered and resolved, Jamal sprung into action. He sprinted towards the last location he saw the shooter. His heart pounded savagely against his chest. Jamal forced himself to calm down and control his breathing. His finger teased at the trigger, ready to pull at the slightest indication of his target's presence.

Two more shots rang in the air. Jamal fell back behind one of the knocked over tables. His jaw clenched. Sweat ran down his temples. He didn't see where the shots had come from but he knew that he was the intended mark. One of the bullets had hit a rail less than two feet away. They'd seen him.

Jamal's nostrils flared as he regained his composure. He cautiously looked up from behind the table and scanned the section of the club where he thought the shots had originated. It was dark but the emergency lights near the exits provided enough light to see bodies moving around. Jamal just couldn't make out whether or not the folks running were the shooters or innocent bystanders.

By now the club was mostly cleared out except for the few stragglers who tried to leave out now that the exits weren't as crowded. There were only two exits in the club and everyone couldn't fit through the doors when the first shots rang through the club. Some folks had hid behind the DJ booth and others behind the bar or tables.

Dark bodies kept darting from corners of the club to the exits and Jamal couldn't make out whether one was the shooter or not. He ducked back behind the table and clenched his eyes shut. He knew if he didn't do anything than the guys would get away. But he wasn't even sure they were still in the club.

Jamal tightened his grip on his gun and pointed it towards one of the speakers. He popped off two shots and ducked behind the table again. He waited, anticipating retaliatory shots. A long moment of silence filled the club. Then three shots rang in the air. Only one hit remotely close to where he was. They didn't know where he was but Jamal was sure he knew where they were.

Jamal took a deep breath and looked towards the second bar. It was the only place where he could get a vantage point of where he thought one of the guys was. Jamal jumped on his toes in crouched position and counted down in his head; *one, two, three.* He sprinted towards a knocked over couch.

He expected and waited for the shots to come. An eerie silence stifled the air around him. Jamal prayed that they didn't see him. A glass hit the ground and shattered less than a yard away from him. Jamal's head and gun swiveled in that direction. The tension in his body eased when he saw the frightened couple.

Jamal exhaled and blinked incessantly. Slowly, he moved his finger from the trigger. He brought his free hand up to his mouth and motioned for them to be quiet. The woman cried and struggled to not make a sound. The man with her had his hand over her mouth and nodded at Jamal. They didn't move until Jamal pointed towards the exit near the stairwell to the VIP rooms.

Sweat beaded on Jamal's forehead as he pressed his body against the couch and peeked over at the bar. Slowly, he leaned over and narrowed the slits of his eyes. The black lights under the bar were still on and offered a limited amount of light. Jamal saw one person behind that bar, hunched over. He saw flesh. It was Smurf.

Jamal's mind raced. The opportunity to get rid of that nigga had presented itself in a gift wrapped present. *I couldn't have planned the shit any better*, Jamal thought. If he shot the boy now it would look like the same cats that shot Diego had got Smurf. It was perfect.

With the calm of a sharp shooter, Jamal planted a knee on

the ground and brought his gun up. He held his wrist with his free hand and took aim at the back of Smurf's head. Jamal curled his finger around the trigger. He took a breath and began to pull his finger back.

Cold steel pressed against the nape of Jamal's neck. He froze. His body went numb and the blood drained from his face. Jamal brought his gun down and slowly placed it on the ground. He closed his eyes and held up his hands. Death had come a knocking and he was ready.

"That doesn't look like the nigga that shot Diego," a familiar voice said from behind Jamal.

Slowly, Jamal turned his head and looked over his shoulder. It was Romeo. Their eyes locked. Romeo still had the gun pressed on Jamal's neck. Time slowed to a crawl as the two of them sat there negotiating life and death.

Anger welled in Jamal as he peered into Romeo's eyes. He couldn't understand why his boy was still holding a gun to his head. Was it because he was about to shoot Smurf? Did he care for that nigga that much? Or was it because of what had happened at Slim's pool hall? Jamal recognized that Romeo faced the same choice he had just a few moments ago; he could kill him and no one would know that he was the one who did it.

"If you going to kill me get it over with, nigga," Jamal said.

Romeo didn't flinch. For a moment Jamal really thought he would shoot him. But then the pressure from the barrel of the gun eased from his flesh. Jamal heard Romeo sigh and sniffle. He looked back at his boy and saw how his eyes were red and watery. They stared at each other for a moment. They'd been on the precipice of death and back.

"Them niggas is gone," Romeo finally said. "That was me

shooting. Go to the truck. My girl has Diego there. I'll go get Smurf."

"Leave that nigga," Jamal said.

Romeo ignored the comment. "You need to hurry up before the police get here. That's unless you want to be sitting up in some jail."

Jamal clenched his jaw. He was about to say something but Romeo stood and sprinted to the bar. Jamal sat there and watched as Romeo hooked his arm over Smurf's shoulder. The two of them embraced. Anger boiled in Jamal's veins. The sight of Romeo consoling Smurf put him in a bad head space. Romeo looked back at Jamal.

If it hadn't been clear before, the look on Romeo's face dispelled any misunderstanding; Smurf was off limits and Romeo would take out anyone, including Jamal, that tried to harm him. Jamal got the message. He stood up and ran to the nearest exit. The truck was still parked in the same spot. Jamal saw the same butch chick from the club leaning against the truck with Diego. She was holding him up.

Jamal ran to them as quickly as he could. A twinge of pain slammed into his gut as soon as he saw the blood staining Diego's shirt. The thought of losing Diego scared Jamal. He ran harder to get to Diego.

"Baby," Jamal said in a labored breath. "Are you okay?"

"I'm good, papi," Diego said.

Jamal's stomach dropped. Diego looked pale. His eyelids drooped and his voice sounded weak. Blood glistened his lips. Jamal thought he'd pass out any moment.

"We need to get him to the hospital," the girl said. "He lost a lot of blood."

Jamal looked at her warily. He was upset that Romeo had

entrusted Diego's life to some stranger he'd met at the club. But then again, if he hadn't tried to go after the shooter and went to Diego first, her presence wouldn't have been an issue. Either way, Diego needed help. Jamal unlocked the truck and put Diego's free arm over his shoulder.

"Help me get him in the truck."

Jamal and the girl eased Diego into the backseat. He coughed up blood as soon as his head hit the seat. Jamal climbed in the back and held Diego's hand. He looked in Diego's eyes, fighting back the tears, and tried to be strong for his boy.

"I'm so sorry," Jamal cried. "This is all my fault. I shouldn't have let that shit between me and Smurf happen. Baby, I'm so sorry."

Diego shushed him. The gesture was weak and depressing. Jamal reached up and caressed Diego's face. Tears welled in his eyes. He could see the life fading from Diego's body.

"Jamal!" Romeo yelled.

Jamal didn't move. He couldn't pull himself from Diego. When Romeo pulled at him, Jamal steeled his body and held Diego's hand more firmly. He shucked Romeo's hand off his shoulder.

"Give me the keys, Jamal!" Romeo said. "We have to go, now!"

Jamal kept his eyes on Diego as he reached in his pocket for the keys. He dropped them on the floor of the backseat. Jamal ignored the sound of doors opening and slamming shut. He noticed the strange girl get in on the other side and place Diego's head on her lap. Jamal felt the truck whip out from the parking lot to the street.

"Is he still breathing," Smurf asked from the driver's seat.

202

Jamal ignored the question. Anger and shock clouded his mind. He wanted to lash out at Smurf for pushing to go out to the club in the first place. Jamal wanted to shoot Smurf for sucking his dick in the VIP room. He wanted to blame Smurf so badly for what had happened but it wasn't working. Guilt had him in a choke hold and he could only blame himself for what had happened to Diego.

"He's still breathing," the girl said, "but just barely."

"Santana, open his shirt," Romeo directed.

She looked up at Jamal before she moved. Slowly, her hand went to the top button of Diego's shirt. Santana opened it, under Jamal's watchful eyes, and exposed Diego's bloody flesh. Red was everywhere. Jamal recoiled at the sight.

"Do you see the bullet wound?" Romeo asked.

"Yea, looks like it hit his ribcage. I think I can see the bullet too."

"Alright, you guys need to put pressure on the wound to stop the bleeding. Jamal, take off your shirt and put it on the wound."

Jamal didn't move. His eyes were transfixed on the blood gushing from the hole in Diego's chest. Santana pulled off her polo and pressed it against the wound. Jamal looked up from Diego and met Santana's gaze.

"Thank you," he whispered.

Jamal turned and looked out the window. They were on the highway. Jamal wasn't from Baltimore but he was sure that there was a hospital somewhere downtown. He jumped up between Smurf and Romeo.

"Why the fuck aren't we going to a hospital?"

"If we go to a hospital we'll all go to jail," Smurf said.

Jamal clenched his teeth. Smurf didn't care about Diego

dying in the backseat. He was only worried about his own ass. Jamal didn't care. He'd go to jail if it meant saving Diego's life. It took all his strength not reach around the seat and choke the life out of Smurf.

"Stop the truck."

"What?" Smurf asked, baffled.

"Nigga, I said stop my fucking truck!" Jamal yelled. "Ya'll can get the fuck out. I'm taking him to the hospital."

"We're going to a doctor," Smurf said. "I already called him and told him what was up. He's ready for us."

Jamal breathed heavily as he eyed Smurf from the backseat. He didn't know if he could trust what Smurf said. Part of him wanted to demand that he pull over again so he could take his chances at a hospital. Jamal looked over at Romeo. He didn't say a word but his expression couldn't be interpreted as anything other than threatening.

Jamal narrowed his gaze and reached for his gun. If he had to press his pistol to Smurf's head to make him stop he'd do it, he didn't care what Romeo did.

Before Jamal could make his move he felt Diego squeeze his hand. He looked down at Diego and saw that his lips were moving. Jamal bent down and put his ear near Diego's lips.

"I love you, Jamal," Diego whispered. "I know you don't believe me but I do."

"I believe you," Jamal said. "I promise I believe you, baby."

He leaned in and kissed Diego. Jamal clenched his eyes shut and fought back the emotions. He had to have some control if he was going to get Diego to the hospital.

Just as Jamal took control of his nerves and reached for his gun, Smurf pulled off on an exit. Jamal looked out the window. Smurf sped down the intersection and ran two lights. That sense of urgency stayed Jamal's hand. For now.

Diego's grip was getting weaker. Jamal felt helpless. He wanted to do something. Anything. Finally, Smurf pulled into a neighborhood. Large houses lined the streets. Smurf raced through the opulent subdivision until they came up to a house that had all its lights on. The truck screeched to a halt right at the driveway. Smurf was on the phone before he burst out the truck.

Jamal's door swung open. Smurf urged him to get Diego and bring him to the house. Without thinking, Jamal got his lover and carried him up to the large house. The door swung open before they reached the stone stairs. A middle-aged man that looked like James Earl Jones filled the frame. He urged them inside.

"Hurry up," the doctor said. "Take him to the study."

Smurf nodded and led the way. Jamal didn't even care that Smurf knew a doctor in Baltimore or that he was familiar with the man's house. All he wanted to do was get Diego the help he needed.

The doctor had Jamal place Diego on a gurney in the middle of the room. It looked like an emergency room with all the medical equipment positioned around the bed. It offered some comfort to Jamal. He looked at the doctor, concern all over his face.

"Is he going to be okay?" Jamal asked.

"I don't know, son," he said. "Right now I need some space to work." He looked at Smurf. "Take your friends to the kitchen."

Jamal reluctantly left the doctor and the woman who he assumed was the man's wife to work on Diego. He dragged his feet behind Smurf and Romeo. When Jamal reached the kitchen he froze. He couldn't believe what he saw. His hand instinctively went to his hip.

Slim sat at the kitchen island eating an apple.

Chapter 21

The kitchen was a powder keg that only required the slightest spark to blow up in everyone's face. A simple gesture, an involuntary movement or a stray gaze would have ended it all and sent the room into a fury of bullets and blood. The only person who seemed oblivious to the tangible tension in the small space was Slim.

Flanked by Bricks and two equally large men, Slim flicked his switch blade open and close as he ate a green apple. The sometime pimp, sometime dealer lazily looked up at Jamal. Their eyes locked for a moment. Yet the flicker of the blade drew Jamal's attention and ire. His gaze strayed erratically.

It was the same blade that had been pressed on his throat the first time he encountered Slim. It was the same blade that Jamal had nightmares about and would wake up in the middle of night with a cold sweat. It was the same blade that Jamal had promised himself to take and slit Slim's throat with when the opportunity presented itself. It was more than just a simple blade.

Jamal narrowed his gaze and forced himself to focus on Slim's face. If he could wish anything at that moment, Jamal wished that looks could kill. The gauntly man took his time chewing as he met the young hustler's look of disgust and disdain. He was unbothered.

Slowly, he ate the last slice of his apple and slammed the blade into the carving board in front of him. Smurf and Romeo's new female friend, Santana jumped back. Romeo looked disturbingly unfazed. Jamal didn't even flinch at the gesture.

"My little stickup crew," Slim began. He opened his hands in a welcoming gesture. "Come in, have a seat and make yourselves comfortable. You all look like you've had a long, hard night."

Smurf, Romeo and Santana all cautiously moved towards the seats circling the large kitchen island. They left the middle seat, the one directly across from Slim, open. Jamal looked at the chair and back up at Slim. The crew leader stood his ground. Hatred flared in his eyes.

Slim motioned towards the food spread out in front of him. "Eat up," he encouraged them, his eyes glued on Jamal. He took Jamal's blatant act of defiance in stride. "Bricks tells me that you all hit the three spots last night flawlessly."

Jamal shrugged. "We got the job done."

"Well, if putting twenty stacks in my pocket along with a grip of dope is getting the job done then I'd love to see what it looks like when you go all out."

"Is that why you're here?" Jamal asked. "You flew all the

way up here to tell us 'good job' and pat us on the back? You could have saved the trip and made a phone call."

Anger clouded Slim's sunken face. Just as quickly as Jamal's antagonizing comment unsettled the man a bright smile covered his face. He snatched his knife and flicked it closed.

"I'm more of a hands on kind of guy, Jamal," he said with a tilt of his head. He grinned mischievously. "You of all people should know that. I like to get in there and dig around for myself, if you know what I mean. That's the only way to find out what a man is really made of."

Jamal clenched his jaw. The tingling in his finger tips quickly turned into a burning sensation. His Glock was calling him and the bullet in the chamber needed release like a virgin teenager playing in pussy for the first time. Jamal desperately wanted to end Slim's life right then and there but he knew that he'd barely be able to take out Slim and Bricks before the other two henchmen sent a barrage of bullets his way.

"Well," Jamal started, desperately trying to control his temper, "Diego is getting patched up by the doctor and I don't think he's taking visitors right now. But I'll be sure to let Diego know that you send your best and well wishes and all that shit."

Slim hung his head and grinned. "You're different," Slim observed, pointing his closed switch blade at Jamal. "It's amazing what a little time, a gun and some bread will do to a young man's pride and confidence. Just be careful."

Jamal looked at the man warily. His eyebrow arched up as he took the bait. "Careful of what?"

"Confidence leads to complacency. And pride," Slim shrugged, "has lead to many great men dying due to their own ignorance. And something tells me that you're not ignorant. Are you, Jamal?" Jamal pressed his lips together. "Good," Slim said. "I didn't think so. Because for a minute I thought you may have become ignorant to the fucking boundaries of this here relationship."

Jamal's stoic expression fixated on his face. "I know my place."

"Good." A broad smile parted Slim's tired face. His eyes lit up like a wildfire. "Since we all know the fucking roles we play up in this bitch, tell me why the fuck you little niggas are up in Baltimore shooting up a fucking club!"

Jamal's eyes darted over to Smurf. Slim jumped up from his stool. "Motherfucker, don't look at him. You're the one in charge, nigga! I asked you a fucking question!"

"It was a last minute thing," Jamal said. His chest burned with the sharp breaths he took. His eyes darted towards the muscle flanking Slim. He began to reconsider shooting the place up. "It was my fault. We shouldn't have risked going out."

"You're right. You're fucking right. It was your fault. How the fuck do you rob niggas one night and hit up a club less than 50 miles away the next? Who the fuck does that? Nigga, are you stupid?"

Jamal's nostrils flared. "No, it was a lapse in judgment."

"Oh, a lapse in judgment," Slim said mockingly, glancing back at Bricks to emphasize the point. "A motherfucking lapse in judgment. So what do you think we need to do about this lapse in judgment, hunh?"

Jamal's body steeled. His eye's pierced through Slim like a dagger to the heart. Jamal saw Romeo react to the exchange for the first time in his peripheral. If Slim thought the same shit that went down at his pool hall in Atlanta a few days was about to happen he was in for a rude awakening.

"I don't know," Jamal said simply. He was ready to pull his pistol if the dealer made a wrong move. "You're the one pulling all the strings."

Slim smirked. "I'm a business man, Jamal."

"You're a drug dealer," Jamal quipped. The words spit from his lips involuntarily.

"No," Slim said firmly. "I'm a man that supplies the demand. I don't run corners up and down the east coast. You know niggas wouldn't go for that shit in their own neighborhoods. Use your head, nigga. Corners and trap house are like prime real estate. If anything, I'm a supplier. And when there's a hiccup in that supply, I have a problem."

An absent glare glazed over Jamal's face.

"Let me put it this way," Slim said. "I can't have you little niggas fucking up and letting cats see ya'll faces. Eventually that shit will get back to me."

Jamal fought the urge to look over at Smurf. There was no way Slim knew the trap boys in DC had seen Diego's face unless Smurf had told him. The crew leader made a mental note to take care of that as soon as possible.

"All I can say is, it won't happen again."

"You're right, it won't," Slim added. "because if it does then we're going to have to revisit that chain of command lesson. Thought I'd schooled you enough the first time."

Jamal's eye twitched at the thought of playing the role of bitch for Slim ever again. Taking his ass out would be his only way to make sure it never happened again. And based on Romeo's response to Slim's words, Jamal knew he had at least one person to back him on that front.

"Are we done?" Jamal asked.

"Almost."

Slim stood up and walked over to Santana. Jamal had forgotten that the girl was even in the room. She had sat on the other side of Romeo, out of his view, quiet as a mouse. She visibly flinched when Slim stepped towards her. Romeo stood up and stared Slim down. The man grinned mockingly at Romeo's chivalry.

"You all need to take care of them niggas from D.C.," Slim ordered as he looked from Romeo to Santana and back. "They need to be dead yesterday. And for now on, if anyone sees any of your faces during a stickup, kill them. Got me?"

"Yea," Jamal answered weakly.

"I want an update when the shit is done. I have a job I need you all on in a couple of days so you may as well stay in town. And make sure to bring the girl. She might prove to be useful. Hell, she might even be able to lead ya'll to them niggas that shot Diego."

Jamal frowned. His gaze slowly shifted from Slim to Santana. Distrust had polluted his mind the moment he set his eyes on the chick back at the club. Now, not only did Slim know who she was but she knew who the cats were that had shot at them at the club.

Aint shit a coincidence, Jamal thought.

Slim rounded the kitchen island, his entourage in tow and began to head for the front door. He ran his finger under Santana's chin as he passed her and shot Romeo and Jamal condescending stares as he left. He looked over his shoulder before he was out of eye sight.

"Oh, and tell Diego I said I hope he gets well soon. His dad sends his love."

A collective sigh enveloped the room. Yet the moment was short lived. Jamal threw himself towards Smurf and backhanded him so hard that the boy crashed to the floor, gripping his face. Santana screamed and Romeo tried to hold Jamal back from pounding Smurf into the ground.

"What the fuck did I do?" Smurf cried.

"How the fuck did he know we were here, nigga?!" Jamal demanded.

"I don't know. I didn't tell him. The doctor probably did."

Jamal balled his fists but held his temper in check as he considered Smurf's words. He pulled away from Romeo and hovered over the likely mole.

"Let me see your phone, Smurf," Jamal demanded.

"What the fuck for?"

"Cause nigga, if I find out you been keeping tabs on us for Slim I'm going to fuck you up. Especially since going to the club was your fucking idea. There's no way that nigga knew about the club, that we was here and that Diego got shot by them DC niggas. How the fuck did he know they saw Diego's face!? You told him."

Fear danced in Smurf's bruised face. It fed the rage Jamal felt from his encounter with Slim. Before Smurf could answer, Romeo reached out and placed a tentative hand on Jamal's shoulder.

"I told him," Romeo said.

Jamal's shoulders slacked. The anger melted from his body. He couldn't believe what he'd just heard. He turned around and looked at Romeo like he was some sort of abomination or aberration walking the earth. Despite all that had happened between them Jamal never thought Romeo would be the one to betray him, especially to Slim. Words couldn't express how Jamal felt at that moment.

He backed away towards the kitchen entrance and just looked at Romeo in disbelief. Before he could gather his thoughts the doctor walked up behind them. A somber expression covered his aged face. The crew collectively braced themselves for the news on Diego.

"You're friend is one of the luckiest young men I've even encountered," the doctor said. The tension on everyone's face eased. "The bullet hit one of his ribs but it didn't do much damage, no more than a really heavy blow to the stomach would have done. If I was a betting man I'd say the bullet went through something or someone else before it got to him."

"Is he able to talk or move?" Jamal asked.

"Yea," the doctor confirmed. "My wife is cleaning him up right now and finishing the stitches. I gave him some pain killers but he should be fine in no time." The man looked to Smurf. "Now, if we could conclude this business."

Smurf pulled out a wad of cash and tossed it at the man. The doctor didn't even bother to count it. He smiled and nodded at the crew before he disappeared back into the living room and headed towards his study.

Jamal looked at Smurf with contempt but felt more pain from what Romeo had done. He took a couple of heavy deep breaths. He was relieved that Diego was okay but there were still a number of issues that hadn't been addressed. He turned and put his attention on Santana, the mystery girl.

"And who the fuck are you?" Jamal demanded of the girl.

"Santana," she answered, her voice low and shaky.

"Don't play games with me, bitch. You know what the fuck I mean."

Santana stepped behind Romeo. "I don't."

"Then why did Slim say you knew them niggas that shot at us from the club?"

"I don't know," she said.

Rage boiled in Jamal's veins. Romeo even flinched at the lie the girl told but he didn't move from in front of her. Jamal pulled out his pistol and leveled it at the two of them.

"If you fucking move I'll take you out too, Romeo," Jamal warned. "Please don't test me."

Romeo's face softened as if he wasn't bothered by the gun being leveled at him. Jamal looked past him once he was satisfied the boy wouldn't obstruct his objective. He looked back at Santana.

"You don't know me. But the nigga you hiding behind can attest that I'm a good ass fucking shot. Now, if you don't start answering me with the truth, I'm going to put a bullet through your head. Believe me when I say I don't give a fuck about you or your life."

Santana gripped at Romeo's arm. Distress covered her soft face as she stared at the ground. Finally she looked up and nodded her head.

"Good," Jamal said. "Now how do you know them niggas from the club?"

"One of the guys, D-Row, is my cousin."

Jamal blinked hard and rolled his eyes. He shot Romeo a hard stare. Romeo got the message. Jamal shook his head. His mind raced. The girl could have been the one that had the guys from DC on them in the first place. There was no telling what Romeo had told the girl at the club that she could have shared with the men to tip them off. Jamal frowned his brow as another question exploded in his mind.

"How does Slim know you?"

Santana's face twisted in fear. "He's my uncle."

Chapter 22

Jamal merged onto the highway and headed back to the hotel in downtown Baltimore. His eyes darted up to the rearview mirror over and over again. He stared at Santana, wondering what else she was keeping from them and whether he'd have to take her out before she could do anything that could put them all in danger. Despite Romeo's inexplicable connection to the girl, Jamal didn't trust her and had made up in his mind to take her out if she gave him the slightest excuse.

If Jamal had had his way, the girl would have been bound and gagged. Romeo, Smurf and even Diego protested, saying that it wasn't necessary. She sat in the back seat, wedged between Smurf and Romeo. Jamal was at least able to get her cell phone to make sure she wasn't in contact with Slim or anyone else.

"How close are you and your uncle," Jamal asked. He

couldn't help but ask.

"I barely even know him," she said. Her voice trembled as she spoke.

Jamal decided not to believe a word she said without reservations. But based on how she acted around him, assuming she wasn't putting on a stunt, at the very least, Santana didn't get along with her uncle.

"What do you know about him?"

Santana sighed. "He's the youngest of eight fathered by my grandfather."

Jamal nodded his head. It explained why he looked young enough to be her older brother. "What else?" Jamal demanded.

"He supplies low level dealers from Boston down to Florida last I heard. Most cats who are trying to come up and get a consistent supply deal with him. Anything that can be smoked, snorted, popped or shot up, he has his hands in. He's the middle man for dudes who can't get a supply from Central and South America themselves because they don't move enough weight."

"That's all he does?"

"No," Santana said as if it were a stupid question. "He pulls money from gambling, running numbers and the tired crack heads he prostitutes. He makes himself out to be some big time pimp. Probably over compensating for all his daddy issues."

"Daddy issues?" What you mean?"

"From what my dad would tell my brothers when we were coming up, Slim was the smallest out of all of them and a mama's boy. My granddad treated him like shit; called him names like faggot and punk. He didn't put him on the family hustle like all the others because he said he didn't have the heart for it. Called him weak and soft."

"So Slim had a little man complex," Jamal observed. "Stepped out on his own despite his daddy to prove a point? That's why that nigga crazy as fuck?"

"I guess you could put it that way."

"What's his name? His government name?"

"Does it matter?"

Jamal flinched at her response. "Not really, but it don't look all that good you don't want to say it."

"That's cause I don't know him by anything except Slim."

"You don't know you're uncle's name?" Jamal asked disbelievingly.

"Calling him my uncle is like calling you my brother. I don't know that nigga from a can of paint. We don't even talk about him after what he did."

"And what was that?"

"He killed his father, my granddad."

The revelation sunk in heavily. Jamal didn't doubt for a moment that Slim was a sick dude but to kill his own father was something on a completely different level. If the man was cold enough to do that to blood there was no telling what he'd do to a bunch of kids that stole from him.

"What about what he said," Jamal pressed. "That you knew the cats that shot at us in the club."

Santana looked down. Her gaze quickly shot over to Smurf and back down. Jamal caught the look and shifted his gaze over to Smurf. The look on the man's face made Jamal suspect he was hiding something.

"Bitch, I asked you a question!"

"Jamal," Romeo began. "You need to calm down."

"Naw, fuck that, this bitch knows something about them niggas that shot Diego. She gonna talk or I swear I'm going to put her butch looking ass six feet under."

"No you're not," Romeo said evenly.

Jamal narrowed his eyes. "If that means I got to take you out too so be it. Don't shit matter if we all end up dead because of that bitch. You need to get a grip on your fucking priorities, nigga! You don't even know this random bitch."

"They're my cousins," Santana whispered.

Disbelief overshadowed the angry scowl on Jamal's face. The realization of what Slim had put him in the middle of shook his very foundation. It was all beginning to make sense. As Jamal began to piece the puzzle together in his head, there was one more question that nagged at him.

"I don't believe in coincidences," Jamal prefaced. "Why are you here? Why did you pick Romeo to latch on to? How did you even know we were at the club?"

Santana's eyes shot up to the rearview mirror and locked onto Jamal's. He saw the red and the tears of frustration coalescing. Jamal didn't care. Finding out everything he could was paramount to anyone's feelings. It could mean life or death for everyone in the crew. He'd fucked up by letting Smurf and Romeo pressure him into a trip to the club. He wasn't about to let anything else slip by him and risk more happening than a simple bullet wound.

Before Jamal could press the issue, Santana balled up and nuzzled under Romeo. The stickup boy shot Jamal a cautionary look, ending the questioning, for now. It wasn't over. Jamal felt the scowl on his face get deeper and harder as he thought about everything Santana had said and all that had went down. Then he felt a gentle touch on his thigh. He looked over at Diego. All the tension in Jamal's face instantly disappeared.

Looking at Diego's beautiful, reassuring face gave Jamal strength. He didn't look as weak or out of it as Jamal had thought he'd be after getting shot, stitched, and doped up on painkillers. The smile on his face hinted at the warrior spirit that wouldn't quit as long as the boy drew breath. Jamal couldn't imagine losing Diego.

There were moments when Jamal thought the thing between them was little more than teenage lust. What he'd felt had happened so fast that it made his head spin. But after nearly losing him, there was no doubt in his mind that Diego was very important to him. He'd even come to terms with never having an intimate relationship with Romeo. He didn't care anymore. Jamal just wanted to be with Diego and only Diego and he'd be damned if he let anyone threaten the boy's life or put him in undue danger ever again.

Finally, Jamal pulled up to the hotel and parked in the back. He made sure to walk behind Santana and Smurf. He didn't trust either one of them as far as he could throw them. Once they made it up to Smurf and Romeo's room Jamal called everyone over to the kitchen near the door. He made Santana stand over near the window and turned the TV on so she couldn't hear what they were saying.

"I don't trust that bitch," Jamal started. "She's Slim's blood. We need to drop that bitch somewhere, check out and get another room."

Smurf shook his head. "She aint like that, trust me."

"The fuck? Trust you? Nigga, we aint even know you knew the bitch until like fifteen minutes ago. Putting on a show like she was a random broad. Speaking of which, how do you know her?"

"When I first got on with Slim a few years ago he had me running supply up through Virginia and DC. Him and the family dealt with each other. They weren't the family reunion type but they didn't mind dealing if money was involved."

"Thanks for the history lesson," Jamal retorted. "But I asked how you knew that bitch."

"I met Santana at one of the trap houses. That was before she started wearing boy clothes. We stayed in contact. At first I was trying to hit but I found out quick that I wasn't exactly her type. But we were still cool. She was like my little sister."

"So you told her about us?"

Smurf nodded. "I told her that Slim had put together a crew and that we were coming through DC."

Jamal shook his head. "You know you could have gotten us all killed, right?"

"Naw, Santana don't deal with her family no more. Not after what they did. When they found out she was gay her dad put her out and her cousins let some niggas they knew from the block rape her. Said it would straighten her out."

Jamal empathized but his concern for his own wellbeing and Diego's safety didn't allow him to give her a pass. All of what Smurf said didn't explain why the two of them didn't just come out and acknowledge that they knew each other from the beginning. The whole thing reeked of shadiness.

"So you trying to put her on with the crew?" Jamal asked, knowing the answer before he asked. "Is that what all the smoke and mirrors is about?"

Smurf nodded. "Yea, when she found out we hit three of her Uncle Damien's corners she wanted in."

Jamal frowned. He kicked himself for being surprised. "So

we're in the middle of a family feud? You knew this before we came here, didn't you?"

"Come on, man. Why else would we go all the way to D.C. to rob some niggas? There are dozens of cities we could have dropped into between here and Atlanta. Shit, why you think Slim is here?"

"Fine. Is there anything else I need to know? Slim got a sister or a brother that you cool with? Are you calling or texting Slim telling him shit?" Smurf shook his head and looked down to the ground. "Good, go tell her if she helps us take out her cousins she's cool in my book. But if she tries some shit I'm putting a bullet in her head and yours."

Smurf gave Jamal a blank look as he backed away and headed for Santana. Jamal watched as the two of them spoke. Romeo started to back away. Jamal reached out and took him by his arm. Their eyes met. The warning Romeo had given Jamal about putting his hands on him was as empty a threat to Jamal as the dude's loyalty.

"Stop telling Slim shit," Jamal said plainly. "If I find out you're still feeding him information I'll deal with you like a nigga I just met that threatened my life. We clear?"

Romeo yanked his arm away and looked Jamal up and down as he walked over to his bedroom. The line between the two had been drawn. There was no more negotiating. No more walking on egg shells. No more feelings.

"Come on baby," Diego said, tugging at Jamal's arm. "I'm tired as fuck."

Jamal smiled at Diego and helped him over to their room. He made sure to lock the door before he laid Diego down. Jamal pulled off Diego's shoes before he pushed his legs on the bed. Diego looked at him with a curious smile.

"What are you doing?"

Jamal looked to the side like it was a trick question. "What do you mean? I'm getting ready for bed."

Diego watched Jamal pull off his shirt and pants before he got in the bed next to him. He groaned just as Jamal reached over and turned off the light. A soft glow from the moon light filled the room.

"You know I sleep naked," Diego said. "I don't know why you playing."

"Babe, I don't know if I can keep my hands to myself if you're lying next to me naked."

Diego bit at his bottom lip and then smiled. "Then don't."

"But you're hurt," Jamal protested.

"Nigga, I aint broke. Just be careful."

Jamal smiled and threw the covers back. He sat Diego up and slowly lifted his shirt over his head. Jamal leaned in and pressed his full lips against Diego's. His tongue attacked his man's mouth like he was a man stranded on the desert for a week who'd just discovered fresh water.

Jamal wanted to reach down and rub all over Diego's body but he kept the urge at bay. He pulled away from the kiss and began to slowly work his way down, planting soft kisses on Diego's neck. The way Diego squirmed and moaned set Jamal's loins ablaze.

"Babe, wait," Diego said.

Defeated, Jamal looked up. He took up at the auspicious look on Diego's face. He looked like he was preoccupied with something on his mind. Too preoccupied to get freaky.

"What? Why?"

"Are you sure you want to kill those guys?" He asked, the question seemingly coming out of the blue.

Jamal sighed and collapsed next to him. "We don't have a choice. They saw your face and mine and tried to kill you. Besides, Slim wants them dead. There's no way we'll get a chance to take him out if we don't do this. He needs to trust us so we can get close to him."

"Can't you just let that shit go?" Diego asked. "Let's just hustle and be done with his ass."

"That's not an option even if we wanted it to be. You weren't there, but when Slim came to the doctor's house and confronted us in the kitchen he was on the verge of trying to bend me over again. I can't live with the threat of that shit over my head. That nigga got to go. Besides, from what Smurf told me at the club, there is no way anyone can pay off a debt to Slim."

Diego visibility recoiled at the mention of the club and Smurf. Jamal saw the look and began to apologize. Diego held his hand up.

"It's okay. I know you were trying to get that dude to talk," Diego said. He let out a heavy sigh and gave Jamal a sidelong glance. "Can't we just go? Just disappear?"

"You and I both know that's not possible," Jamal answered. "What about your grandmother and all you brothers and sisters? We have family that Slim can reach out and touch, literally. This nigga killed his own father. What do you think he'd do to our families if he felt like we tried to get over on him?"

Diego nodded. "You're right. I'm just worried. Taking a bullet puts things in perspective, papi. I'm not trying to die."

"Yea, I know. But I don't want you to worry. I got your back," Jamal said. "And your front"

Diego laughed and nudged Jamal in the side. "You right,

nigga. Don't think I forgot. You owe me some of that chocolate ass."

Jamal shook his head. "You need to get some rest. We got shit to take of tomorrow and I need you on your A-game."

"Oh naw, you aint getting away that easy. You going to ride this dick til I bust. Now get down there and suck my shit so I can get hard."

Jamal looked over at Diego biting his bottom lip. He shook his head as he moved down to Diego's shorts and pulled them down to his ankles. He looked up at Diego. The El Salvadorian motioned at his thickening manhood. Jamal pulled his boy's boxers down and took Diego in his mouth.

Chapter 23

Jamal couldn't sleep. He lay in the bed, Diego nuzzled up under him, looking blankly at the ceiling. The paranoia fueled insomnia had his nerves wrecked. He couldn't get a grip and his only anchor was Diego. He looked down at his Latin lover. Jamal wondered if he would be enough. He doubted it. Diego's presence was a much needed comfort but Jamal just couldn't shake the feeling that the fragile world he'd thrust himself into was collapsing around him.

He felt small and insignificant. Diego, Smurf and now Santana had all attested to the reach and power that Slim wielded. His control extended up and down the east coast. Jamal knew he had to be paid if he was supplying drug dealers and had a direct line to cats down in Ecuador, Peru or where ever he got his dope from. Thinking about it was mind boggling.

Jamal couldn't fathom why a man so paid would be pressed about the couple of thousands that a stick up crew could bring in. $20,000 would change Jamal's and every cat in the crew's life but it was just a piss in the river of revenue for Slim. Recruiting Jamal, Romeo and Diego was more than trying to make more money. Slim had a personal vendetta to settle and the crew was just a pawn in the grand scheme of the man's plans. That much was obvious.

Jamal pulled Diego's heavy arm from over his chest and sat up on the bed. He threw his legs over onto the floor, pressed his elbows in his thighs and placed his face in his palms. Jamal had gone over everything that had happened over the last week and still could not seem to put everything in perspective. From the outside looking in, it seemed like Slim was just a demented asshole who got his rocks off by toying with people's lives. That would have been a good enough explanation before Jamal realized that the man had him and the crew robbing his family.

What kind of shit happened for a man to want to rob and kill his own blood, Jamal wondered.

He stood up from the bed and went to the window. Jamal looked out and took in the scenic view of Baltimore. It was a city near water. Jamal liked that. He had love for Atlanta but a change of pace had been nice. The unfamiliar city had offered a break from the daily shit Jamal had dealt with in his hometown even if he was up there to hustle and rob dudes. Jamal looked back over his shoulder and stared at Diego, still asleep.

Jamal wondered if he was really in love with the boy. Doubt lingered. The idea of loving a man still seemed foreign to him even if being in Diego's arms; holding him, kissing him and making love to him, came as natural as breathing. If nothing else, Diego was convinced that Jamal was worthy of his love. That's at least what he had said with his mouth. Jamal was still waiting for his actions to speak that truth. If that was the case, then moving from Atlanta to somewhere up north or out west would be a great way to start afresh.

But Jamal wasn't delusional. There would be no future with Diego while Slim still walked the earth and drew breath. The thought of the man made Jamal's blood boil. His fantasies were dominated by two images: making love to Diego and putting a bullet through Slim's forehead. There was no sleeping moment where Jamal did not conspire to end Slim's life. And with the arrival of Santana, Slim's estranged niece, he thought he finally had a means to get the deed done.

Jamal moved from the window to the door separating his room from Romeo and Smurf's. He stood there, mentally picturing them and Santana sleeping the night away, as he should have been doing. *Hungry niggas never sleep*, Jamal thought. It was a mantra that his father had said over and over when Jamal was too young to understand what it meant. Until now.

A frown formed on Jamal's face. He wondered why thoughts of his deceased father had suddenly entered his mind. While Jamal only had fond memories of the man, he hadn't really thought of him much for years. When he was murdered, Jamal was too young to see him for the drug kingpin he'd been in Atlanta. That hadn't been an accident.

Jamal's mother had made it her top priority to grind in his young head that he was going to be more than "a nigga in the streets." But as much as she had tried to shield him, there wasn't anyone in the game who didn't know Jamal's father.

Many of the old heads had said it was in his blood to be a hustler, "a nigga about that work." It was a phrase which men that had known Jamal's father heard the legendary kingpin say over and over again when he was on top. Jamal wondered if that hustler mentality he adopted was in fact in his blood.

Jamal knew that he had the instinct and go get it attitude of a hustler. He'd never been scared of the streets. Jamal had hungered for the cold concrete jungle filled with opportunity and danger. And knew that any dude that picked up a gun and was ready to take what he wanted lived on the edge. The threat of jail and death was a constant one. But the rewards somehow made it all worth it in his mind. Jamal only realized that recently.

Having a name on the streets was what got many dudes hard like a porn star. Others got off by stacking guap like Leggos. But Jamal knew that the few that stayed true to the hustle were the ones that were in it to make something bigger for them, the one's they loved and their progeny. Jamal was his father's namesake and his legacy. Jamal intended on living up to that legacy and being under the heel of a man like Slim was unacceptable.

A sound from behind the door grabbed Jamal and took him from his thoughts. He was sure it was a moan. Whether it was from pain or pleasure was unclear. Tentatively, Jamal placed his ear against the door. Silence. He stood there and waited. It was still quiet. Too quiet. Jamal stepped back, placed his hand on the handle and turned it down ever so quietly.

Slowly, Jamal pulled the door open just a crack. He let the handle go, not letting it make a sound. With the stealth of a panther, Jamal laced his fingers between the small crack of the door and frame. He eased the door open. The second door, the one on Smurf and Romeo's side was already open. Jamal had a clear view of the room. What he saw baffled him.

Santana, Romeo and Smurf were all lying in one bed, spooning each other like lovers. Romeo was in the middle. Jamal tilted his head and looked at the trio queerly. He was at a loss for words. Had there not been so much baggage between him and each of them, it would have been one of the most erotic things he'd ever seen. But looking at the three of them linked together in such an intimate position just complicated things that much more for Jamal.

Smurf had been on Jamal's short list from the get go. Santana was a new face that Jamal wanted to see gone. But Romeo was his boy. At least he had been. At one time the two of them were as inseparable as brothers. Jamal understood that Romeo was mad at him for what had happened at Slim's pool hall but couldn't see how he could still hold that hate, especially after Slim had just threatened him with rape a few hours ago. In Jamal's mind, Romeo had sided with the enemy. He shook his head and began to turn around until he saw movement out the corner of his eye. It was Santana.

Her head peeked up from the mass of pillows and blankets. She turned towards Jamal's direction. The steady stream of moonlight coming through the window cast a sobering glow on her soft, beautiful face. Santana's large, almond shaped eyes stared at Jamal's silhouette of a figure. There wasn't enough light for Jamal to read the expression on her face. He wondered if fear or indignation flared in her hard gaze as their eyes locked. The two of them were still as a picture; unflinching, unmoving.

The list of reasons Jamal had come up while laying in the bed looking up at the ceiling on why Santana couldn't and shouldn't be trusted ran through his mind, demanding his attention like a train wreck. Jamal wondered what thoughts ran through her mind.

Santana was the first to move.

She eased her petite yet curvy body from Romeo's grip without waking him and got out of the bed. Her eyes were glued on Jamal as she moved to the other bed in the hotel room and carefully snatched the covers off. She wrapped the blanket over her shoulders, covering herself and the form fitting t-shirt and boy shorts she had worn to bed. With the grace of a swan and the confident stride of an undefeated boxer, she made her way over to the door, where Jamal stood.

Although the top of Santana's head only came to Jamal's chin, the masculine vixen stood toe to toe with the crew leader, the two of them leaning against opposite ends of the door frame. Jamal looked at her face, unable to not admire the simple beauty of her simple, smooth face. Her eyes, feigning innocence, moved from Jamal's face to his room. They settled on Diego's sprawled body on the bed, then over to the empty, undisturbed bed. She looked back at Jamal. Some of the tension in her face had left.

"You don't trust me, do you?" she asked.

Jamal eyed her suspiciously. "Why should I?"

"You shouldn't. You have no reason to." She looked back over towards Diego. "He means something to you?" Jamal heard the question but recognized that it was more an assertion than an inquiry. He crossed his arms over his chest and pressed his lips together. Santana looked back at Jamal. "He kept asking for you when I helped him outside of the club."

"Why are you here?" Jamal asked, narrowing his gaze and reigning in his growing anger. He looked towards Romeo and Smurf. "I know you're not here for them."

"I'm not," she confirmed. "And they know that."

"Then why are you here?" Jamal pressed, not so sure Romeo felt the way she did.

"Revenge."

"Against?"

"Everyone."

Jamal considered her vague words. She barely answered but had said everything that needed to be said to make Jamal understand even if he wasn't fully convinced of her motives.

"What did they take from you?" Jamal asked. "And don't say 'everything'?"

A small smirk curled at the corners of her mouth. Then a somber expression clouded her face almost instantly. "They took my innocence; my will to live for myself and my ability to love."

"You're cousins?"

She nodded. "And uncle."

Jamal frowned. He wouldn't put it past Slim to rape his niece but reserved his opinion on believing Santana because it was the first he'd head of it. Santana straightened and stared harder at Jamal. She'd seen his brief change of demeanor.

"Don't think you're the only one he's tried to control with the threat of rape and humiliation," she asserted. "Mr. Avant "Slim" Monroe is a sick fuck and deserves everything that comes his way."

"You said you didn't know his name."

Santana shrugged. "I lied."

"So how am I supposed to believe anything you say?"

"What you believe is not important. At least not for what I plan on doing. But trust that I will say what needs to be said for me to do what I need to do."

"Big words from such a little girl."

A vicious smile parted Santana's full lips. She slipped her hand from under the covers that draped over her small frame. Her small hand was wrapped around an equally small gun. Jamal froze up as soon as he saw the heat she'd been carrying. She pulled it back just as quickly.

"Relax," she said. "I took my finger off the trigger as soon as I saw your boy in the bed. I thought you were going to try and hurt me like all the other men I've run into in my life."

Jamal let out a heavy sigh of relief. "Is that why you're a lesbian?"

"No. I just like pussy."

The two of them fought back stifled laughs.

"So level with me," Jamal started. "Are you really here to kill your own blood?"

"If they were blood then they wouldn't have violated me the way they did."

"You didn't answer my question."

Santana let out a sigh and licked her lips. "I'd be lying if I said I was a killer. I'm not, Jamal. I just want a chance to make them all pay for what they did. If that means a bullet in the chest or in the balls, so be it."

"Fair enough."

"So you believe me?"

"No."

"Do you trust me?"

"Hell no."

"Are you going to let me help you guys tomorrow?"

"Go to bed and we'll find out when we get up."

Santana opened her mouth like she was about to say something, then quickly snapped her jaw shut and nodded. Slowly she took the door and closed it as Jamal did the same.

For a moment, Jamal just stood there, thinking about what Santana had said. His opinion about her hadn't changed. She was trouble, just like Smurf and like an increasingly unreliable Romeo. But for now, he'd use her to and what she knew to take out the cats that had shot Diego and appease Slim.

Jamal dragged his feet and headed for the bathroom. He looked over at Diego. The Latin sensation was still knocked out. Jamal shifted his gaze towards the alarm clock. It was still dark outside but it was almost six in the morning.

Jamal hit the shower as soon as the water was warm enough. He leaned under the shower head and let the warmth of the water relax some of the tension in his body. Worry and concern had not only taken a mental toll but a physical one as well. Before he could busy his mind with more plots and schemes, he felt the familiar touch of Diego at his back. The Spanish thug pressed his naked flesh onto Jamal's back.

"You didn't sleep last at all, did you?"

Jamal turned around. He reached up and held Diego's face in his hand. "No."

Diego shook his head and looked at Jamal with the shadow of concern darkening his expression. "You know you need to sleep."

"I know."

"Still thinking about ways to kill Slim?"

"Always."

"Well," Diego started. He placed his hand on Jamal's chest. "You need to rest if you want your mind and body to work right. Maybe you just need some tension relief."

"That's why I was taking a hot shower."

Diego smiled and began moving down Jamal's body, before the crew leader could utter another word, kissing and sucking all the way down. Jamal thrust his head back and clenched at the shower curtain and wall as his man took him in his mouth and gave him the much needed relief denied him by his own thoughts.

Chapter 24

"That's my cousin Tay with the black fitted," Santana said. "He's the one that runs the trap house ya'll robbed the other night. The fat boy with the baby face and the forty in his hand is C-Note. He's dumb as fuck but he's Tay's muscle. He's the one that shot Diego in the club last night. That nigga is slick reckless."

Jamal's eyes followed where she pointed at through the tinted window of the black SUV Romeo had boosted just an hour ago. Three men huddled together outside of a convenience store, laughing. His gaze settled on the chubby, would be killer and committed the man's face to memory. Jamal promised himself that the last thing C-Note would see would be the barrel of a gun lodge in his fat mouth.

"C-Note?" Smurf asked from the third row of the vehicle. "How the fuck that fat nigga get a name like that?"

"How does anyone get a nickname running the streets?" Diego asked. He turned from the front passenger seat and looked back at everyone. "Shit, why does everyone call you Smurf?"

"Do you really want to know why they call him C-Note?" Santana asked.

"Fuck that," Jamal said. "It won't matter what they call his fat ass after I put a bullet between his eyes. They'll just call him dead."

Jamal's words had had the intended affected. The somber silence that pervaded the small space reflected on everyone's expression. Jamal wasn't interested in anecdotes or jokes. The only thing on his mind was figuring out how to deal with the dudes that had tried to take Diego's life. Nothing else mattered at that moment.

Tay and C-Note had looked familiar to Jamal. He even recognized the tall, dark skinned skinny dude standing with them. The first stickup the crew had run had been botched. It was by pure luck and the grace of God that they all walked out of there unscathed. Mistakes were made. That was Diego's first brush with death. Last night at the club would be his last if Jamal had anything to do with it.

"Who's the skinny dude with them?" Jamal asked.

"Keyon," Santana answered. "They call him Black, for obvious reasons."

"I remember that nigga," Diego said. "He's the runner that we caught outside the trap house with the females from the first house we robbed."

"Yea," Jamal confirmed. "And the fat boy is the nigga that answered the door."

"You remember Tay, don't you Jamal?" Romeo asked. He

didn't wait for a reply. "You put a gun in his mouth after you slapped him. That was right before you were about to put your dick in his mouth. Remember that?"

Jamal slowly turned from the window and looked at Romeo with a stare that could almost kill. He ignored the shocked looks on Smurf and Santana's face. Diego's hung head offered him no consolation. Jamal zeroed in on Romeo. The overwhelming urged to slap the spit from the boy's mouth pulsed at Jamal's finger tips. But the feeling was fleeting. His guilt was too overwhelming.

Nothing Romeo had said was untrue. Hearing it now had stung him almost as deeply as when Romeo called him 'Slim' when it had all went down. Jamal wasn't Slim. He loathed that man. Jamal refused to become the monster Slim was. Slowly, the anger that had flared like a wildfire had subsided to a smoldering ember. He was still pissed but more so at himself.

Santana squirmed uneasily, wedged between Romeo and Jamal. The tension in the car cut through the prevailing silence. It was only when Jamal shook his head and pulled his eyes from Romeo that the crew let out a collective sigh of relief. They'd recoiled from the precipice of pure chaos that could have easily enveloped in the SUV. The growing tension between Jamal and Romeo needed only a spark. Anyone near the two of them felt the beef stewing between them. It was only a matter of time.

"So are we actually going to kill all them niggas?" Smurf asked.

Jamal sighed. "They saw our faces. Slim said that he wanted them dead. You gonna run and tell that nigga you aint going to do it? Besides, when was the last time you did anything besides drive the fucking car? Do I need to remind you about the sawed off shotgun and Romeo shooting you in the leg?"

Smurf shook his head. He turned towards the windshield, facing away from everyone, and sulked in the driver seat. Jamal smiled. Finally, he was able to hit below the belt on Smurf and Romeo.

"He has a point, Jamal," Diego chimed in. "Do we really have to kill them?"

"Are you serious?" Jamal asked. He felt a tinge of betrayal. *We talked about this shit last night*, he thought. "You don't want to take care of the motherfucker that shot you?"

"I'm just saying, I'm not dead. I'm still breathing."

Jamal sighed. He was annoyed. He honestly didn't care if they killed the three trap boys or not. Especially since Diego wasn't too pressed about it. But he knew that if he didn't do what Slim wanted then he would be on the man's shit list. Going against an order from Slim almost guaranteed that he'd never get the chance to finally take him out.

Jamal looked over at Romeo. "What do you think?" he asked. "Should we take him out execution style like you did that big swole nigga at the trap house?"

The flash of emotion that hit Santana's face caught Jamal's eye as Romeo shrugged nonchalantly. It was gone in a fraction of a second. Jamal was sure that he was the only one that had caught it. Her momentary relapse had pique Jamal's interest.

"What about you, Santana?" Jamal prodded. "You want any of them taken out?"

Jamal watched the girl's face as she stared back at him. Jamal was sure everyone knew by now what Santana had gone through with her cousins. Or at least what she had suggested. If she had wanted blood, there was a reason. The question also poked at her relevancy. She'd taken the crew to where the guys who shot Diego hung out. Her usefulness seemed to have run its course and Jamal saw no need to keep her around.

"I'll do it," Santana said, her voice a whisper.

"Do what?" Jamal asked.

"Kill em'."

"Just C-Note or all three of them?"

Santana narrowed her gaze. "I'm going to need help."

A coy grin curled at the corner of Jamal's mouth. "Is everyone willing to help out the latest addition to the crew?"

Looks of surprise were coupled with shrugs of affirmation. None of them really wanted to kill anyone but with the pressure on their backs from Slim and the resolve from Santana, they all had begrudgingly come around to getting the task done.

"Great," Jamal said, sarcasm tainting his tone. "Now all have to do is figure out how to off those niggas."

"Well, we can't exactly shot them now in broad daylight," Smurf said, still staring straight ahead. "We'd have the feds all over our asses."

"I'm sorry, you have a gun?" Jamal quibbled. "I thought you were just the fucking driver. How bout you focus on that? Fucking clown."

"We need to get them somewhere alone," Diego said, cutting the back and forth between Jamal and Smurf short.

"Alright," Jamal said, looking back out the window. "But them niggas don't look like they're going anywhere anytime soon. Guess we have to wait until they make a move."

"Actually," Santana said. "Can I have my phone back, please?"

Jamal eyed her suspiciously. "For what?"

"Do you want to get this shit done quickly or not?"

Despite his reservations and mistrust of the tomboy, Jamal reached in his back pocket and pulled out the cell phone. He reluctantly handed it over, watching her with a wary eye as she punched away at the device. When she was done she placed her hands on her lap and stared blankly at the seat in front of her. Jamal leveled a hard look at her, demanding an explanation. She stared back at him indifferently and then averted her eyes. The message was clear: wait.

After what seemed like forever but was actually little more than five minutes, Tay was on his phone talking. Soon after, the trio piled into an Impala and pulled out of the parking lot. They were halfway down the street and almost out of sight when Smurf revved the SUV up.

"Should I follow them?" he asked, his voice laced with uncertainty.

"Yea, should we follow them?" Jamal echoed.

"No," Santana replied curtly.

Jamal bit his lip and balled his fist. His patience was running thin. The smug look of satisfaction on Santana's face beckoned at him and his knuckles. He'd never struck a female but the satisfaction he knew he'd get from crushing her pretty little face teased him like preteen virgin pussy for a pedophile.

"I'm going to say this one time, Santana," Jamal began. "This is not a game. If I think for one minute you're fucking around and putting our lives at risk, I will end you. No questions asked. I will put a bullet through your skull. I'm not trying to threaten you but you clearly need to get a clear picture of how real this shit is. Now explain what the fuck is going on and what you just did."

"Fine, I'm sorry," Santana offered. Her voice conveyed understanding of the gravity of the circumstances. Yet there wasn't a lick of fear to be heard. "What is almost every man's weakness?"

A smile formed on Jamal's face. "Pussy."

"Exactly. I just texted my girl that Tay has been fucking with for the last couple of months. She hit him up and offered the pussy up. Promised to ride his dick like an all-star jockey."

"She going to let all them niggas hit?" Smurf asked.

"No, stupid. She has her own spot. One of her old boyfriends left his PlayStation at her spot. Black and C-Note will probably be on the game while they are in the back fucking."

"Tay doesn't know that ya'll are cool?" Jamal asked.

"Yea, he do."

"Then why the fuck is he still dealing with her?!"

"LaQuita is the first female I fucked with," Santana explained. "I met her through Tay. He's the one that outed me. LaQuita doesn't fuck with females anymore. But we're still cool. Tay doesn't know that we still talk."

"You still aint explain why this broad would help you set that nigga up?"

"She's my friend and she's a woman." Santana looked down. Her voice became a whisper. "She understands."

Jamal clenched his mouth shut. His skepticism nagged at him like an addict begging for his fix. He wanted to take the girl at her word but something in him wouldn't let him accept her explanation at face value. But he didn't have room to question her; at least not now. He decided to go along with her explanation, until he could prove otherwise.

"Alright," Jamal relented. "Your girl LaQuita is going to just let us waltz right in when Tay has his pants down with a hard, wet dick and his boys are stuck on stupid playing the game."

"I have a key to the apartment."

"Well that's convenient," Jamal said sarcastically. "So run down how this shit is going to work."

"The apartment has two entrances. We're going to come in through the back, in the kitchen. Creep in and catch them niggas off guard. Simple."

"We can't kill them in the apartment," Romeo chimed in. "Be too messy."

"How much does this LaQuita know about what we're doing to them?" Diego asked.

Santana shrugged. "Nothing specific. But she knows wassup. She's from the hood. She's good. She ain't no snitch."

"We still need to wear masks when we run up in that bitch," Diego offered.

"True," Romeo agreed. "But how are we going to get three niggas out of the apartment?"

"Shit, just get them high," Smurf said jokingly.

"Damn, that's actually not a bad idea," Jamal said.

"Really?" Smurf asked.

"That should work," Romeo said. "We can cop some pills and get them doped up so that they don't put up a struggle when we bring them to the car."

"Alright, so where to?" Jamal asked.

Smurf pulled out and headed to a local dealer he was

familiar with to get the dope. Santana gave him LaQuita's address to GPS. They were on their way to do Slim's bidding and the knot in Jamal's stomach couldn't have twisted any harder than it was during the whole ride.

Something about the whole scenario seemed too easy, too convenient. Slim had been the one to suggest having Santana assist in the murder of the trap boys. Regardless, Jamal didn't even trust her with that task despite her supposed misfortunes with her family. The whole thing reeked of a trap. For a moment, he thought that waiting for the trio to emerge from the apartment and opening fire on them would be a better plan. But the idea of a shootout in broad daylight made him cringe.

When they pulled up to the apartment building the crew collectively prepared for the assault. Diego tucked his two pistols in his pants and stuffed some zip tie in his pockets. Romeo slid his gun down the front of his pants and took the pills to drug the men up from Smurf. Even Santana had her little gun tucked between her breasts.

Jamal made eye contact with everyone, making sure they were ready to roll out. He was the first one out the SUV. They moved swiftly and quietly. Once they made it to the apartment they huddled at the door, pulled on their masks and waited as Santana quietly put the key in the knob and turned.

Everyone had their guns drawn. Santana and Diego were the first ones inside, then Jamal and Romeo in the rear. As expected, the sound of the game and the complementary shit talking rumbled through the apartment. Santana held up her hand and motioned for Diego to take the lead. He obliged and stepped in front of her. As one unit, they moved from the kitchen into the living room. Black and C-Note were caught off-guard.

Diego pointed both his pistols at them as Santana had his flank and motioned for them to be quiet. The pair thrust their hands in the air and angrily eyed the crew. Diego moved to zip tie their hands and feet. Once they were secured it was onto the bedroom.

Santana looked back at Jamal and motioned for him to go to the bedroom with Romeo. Jamal shot her a hard look before moving. His stomach twisted but he pushed on. He stepped to the hallway and waited until Romeo had his back. The two moved to the door. Jamal looked back at Romeo before reaching for the knob. Romeo nodded. They moved.

Jamal snatched the knob and thrust the door open. He charged in with his gun raised. He caught sight of the bed and aimed. It was empty. Panic gripped him. He turned and looked behind the door. He stood there, frozen, staring down the barrel of a gun.

"Put that shit down, nigga," Tay ordered. "Unless you wanna suck on this steel. I hear your faggot ass likes putting things in your mouth."

"Bitch," Jamal mumbled as he lowered his pistol.

"You too pretty boy," a female voice said.

Jamal looked over his should and saw who he assumed was LaQuita with a Glock pressed against the back of Romeo's head. Without pause, Romeo put his gun down too. The Bonnie and Clyde pair escorted them back to the living room. Jamal wasn't the least bit surprised at what he saw.

Diego was on the couch, his hands and feet bound. Jamal looked over at Santana. She stood in front of the flat screen, her hands on her hips, flanked by C-Note and Black. Santana didn't smile. There was no hint of gloating. Still, Jamal fumed. He'd seen the deception from the start. He'd let Smurf, Romeo and Diego to a lesser extent, cloud his judgment and go against his instinct.

Before Jamal could utter one of the half dozen threats dancing on the tip of his tongue, the front door opened. Jamal wasn't surprised. Smurf waltz through like it was his apartment. He walked over to Santana and stood next to her.

"I promise you two one thing," Jamal said. "You'd better kill me if you plan on breathing another day."

A tight lip smile creased Santana's face.

Chapter 25

"Calm that shit down and take a seat," Santana said. She motioned towards the couch where Diego sat. "No one is going to kill anyone as long as no one does anything stupid."

No sooner had the words left her mouth that Tay barreled towards the trio and brought the butt of his gun down on Romeo's face over and over again. Jamal moved to stop the assault but C-Note's cocking of his gun had him reconsider the move. Blood was everywhere. Yet, surprisingly Romeo didn't cry out or fight back. He just took it. It took Santana to get Smurf, Black and C-Note to pull Tay off Romeo for it to end.

"What the fuck was that for?!" Jamal demanded. He looked up at Santana angrily. "I thought you said aint shit was going to happen?!"

Santana shook her head. "I said no one would be killed."

She looked over at a fuming Tay. "And I'd guess that Tay is still mad about Romeo killing his best friend, Boi Boi. Remember, the big linebacker looking dude that had your boo thang yoked up at the trap house?"

Jamal looked at Tay and saw the anger flaring in his eyes. He was a pit bull on a tight leash that could snap at any moment. Jamal reached over to help Romeo but was angrily shrugged off. Hurt or not, Romeo still had a deep rooted contempt for Jamal. Even with guns pointed at them and death a few breathes away, that wasn't going to change. Jamal looked over at Diego.

His teenage love was scared. Jamal could tell even though there wasn't a lick of fear on his face. He was ready to look death in the eye and welcome it with a warm embrace. Jamal felt the same way. He looked up at Santana.

The cold, calculating eyes gave the stickup boy pause. Part of him wondered why she still let them breathe and why she'd promised that no one would get killed. Again, Jamal felt like he was simply a pawn in a much larger scheme.

"If you're not going to kill us, what do you want? Money?" Jamal asked.

Tay and LaQuita laughed like it had been the funniest thing they'd ever heard. A quick, hard stare from Santana instantly quieted them. It was obvious who was in charge. She moved to the coffee table in front of the couch and sat down. She crossed her legs and leaned in as if she were about to explain something very complex in simple terms for a child.

"We have money, Jamal," she began. "The couple of stacks you could get with your little stickup hustle aint shit, trust me. No, I have bigger plans for you. I need you. I want you to be my partner, for now. I got a job for you and your little crew."

Jamal frowned. "Partner? How the fuck would that work? You just beat in my boy's face and you have four guns pointed at me. Where the fucked they do that at? Must be a D.C. thing. Negotiating deals at gun point and shit."

Santana smirked. She looked over her shoulders and gave a quick nod, gesturing for C-Note, Tay, Black and LaQuita to put down their guns. Slowly they obliged. Jamal pounced.

The crew leader sprang to his feet and had his forearm and bicep snugly placed on Santana's throat. His free hand gripped the back of her skull. With enough pressure, he'd snap her neck and crush her wind pipe before any of his captors could end his life with a bullet.

Struggling to breath and on her tippy toes, Santana didn't even fight Jamal. She demanded that everyone put their guns down. She tried to say something but Jamal's grip was too tight. Santana tapped his strangling bicep. The only reason he let her speak was because everyone's gun was pointed at the ground.

"Bitch, you better give me a good reason why I shouldn't snap your neck before your goons fill me bullets. I'm ready to die, are you?"

"I have a way for us to get rid of Slim."

Jamal's throat constricted. His breathing became shallow. The titillating thought of Slim dead yanked at him. Nothing Santana had said before was true. She'd lied, deceived and plotted to get Jamal and the crew where they were now. Yet despite all that, Jamal hoped that there was a drop of truth in her words. He figured there was no other reason for him to still be alive.

"Why the fuck should I believe anything you have to say?"

"If this was about killing you, all of you would be dead right now. Tay wouldn't have hesitated to put a bullet in ya'll hearts. Trust me when I say he's itching to kill all of you."

Jamal looked over at Tay and saw the truth in Santana's words. The boy wanted blood but there was something restraining the inner urge of murder and revenge. Something larger than him was going on. Jamal decided to play along. He had nothing to lose. From the moment Tay had a gun to his head back in the bedroom he knew he wouldn't be leaving the apartment alive anyways. Jamal was on borrowed time.

"Partners, hunh?" Jamal echoed. Skepticism lingered in his voice. "Then why don't you give Diego and Romeo their guns back so we can be equal in this fucking union."

Without hesitation, Santana motioned for Smurf to give Jamal's crew their guns back. A wary expression hunkered on his face but he did as he was instructed. Locked and loaded, Romeo and Diego held their gun at their hips and stared down Santana's gang of thugs.

"You going to let me go now?" she asked.

A million and one thoughts ran through Jamal's mind. It was a real possibility that Tay, C-Note, Black or LaQuita would put a bullet through his chest the moment he released Santana. He just hoped that Diego and Romeo would be able to get off a couple of shots and go out like soldiers. With nothing to lose but a life that was forfeited the moment he picked up a gun back in Atlanta, Jamal let Santana go. He closed his eyes and waited for the barrage of bullets to rip through his body.

They never came.

Jamal opened his eyes and looked from Santana's goons to Romeo and Diego. Only a slight misstep would plummet the room into chaos. But for now, there was room to talk; room to negotiate.

"Sit down, Jamal," Santana said. "We have a lot to discuss."

Jamal obliged. "You lied about everything."

"Not everything."

"Did Slim really do all the things you said he did? Did Tay and your cousins really rape you?"

"None of that matters," Santana said. Her dodging the question didn't matter. Jamal saw the look on Tay's face at the sound of his name being attached to the act of rape. "What matters is that we have a mutual interest: killing Slim."

"Why do you want him dead? Why is it so important to you? Why go through all this bullshit to kill a man that that bitch nigga over there could have taken care of before we even entered the picture?"

Smurf visibly shrunk back from Jamal's accusatory finger leveled at him. Tay gave the boy a sidelong glance that only confirmed that the sentiment had been mutual across the table. Santana waved off the accusation.

"You're focusing on the wrong shit right now, Jamal."

"Please, enlighten me as to what the right *shit* is."

"How we're going to kill Slim."

"Fine, but tell me one thing," Jamal began, "why couldn't you do this on your own? Why couldn't Smurf take Slim out on his own? The two of them are close enough for him to get the opportunity."

Santana looked back at Smurf and gave him a motherly smile. "You're right. Smurf is very close to Slim. Maybe too close. He's in love with the man. In some disturbing way, he has very strong emotions for the man that abused and repeatedly raped him and can't bring himself to pull the trigger."

"Then why is he here?" Jamal asked.

"He may have a twisted infatuation with the man but he isn't loyal to him. And he knows shit about Slim that none of us would have found out if it weren't for him."

"Like?"

Santana smiled. "How about I explain our little plan?"

"Let me guess. You want to go Slim's house, guns a blazing?"

"No, you're going to deliver Tay, C-Note and Black up to Slim as planned."

Jamal frowned. He blinked incessantly, not believing what he'd just heard. He looked over at the gang of thugs and didn't see one of them flinch. Jamal looked back at Romeo and Diego. They looked equally baffled by Santana's supposed plan. Like a mad man, Jamal began to laugh uncontrollably. Santana sighed and crossed her arms over her chest. She waited until he calmed down before she spoke again.

"Are you done?" she asked, annoyed.

"Am I done? Bitch, are you crazy?" Jamal shook his head and buried his face in his hands. "That nigga is expecting three dead bodies. How the fuck we going to fake that?"

"You're not. You already said you aint want to kill them. Smurf had his phone on with Slim listening while we were in the car. Slim heard the whole thing."

Jamal looked over at Smurf. "You're a sneaky motherfucker."

Contempt and rage tugged on Jamal's spirit as he looked at Smurf. The would-be stoner had played him from the get go.

Jamal couldn't help but wonder what role he had played in getting Diego shot or having the first stick-up go south. There was no telling how deep that nigga's treachery went.

"I only did what I had to do," Smurf offered.

"And I'm only going to do to you what I think you deserve," Jamal threatened. He looked at the boy wondering if he had his phone on again.

"Once this is all over everyone will go their separate ways," Santana interceded. "Right now we have something we both want: Slim dead. Let's focus on that, please."

"Fine," Jamal said, his gaze stuck on Smurf. "How are we going to serve up some not so dead bodies and find a way to take Slim out?"

"We're going to act like everything worked out. You'll escort the three of them back to the SUV, one by one, call Slim and tell him that you're not going to kill them. That he has to do his own dirty work."

"And you think that shit is going to work? You and I know damn well that nigga is going to be on some discipline hierarchy bullshit. I promise you I'm not going to let that nigga near me."

Santana stood up. "You're going to do whatever it takes to do this right. You understand?!"

"Bitch, what?" Jamal looked up at the girl like she was a piece of shit on his shoe.

"Or doesn't it matter what he did to you and made you do to your best friend and boyfriend?"

Jamal sank back and hung his head, not wanting to look at Diego or Romeo. Slim's death was a harrowing preoccupation for Jamal. He wanted nothing more than to have the chance to end the man's life for what he did. And as much as he hated to admit it, he'd do almost anything to see that fantasy become a realization.

"Slim never goes anywhere without his goons," Jamal said. He sighed as he gave the plan consideration. "And if he has us meet him somewhere they'll probably take our guns. Your cousin and his little entourage would be killed on the spot and we'd still be stuck working for that nigga. That's assuming he doesn't catch whiff of this little meeting right here. I'm not seeing how this shit could possibly work."

"It's not rocket science, Jamal. And it's not a plan etched in stone without risks. We only thought it up when we found out Slim wanted you guys to hit up Tay's trap house."

"Who thought it up? You and Smurf? He's the one that told you we were going to hit the house up first?"

Santana pursed her lips and shook her head. "You are dedicated to focusing on the wrong shit, aren't you?"

"I don't trust you," Jamal said, spitting the words out like venom. "I'm not even sure that you know where the lies end and the truth begins. You're fucking delusional."

"Alright, let's get something clear. The truth of the matter is you're alive because *I* say so. Period. Nothing else fucking matters. Truth; beings that I thought you'd jump at a chance to kill Slim and gave your boys their guns back we're at a crossroad right now. Truth; we can all shoot each other and hope to be the last ones standing or we can walk out of here like everything went according to plan, take Tay, C-Note and Black to Slim and kill the son-of-a-bitch."

Jamal took a deep breath and weighed the girl's words. He'd been burned too many times to just go with what she said but he had a hard time seeing any type of alternative. Jamal knew that the bullshit plan Santana had concocted wouldn't work. Slim would see right through it and kill them all. Hell, with Smurf's disloyal ass, Slim could have been listening to the conversation right now. The only thing that gave Jamal hope was the fact that he might have a chance, however remote, to kill Slim before he was gunned down himself. It was an acceptable risk.

"Fine," Jamal said. "We'll do it how you say. But your little crew is going to have to give up the guns and let us wrap those zip ties on their wrists."

Santana looked at Jamal with a wary expression full of mistrust and apprehension. Regardless, she got up and took the guns from Tay, Black and C-Note. She motioned for LaQuita to bind their hands up. Once that was done, she stared at Jamal, waiting.

"You're serious," Jamal said.

"As death."

"And what if this shit doesn't work?"

"Then everyone dies," Santana said. "And hopefully Slim goes out in the process."

Jamal nodded. If nothing else, the two of them were in agreement on that one issue. The crew leader looked towards Diego and motioned him to step forward.

"You and Smurf take that big gorilla looking nigga first."

C-Note shook his head as he was escorted out the apartment. There was no love lost. And even less was gained. After about five minutes it was on to the next. Jamal had Romeo take Black to the SUV. Jamal stared at Santana, racking his mind as to what the girl's end game was. Slim's death meant the end of a constant threat to Jamal's manhood. What it meant to Santana was still very much unclear.

"What if they're watching?" Jamal asked.

"They are."

Jamal simply nodded. He'd expected as much. He imagined Bricks tailing them and watching them take the dope boys out one by one. It didn't matter. Jamal doubted the rouse would work anyways. His only hope was that his last breath came after Slim's. Jamal stood up and motioned towards the door. Santana was the first one out. Tay and Jamal followed behind. LaQuita stayed behind.

Once they were huddled in the SUV, Smurf passed his cell phone back to Jamal. "Slim wants to talk to you."

Jamal shot the boy a hard stare and snatched the phone. "We have them niggas that tried to kill Diego at the club. But I aint killing no niggas for some shit that aint end in a nigga six feet under. You going to have to take care of that shit yourself."

Everyone in the SUV got quiet. Jamal just listened. He didn't say another word. Just as quickly as he had spoken, he hung up the phone.

"What did he say," Smurf asked, everyone wondering the same thing.

"Not much," Jamal said.

"Now what?" Santana said.

Jamal looked at her blankly. "We wait."

Chapter 26

Jamal paced back and forth in front of the hotel room window. It had been six hours since he'd spoken to Slim on the phone and he hadn't heard a word back yet. They all had waited in the SUV for an hour before he and Santana had decided that it would probably be a good idea to wait at the hotel. Everyone was hungry and getting antsy cooped up in the SUV.

Now it was getting dark. Anxiety had wrecked havoc on the young stick-up crew leader. Jamal looked back over his shoulder at Diego. A calm storm seemed to encompass the boy's face. It was a look Jamal had seen many times on the faces of men about to enter the ring with a man they knew was stronger, faster and more than likely to knock them out. It was an expression that belied cowardice and faced the impeding danger ahead. It was a look of resolve.

No other moment in the brief time Jamal had known Diego was he more proud of him. The urge to go over and sit next to Diego on the bed was nauseating. Jamal almost gave in to his bodily urge but then he looked beyond the young man that made his heart weep with joy to the other side of the hotel room.

Black and Smurf lay across the other bed, laughing and chatting like little school girls. A few times Jamal was sure Smurf was talking to the dope boy about him and Diego. With Tay and C-Note in the other room with Romeo and Santana, the pair were like cackling hens gossiping in whispered tones. Waiting was unbearable. Waiting with a snake like Smurf a few feet away was insufferable.

Jamal was going through an internal struggle the moment he stepped into the room. On one hand he wanted to be there for Diego. On the other he wanted to rip Smurf's heart from his chest. And on top of it all, he needed to come to terms with the fact that his life would very likely come to an end in a few hours. Accepting his fate had been the most difficult thing imaginable.

Diego stood up and placed his hand on Jamal's shoulder. The gentle touch grounded him. If only for a moment, the world seemed to not be collapsing around Jamal. He looked over at Diego and saw the comfort and love he so desperately needed.

And I'm supposed to be his rock and protector, Jamal thought. I'm leading this boy straight to the grave.

"If you keep acting like the weight of the world is on your shoulders those frown lines will become permanent," Diego teased. "You need to keep sexy for me, papi."

Jamal smiled at his teenage love. He searched the boy's

eyes and wondered how they'd come so far in such a small span of time. The way they'd met would have left any other pair ready to jump down each other's throat with a Berretta. Jamal imagined that the years of friendship between him and Romeo was the only thing that had kept the two of them from travelling down that path even though Jamal thought it was an inevitable fate. But Diego was different.

Jamal had followed orders given by a mentally disturbed man. Diego had followed something else. It was that 'something else' that had made him invite Jamal back to his grandmother's house. It was that 'something else' that had made it possible to look beyond the forced sex and encouraged Diego to have Jamal in a way that no other man ever had. Jamal was sure it was lust or simple sexual infatuation at first. But it had grown to be so much more. *They* were so much more.

"You act like we'll have a chance to grow old enough to have frown lines," Jamal said. His voice was barely a whisper. "That's a luxury that cats like us don't have."

"I have faith that you'll see us through all this shit," Diego said.

A weak chuckle shook Jamal's chest. "Your faith might be misplaced, pimpin'. If it wasn't for me you wouldn't have gotten shot at that fucking club. And we wouldn't be taking orders from some psycho bitch that has a death wish."

"If it wasn't for you I would have died in that club."

Jamal shook his head. "As much as I hate to admit it, Smurf did that."

"Only because he knew he would have been staring down the barrel of a gun if he didn't call that doctor."

"Hmm, maybe," Jamal relented. "Still, all this shit is my

fault."

Diego frowned. He wrapped his arm over Jamal's shoulder. "I hope this isn't some lame ass pity party. You're too strong to start doubting yourself. We need you. I need you."

Jamal looked up and saw the concern all over Diego's face. He was more worried about Jamal's feelings than the impending bout with the Angel of Death. That dedication actually scared Jamal.

"I'm not sure that I'm enough. I'm not sure that I can see us through this shit."

"I'm sure."

Diego leaned closer and placed his head onto Jamal's shoulder. The two of them looked out the window at the Baltimore harbor, savoring the sight, both knowing it might be their last. There was so much that Jamal wanted to say to Diego. So much he wanted to share with him. He didn't want to say anything he wouldn't have said if they weren't facing death but what he was feeling at that moment felt overwhelmingly genuine. He doubted words could begin to describe how he felt. So he stood there, quiet, in a small embrace with the man he loved.

"Jamal," Diego began. "I need you to do me a favor."

"Anything," Jamal said without hesitation.

"If I don't make it out of this—"

"Either we both walk out or neither one of us do," Jamal said firmly.

Diego smiled. "Make sure my *abuela* is taken care of. She needs me. My brothers and sisters need me. I need to know that they will be okay however this shit ends."

A solitary tear ran down Jamal's cheek. "I got you."

Diego nodded and placed his head back on Jamal's shoulder. They stood there comforting each other as much as they could given the circumstances. After a few minutes Jamal noticed how quiet it had gotten in the room. He looked over his shoulder back at the bed. Smurf and Black were nowhere to be seen. Jamal's eyes shifted to the bathroom. The door was closed. He heard the shower cut on. Jamal shook his head.

Before Jamal could give anymore thought to the idea of Smurf and Black fucking around, Diego stepped in front of Jamal. He looked up into Jamal's eyes as he caressed the crew leader's face. Jamal saw want and desire intermingled with despair; the need for comfort and affirmation radiating from the young stick-up boy's body.

"Do you love me, Jamal," Diego asked. He studied Jamal's face unhurriedly, feature by feature. "Tell me that you love me as much as I love you."

Jamal stared back in waiting silence. He wondered where the need for a declaration of love had come from. Jamal couldn't help but feel that the question was grounded in fear of what lay ahead. There was no time for reflection and deep thought. Diego's eyes darkened with emotion. His thick brows and brown eyes were startling against his light skin and dark hair. Despite the reason for the question, an answer was needed.

Taking a deep, unsteady breath, Jamal stepped back. A frowned covered his face as he narrowed his gaze and focused his eyes on Diego's until they locked their sights on each other. Jamal had to fight his overwhelming need to be close to Diego. It was a losing battle. Jamal pulled him roughly, almost violently, to him. He pressed forward and kissed Diego like it was the last kiss they'd ever share. His lips were firm and sensual.

"Yes," Jamal said between shallow, quick gasps, "I love you."

The corners of Diego's mouth curled into a devilish smile. "How much do you love me?"

Jamal pulled his lips back just an inch to answer. "So much that it fucking hurts thinking about being without you, nigga."

Diego reached up and gripped Jamal by the neck. His thumbs pressed roughly into Jamal's jaw bone as their foreheads meshed together. Jamal's muscles tensed suddenly under his fingertips. Diego's hands were rough and gave him a sense of protection. For a moment, the impending meeting with Slim didn't strike a chord of fear in his body.

"Prove it," Diego demanded.

He moved in and forced his tongue into Jamal's mouth before the words sunk in. The Latin lover's tongue darted into Jamal's mouth like a piston fucking his face. Their tongues wrestled like two heavyweight champs vying for a championship belt. Diego didn't pull back until the two of them were nearly out of air.

Huffing and puffing like they'd run a mile in under six minutes, Diego and Jamal stared each other down like two warriors ready to engage in battle. Only, the weapons of choice were not guns or knives. Something more physical and sensual was the more desired tool.

Jamal stepped back, still gasping for air, and collapsed on the bed. A raw sensuality flared in his eyes. Diego saw the burning desire. As if his clothes were ablaze, he began to strip until he stood there, stark naked, with his dick raging hard and jutting from his body proudly. Jamal's eyes drank in the sensuality of Diego's physique.

"Bring that ass over here," Jamal said with a huskiness that lingered in his tone.

Diego smiled. A spark of eroticism brightened his face as he slowly made his way toward Jamal. Even though he was just a few paces away, Jamal couldn't help but feel empty as a bottomless pit waiting for Diego to come within his grasp.

The air crackled from the heat and electricity radiating from Diego's body. Jamal felt the sensation on his lips as his lover stood between his legs, his manhood just a few inches from his mouth. Like a flash flood, his tongue gushed with wetness. Jamal felt the overwhelming urge to take Diego in his mouth. His eyes zeroed in on the one-eyed snake, hypnotized.

Diego reached down and took Jamal by his chin and forced him to look up. With his bottom lip wedged between his teeth and his chest heaving with heavy breaths, Diego squinted his eyes and forced Jamal's head down on his thick pole.

There was no slow, steady stroke. Diego was driven by a carnal desire that needed to be quenched and could only be tamed by Jamal's submission. He pressed the thick head of his dick through the tight 'O' Jamal made with his thick lips all the way to the back of his throat. Diego thrust his thick stick in and out of the wet, warm hole at a pace that only forced Jamal to gag.

Then suddenly, Diego pulled his sloppily wet dick from Jamal's mouth, bent down and swallowed the stick-up crew leader's lips with his mouth. He kissed, licked and sucked Jamal's orifice with all the raw sensuality that had built between then from the moment they met. Jamal was caught up in the rapture.

His eyes clench tightly and he leaned forward so hard that he would have hit the floor face first if Diego had not steadied him. He wanted more. He wanted Diego. Then, out of nowhere, he was halted by an iron grip on his waist. Diego pulled back and gave him a look that sent shivers up his spine and made his dick harden to the point of near pain.

Diego pushed Jamal up on the bed and spun him around onto his stomach. The crew leader barely caught his breath before he felt Diego's tongue plunge into his round, muscular ass. Instinct kicked in. Jamal clenched his cheeks hard, pushing Diego from his hole. A hard, heavy smack to his right cheek made Jamal relax and submit. The stinging pain that burned on his flesh from the heavy hand made Jamal crave Diego's touch. He ached for it.

Jamal felt like he'd been possessed. His body squirmed beneath Diego. His back arched and his ass pushed into the air. Jamal's ass shook uncontrollably as he pressed back, searching for Diego's firm touch. The Spanish thug obliged.

Diego grabbed each muscular mound of ass flesh and peeled them back until Jamal's brown rosebud was exposed to the elements. His eyes raked boldly over Jamal's flesh. Again, he dove in and ate Jamal's ass without restraint or inhibition. He licked and sucked until his lips and chin were glistening with spit and ass juices.

"Damn that feels so fucking good," Jamal said. The words were caught between moans and mostly muffled into the sheets. "Eat that shit, boy!"

No sooner had the words left Jamal's lips that Diego was reaching over to the nightstand. Jamal looked up and caught himself and Diego in the mirror. He watched the boy strap up and squirt so much lube on his meat that it glistened. Jamal's body shook uncontrollably. Up until that very second he'd been caught in the moment. Now, with Diego's dick just inches from his hole he was having second thoughts.

"Baby," Jamal started. He tried to turn on his back but Diego planted a heavy hand on the small of his back. "Let's just jack-off and make out. I don't think I can take it."

Diego frowned at the reflection of Jamal in the mirror. He leaned down and pressed his slim, toned body onto Jamal's, the length of his dick rubbing on Jamal's hole. Diego leaned in, reached around and wrapped his free hand around Jamal's throat. He nuzzled close to Jamal's ear and whispered in a labored breath.

"Nigga, you're mine, forever," Diego said. The authority in his voice sent tremors of fear through Jamal. "This ass is mine. This dick is mine. Right now, I'm going to enjoy this fat ass. And you're going to love every minute of it because you love me and you love this dick. Understand?"

It wasn't really a question. Jamal knew that. He buried his face into the bed. Despite the overwhelming fear there was an equally if not more compelling urge to feel Diego deep inside of him. He clawed at the bed and braced himself for the penetration.

In one smooth stroke, Diego lined his rigid pole directly for Jamal's tight hole. He pushed the tip of his dick in on the first try and pressed forward inch after, slow, painfully blissful, inch. The Latin thug's body shivered as he impaled his dick deep inside of Jamal.

The pain that came with the dick wedged between his cheeks, abusing his hole, carved merciless lines of pain and pleasure on Jamal's face. His sphincter clenched and pulsed with the rapid beat of his heart. Jamal gasped in sweet agony as he reached down and stroked his dick between his taut flesh and the tangled covers.

"Fuck," Jamal nearly screamed into the sheet. "Damn boy!"

He clenched his eyes shut and concentrated so that he didn't cum too quickly. The pain intertwined with the pleasure. He could only bear the anal assault by stroking his own dick without regard to his own impending orgasm.

Diego grinded his hips into Jamal like he was on the dance floor. He pulled Jamal's by the throat, forcing his head back, as he nibbled hungrily at his lobe.

"Look at me while I fuck this ass," Diego demanded. "I said look at me, nigga!"

Jamal forced open his eyelids and looked at the reflection of Diego dicking his ass down with little restraint. It was the most erotic thing he'd ever seen. His young body wrecked with tremors. He felt every single nerve ending in ass explode with agonizing pleasure as Diego's dick pounded into him.

Slowly, the pain he had felt at first began to melt into a lingering, mind numbing sensation of arousal and lust zeroed in on his swollen hole. The thought of dick penetrating him scared Jamal. But with Diego thrusting his brick hard meat into a special spot within his bowels, the urge to push back beckoned. Jamal couldn't help but move faster and faster as Diego slammed harder and deeper inside of him. Jamal knew he couldn't last much longer.

Jamal pushed back forcibly and squeezed his anal muscle with all his strength. Diego met each backward push with an equally, earth shattering lunge forward. Jamal cried out each time. The sound got caught in his throat as he slammed his ass back over and over again. All that emerged was a silent stifled moan.

The raw sound of wet flesh smacked against the walls of the small hotel room. Diego's dick strained until it was impossibly hard. Jamal felt every vein of Diego's dick swell in his ass and brush against the ring of his hole. Diego's back straightened. His nailed racked down the middle of Jamal's back as he repositioned himself to long dick Jamal's hole. Diego's balls drew tight against his sweat covered body. He pounded inside Jamal's ass twice more before stiffening in the stick-up boy's ass and shot load after load into the rubber.

Diego collapsed atop Jamal just as he busted a fat nut into his hand and on the sheets. The two of them lay there spent. Somehow, Diego managed to press his body around and plant a hard kiss on Jamal's lips.

"Goddamn that was hot as fuck," Smurf said.

Jamal and Diego looked up at Smurf and Black. The two of them had towels wrapped around their waists but even that couldn't hide their hard-ons. Jamal was too tired and worn out to say anything. He reached down and pulled the covers over him and Diego as he shot a look of anger at the snake nigga.

A gentle knock on the door between the two hotel rooms interrupted the awkward moment between Jamal, Diego, Black and Smurf. Smurf unlocked and opened the door, his eyes still glued on Jamal. It was Santana. Surprisingly, she didn't even flinch at the sight or smell in the room. She looked at Jamal.

"Slim just called," she said. "We need to move, now."

Chapter 27

Jamal eyed Bricks as the beast of a body guard roughly grabbed and patted him down. Slim's right hand man along with three other equally large men dressed in all black had stripped him, Romeo, Diego and Santana of their guns. Smurf wasn't even touched. Even though Jamal never knew the boy to carry any type of a weapon, he thought it odd that he wasn't even searched. Jamal made a mental note.

"Your boss scared that his crew might snuff his ass out?" Jamal asked gaily. "I thought we was his handpicked golden boys and shit."

Bricks ignored the comment and visibly clenched his jaw. He laid a heavy hand on Jamal's shoulder and pushed him through the large foyer where they had been stopped and frisked into an ornately decorated living room. Jamal hadn't seen it at the pool hall back in Atlanta but sitting in what

Santana said was one of many homes Slim owned, he saw just how deep in cash the drug dealing rapist was.

Bricks and his goons had the crew and Santana sit down on a large couch near the fireplace. They removed the zip ties from Ty, C-Note and Black's wrist and ankles and replaced them with handcuffs. The trio was pushed down onto the ground with one of the bodyguards hovering over them with what looked like a semi-automatic pointed at them.

How the fuck we going to pull this bullshit off, Jamal thought. We aint got no fucking guns and these niggas got oozes and shit.

His eyes darted over to Diego. He was like a stone; hard, rough and unmoved. The look in his eyes showed he was ready for death. Romeo looked as if he didn't have a care in the world. There was neither concern nor resolve; just nothing. He looked empty as ever. Then there was Santana.

Jamal watched her eyes move from guard to guard and from window to door. Then she looked forward as if not focusing on anything. It was a calculating gaze. She was plotting. After a moment, she looked up and met Jamal's eyes. He was no mind reader but Jamal knew exactly what she was saying with those cold and calculating, piercing eyes: *hold your shit.*

Jamal intended to do just that. He'd prepared himself during the ride to the Fort Washington, Maryland house for the worse. Jamal had convinced himself that he was ready to go out like a soldier, guns a blazing, and meet his maker. But now, as he looked at his crew and felt the nakedness of not being strapped, he wasn't so sure.

Jamal had imagined all of them storming the house shooting everyone in sight. He even kept that hope alive when he saw Santana binding Tay, C-Note and Black with the zip ties back at the hotel. It wasn't until they reached the gate of Slim's house with all the cameras that the hope for a bloody assault had faded along with the remote hope that he might walk away from the ordeal with Diego by his side.

The last drop of hope evaporated when they made it to the door and Santana handed over her two guns to Bricks without complaint. Jamal had struggled to maintain his demeanor and not let the shock he felt when she just gave over her only means of defense. At that point it all seemed hopeless. Jamal was like a robot going through the motions.

Jamal pulled his eyes from Santana and her cold gaze and looked down at Tay, C-Note and Black huddled together on the floor like some kindergarteners. He didn't see fear in their eyes. There wasn't even a hint of concern. Jamal wondered if they knew something that he didn't. He was almost sure that they did. If they didn't, they were surely placing a lot of trust in Santana.

The fact that Santana and her crew didn't seem the least bit concerned about not being armed and three of them cuffed and guarded had given Jamal a sliver of hope. Despite constant questioning in the SUV, Santana outright refused to say what she had planned besides them getting close enough to Slim to somehow kill the man.

Soft music cut into the air and tugged Jamal from his thoughts. It was opera. Jamal and everyone else turned towards the sound and faced what looked to be a study. Jamal could see shelves of books from his vantage point but nothing else. Then, the tip of a shadow slithered beyond the threshold of the study. Jamal's stomach hardened. Death was coming.

Slim glided in the room like royalty, dressed in a large, plush white robe. A sinister grin spread on his haggardly looking face. Jamal recoiled in disgust. The blood shot eyes and the sweat lining the man's temples became more prevalent the closer he got to the crew. Even Slim's own men looked turned off by his display. With the bottle of Hennessy clutched in his fingers and his appearance, it didn't take a rocket scientist to see that Slim was drunk off his ass.

"Look at what the fuck we have here," Slim said, his words painfully slurred. "Got these little niggas all tied up like presents under a fucking Christmas tree!"

No one spoke. Everyone just watched the train wreck of a man stumble over towards Tay, Black and C-Note. He looked at them, sizing them up as if they were slaves being auctioned off. Then he spun around, almost dropping his bottle, and leveled a mean, drunken stare at Jamal.

"Why didn't you kill these little niggas like I said?" he asked, pointing and spilling his liquor. "I gave you a fucking order and I expected you to carry it out."

Jamal clenched his jaw and took a deep breath. "Revenge and getting even is one thing," he began, "murder is something totally different. I'm not some gun for hire that you can point in a direction and command me to off some nigga. Not how I operate, man."

Slim frowned. He looked at Jamal like the boy was some deformity of existence. Then his right eye twitched. The man had gone from shock to anger in a split second. Finally, a baffling grin creased his face. Slowly, a maniacal laugh erupted from Slim's small frame. He clutched his gut, arched his back and laughed towards the ceiling. Everyone squirmed in their skin from the disturbing display. Even Romeo eased further back in the couch.

In a flash, Slim transversed the span of the room and was staring down at Jamal, less than a foot from the crew leader's face. The acrid odor of liquor oozed from his pores. A plastic, ominous expression replaced the grin. Jamal struggled to maintain. If nothing else, he was grateful for not pissing on himself.

"You still think that this arrangement is open for interpretation or some type of fucking negotiation," Slim said. Spittle erupted from his mouth like a volcano as he spoke. "You still think that you have some type of fucking control over shit. Nigga, you don't. You don't motherfucking control a Goddamn thing!"

Slim stuck his hand in the front pocket of his robe and pulled out his switch blade. Jamal's eyes fixated on the knife. The young crew leader didn't feel fear from seeing the blade. No, he felt anger. It was a white, hot anger that that burned hotter and brighter than a thousand suns. It was a drowning anger that had him pinned a thousand leagues under the ocean. It was anger that if unleashed, there wouldn't be much of a soul for even God to redeem.

That blade was the same one Slim had pressed on Jamal's neck when they first met. It was the same blade Slim had threatened him with as he demanded him to penetrate and violate Romeo and Diego. It was the same blade that he had pulled on Jamal at the doctor's house when Diego was on his death bed. And now, it was the same blade the woefully well connected dealer pulled as he made his point on how things worked under his leadership.

Slim brought his hand up and dug the edge of the blade against Jamal's throat. "Little nigga, when I say do something

I want it done. Right now, you should be tying cinder bricks or chains to these nigga's ankles and knocking them into the harbor. Why the fuck are they sitting in my fucking living room still breathing!"

Jamal felt the blade break his flesh as Slim yelled. His hands were unsteady; guided by blind, mad rage and liquor. It was a potentially fatal combination. Jamal focused on his breathing as he slowly looked up at Slim. He tried to bottle all the hate he had felt for the man. It wasn't time to smash it over his head. Not yet.

"Give me my gun back and I'll finish it," Jamal said. "Right here, right now."

Slim's face scrunched up like a child who had been given liver to eat. He looked at Jamal thoughtfully and then shook his head. "Naw, you said you weren't a killer." Slim pulled the knife from Jamal's jugular. "Do you believe in an eye for an eye?"

Jamal reached up and rubbed his neck. He felt the wetness of blood on his finger tips. Jamal blinked incessantly as he tried to take deep breaths and calm his nerves. "I don't have a problem with getting even with a nigga." Jamal said the words and meant them. He only wished he could apply them. "So yea, I guess so."

Slim swiveled and directed his gaze to Diego. "Show me your gunshot wound."

Diego kept his eyes on Slim as he reached for the bottom of his shirt and lifted it just enough for the bruised, stitched flesh to be visible. Once Slim nodded Diego dropped his shirt and hung his head. Slim reached into the other pocket of his robe and pulled out a .9mm. He walked over to C-Note and shot the man in the gut at point blank.

C-Note doubled over, placing his hands over the wound. Black and Tay moved to help him but Slim waved his gun, warning them to stay where they were. The burly baby faced man wailed in pain.

Jamal felt his chest burn. It felt like someone had knocked the wind out of him. There was no love for C-Note and Jamal had wanted to kill the man just few hours ago but how Slim had shot the man so unexpectedly had ripped through him like the cry that screeched through the room from Santana.

"Bitch," Slim said as he stampeded towards Santana. He backhanded her, hard. "Shut that shit the fuck up or I can give you something to really scream about."

Santana clamped her mouth shut and held the side of her face where slim had violated her. Tears of anger streamed down her cheek. Her eyes were red with rage and pain. Jamal saw the way she looked. For a moment he was more afraid of her than Slim. She was holding something back. Slim shook his head at her and then frowned as if a sour thought came to his mind. He turned and looked at Jamal.

"I'm guessing you know this is my niece, right?" he asked, his tone oddly bright. "And Tay over there is my nephew. Both by blood."

"Hell of a way to treat blood," Jamal said. The words left his lips before he had thought.

Slim smiled. "You right, young nigga. Just watch that tone before I take that tongue." Slim walked over to the chair opposite Jamal and the crew. He sat, spread eagle, his manhood in full view. "Did she tell you anything else about the family?"

Jamal shook his head. "Nothing important."

"Really?" Slim asked as he looked from Jamal to Santana and back. "Little bitch is good with her whole rape story. Shiiiiittt, she told it to Daddy Knight years ago. Made the old man turn on me. Been trying to kill me since."

Jamal didn't respond. Now he knew she lied about Slim killing his own father. He knew Santana had lied about her cousins raping her. Still, Jamal wasn't convinced that Slim hadn't done the same despite Santana's propensity to lie through her teeth. Slim was a predator and a proven rapists. Jamal only needed to hear the accusation towards the man for it to have weight.

Slim looked over at Santana. "How is the old man?" he asked. "He still trying to work over my connects and dip into my money?"

Santana didn't say a word. Her eyes stuck to the ground. She held her face and didn't make a sound. Jamal was surprised. He didn't think a slap to the face would have quieted Santana. She seemed like she was built a little tougher.

"Jamal," Slim started. "Who picked the houses for you to rob a couple of days ago?" Jamal shot a hard look at Bricks. "Good," Slim said, acknowledging the response. "And why do you think I had you hit those particular spots?"

Jamal shrugged. "Boredom?"

"I told you to watch that tongue," he warned. Slim waved his gun tauntingly. "Now answer the question."

Jamal shook his head. "I don't know. The first house was them niggas over there on the ground, your kinfolk. Revenge I guess."

"If you ever want to be more than someone's fucking foot soldier you need to start using your head, nigga. Tay knew ya'll was coming."

"Then why did you send us there in the first fucking place?" Jamal asked. Anger singed the tip of his tongue. "You wanted us dead, didn't you?"

"To be honest I really don't give a fuck what happens to you? You really think I give a fuck about the money you tried to take? I make that in under an hour. I can wipe my ass with the cash ya'll sent me and flush it down the toilet without a second though. Honestly, I was hoping that you all would have killed each other. I was going to send Bricks and my boys in to clean up the mess left behind. Take care of the loose ends."

"You mean kill whoever was left standing."

"Apples and oranges, nigga, apples and oranges."

"So we robbed them other two spots for no reason?" Jamal asked.

"There's always a fucking reason. But that's not important. You little niggas did better than I could have ever hope. That's the only reason you're still fucking breathing. But don't push me. You already got my trigger finger itching."

Jamal's nostrils flared. "I don't understand how you told Tay we was coming and shit went down how it went down. It didn't seem like he knew."

"You're right, it didn't," Slim admitted. "But I'm not the one that told Tay." Slim's eyes went to Santana then Smurf. "Bring your little ass over here, boy."

Smurf hung his head low and got on his hands and knees. He crawled over to Slim like a dog. Jamal looked at the boy with disgust and, for the first time, pity. The level of degradation reached an all time high when Smurf rested his head on Slim's thigh and started sucking the man's dick. Anger welled up in Jamal. The ebb and flow of the emotion was becoming nauseating. He was still mad at Smurf for being a snake but he finally understood how fucked up in the head Slim had the boy.

"You knew he would tell Santana?" Jamal asked, his eyes avoiding Smurf between Slim's legs. "You knew they still talked?"

"Yea, just like I knew that Santana would tell Tay and just like I know that you little niggas came up in my motherfucking house plotting to kill me. Trying to do what my old man hasn't been able to do since I became his only supplier."

Jamal shook his head. "I don't understand why we're here."

"Ask Santana."

"No, I mean me, Romeo and Diego. We was supposed to repay a debt; not get involved in this family feud shit ya'll got going on."

"Weren't you listening?" Slim asked. "I aint worried about no fucking money you niggas tried to take from one trap house in fucking Georgia or some debt that Spanish bitch's daddy got. You fuckers was dead the moment ya'll crossed me. You eat, breathe, shit and fuck on my convenience. And I wanted them niggas dead." Slim shrugged. "I guess you can never send a boy to do a man's job."

Slim pulled out his gun, leveled it at C-Note and pulled the trigger.

He may have been drunk but the man's aim was impeccable. A bullet hole went from the front of C-Note's forehead to the back of his skull. His large body fell limp to the ground. Slim aimed at Black.

Before he could pull the trigger, Santana jumped up from

the couch, gun in hand. "Put your gun down or I swear to God I will blow off your fucking head!"

Jamal blinked incessantly. He hadn't even seen the girl jump up. His eyes had been glued on C-Note's lifeless body. Everything was happening so fast. Jamal wondered how the hell she managed to get a gun. Bricks had patted her and him down. The man had been thorough. Jamal's ass and balls could attest to that.

Slim held his hands in the air and laughed that said haunting laugh. "Whoa, whoa. Calm down baby girl. Is this how you planned on killing me? Hiding a gun in that pussy that's been raped by uncles and cousins? Before you pull that trigger, just hold on. I got someone I want you to see." Slim winked at her and whistled.

Another guard came in with a handcuffed woman. Her face was badly beaten but Jamal recognized her. It was the same woman he'd seen at the motel room with Bricks. The same one that had made the hair on Jamal's neck stand at attention. The woman Bricks had said was his ex-wife. Santana's arm shook as she looked at the woman.

"Mom," she whispered, fighting back tears.

Chapter 28

"Just one big ass family reunion, hunh?" Slim asked. He pointed his pistol at Santana. "Put your gun down or I'll have my boy put a bullet through the back of your mother's skull."

Santana dropped her gun. She looked at Slim like the man had already killed her mother. "You'd kill you own sister?"

"Without a second thought," Slim affirmed. "Drop her like the bitch she is. I've killed women better than her. Ask your father."

"I can't," Santana said. "You killed him a month ago. I know you did."

"That wasn't your father," Slim said.

Santana frowned. She looked from the mangled hunk of beaten flesh that was her mother back to Slim. The man laughed maniacally again. Jamal saw that he was getting a perverse pleasure from the whole scene developing right in front of his face.

Jamal looked to Bricks. The man looked like a rock, as always, but his eyes were like a caged animal demanding release. Jamal wondered if the woman really was Bricks ex-wife and if she was, how Slim could handle the woman, even though she was his sister, in such an inhumane manner. There was no way Bricks wasn't aware of her being beaten in the house. Jamal had it figured out. She wasn't Bricks' ex-wife. That had been a lie. And up until that very moment, Bricks believed that even Slim didn't know about his dealings with his sister. Bricks was Santana's father and she didn't even know.

"I'm not going to sit here and play these games with you, uncle Avant," Santana said. "Please let my mother go. She has nothing to do with this. Grand daddy put this whole thing together."

Slim shook his head. "I know damn well my sister isn't innocent in all this. Eve has a way of putting herself in shit that has nothing to do with her."

Eve, Jamal thought. Her name's not Shonda like Bricks lied and said.

Jamal racked his mind on how he was going to get the hell out of the family mess that was engulfing the room. Diego and Romeo looked as if they were captivated, watching some soap opera. Jamal looked back at Bricks. The man had to know that Slim was on to him.

Bricks eyes settled and narrowed on Jamal. The two held each other's gaze for what seemed like an eternity. Words weren't needed. The motion of Bricks eyes, the flare of the man's nostril and the way his forearm tensed signaled all the information Jamal needed. The young hustler slowly slid his hand into the plush cushion of the sofa. He pressed his finger down, further and further until he felt the familiar touch of steel against his palm.

"Are you really going to kill me and my mother?!" Santana said. Her voiced strained to the point where her words were barely recognizable. "Are you that fucking cold hearted?"

Slim kicked Smurf from his engorged manhood and walked over to Santana's mother. He gripped a handful of his sister's hair and pulled the woman next to him. A loud, sickening cry bellowed through the woman's bloodied lips.

"You all came in my house planning to kill me, right?" Slim asked. "Well fuck it."

Slim brought his gun up. Before he could place it at Eve's head, Jamal yanked his gun from the couch. Santana dropped to the floor for her piece and Bricks had pulled out two Berettas. Four guns pointed at Slim. In the blink of an eye, the drug dealer yanked his sister's head back by her hair and kicked her in the back. He shot her in the back. He let of one more shot as he back peddled yelling, "Kill those motherfuckers!"

Bullets ripped through the small space. Screams of pain from getting shot coupled with the sound of hot lead ripping through wood and fabric. Blood was everywhere. Slim was nowhere to be seen.

Jamal had pushed the sofa he, Romeo and Diego had been sitting on back with all his strength. He shot off two rounds and dropped the man that had brought Santana's mother in the living room. Jamal pulled back behind the sofa to check on his crew.

"Are you guys alright?" he asked

Romeo nodded. "Yea, I'm good."

Jamal's eyes darted to the bullet wound he was nursing. It was a graze; a simple flesh wound. Jamal turned and looked at Diego. The world went silent. Jamal's heart slowed to a snail's crawl and beat so loudly that it was deafening. He didn't even hear all the gun shots being rattled off. His eyes were glued on the empty, dead face of Diego.

Jamal couldn't move. He sat there in shook, looking at Diego's lifeless body. One bullet hole right in the middle of Diego's forehead was what did it. Jamal's heart burned to a crisp. Every muscle in his body began to jerk involuntarily. He was convinced that his mind was playing a trick on him. Jamal reached out to touch Diego, to see if the corpse in front of him was real.

Romeo gripped Jamal's hand before his fingers touched his dead lover's flesh. "Don't, just don't." Romeo said, hugging Jamal from the back. He held his best friend from another lifetime in a vice grip as he reached out and closed Diego's eyes. "We have to get out of here, Jamal."

The tears came. Jamal rocked back and forth like he was having a seizure. Romeo struggled to hold him down from the gun fight surrounding them. The crew leader wailed and hollered. An unearthly sound erupted from his stout frame and echoed through the house until he was out of breath. Jamal inhaled and exhaled rapidly.

Images of Diego flashed in Jamal's mind. The feeling of utter lose welled inside of the young hustler and poured out like the Niagara. He looked down at Diego again. This time he only saw the bullet hole. Jamal's body went rigid. His jaw clenched so hard it felt as if his teeth would crack. One thought ran through his mind: *Slim.*

Jamal looked back at Romeo and whispered, "Get off

me."

The words were low but forceful enough for Romeo to know not to ignore them. Jamal gripped his gun and stood up from behind the sofa. A guard saw him and pointed his gun. Jamal shot him first. He planted three bullets in the man's chest without blinking.

Jamal looked around. All the guards were dead. Blood covered the broken furniture and the large oriental rug in the middle of the floor. Jamal looked over to where C-Note had been murdered. Black was dead. Tay was under C-Note's dead body but looked to be alive. Jamal turned and looked for Smurf. The boy was lifeless on his back in the middle of the living room. Santana was just a few feet away. She was hunkered over her mother, praying.

Jamal looked around and caught sight of Bricks leaning on the wall separating the hallway and living room. He clutched his chest as he slid down to the floor. Jamal rushed over to the bald brute. The first thing the young hustler noticed was the streak of blood on the wall where Bricks had been leaning.

"Where is he!" Jamal demanded. "Where the fuck is Slim!"

"Garage," Bricks answered. Blood oozed from his mouth as he spoke.

"Fuck!"

Bricks started laughing. He reached up and grabbed Jamal by the shirt. The stick-up boy looked at the man warily. Bricks reached into his pocket. He pulled his hand out, balled into a fist and held in the air. He opened his hand and a half dozen car keys fell to the ground. Bricks started laughing again and pointed down the hall.

Jamal sprang to his feet and sprinted down the hall to the

kitchen. It was dark. He held his gun close to his chest as he switched the lights on. Jamal circled around the kitchen island. Nothing. He went for the door in the corner, near the counter next to the stove.

Jamal placed his hand on the knob and slowly turned it. He snatched the door open and let loose a torrent of bullets into an empty pantry. Jamal kicked the baseboard and cursed under his breath. He was convinced that Slim was long gone.

The laundry room was empty. So was the formal dining room. There was no way he could have left through the front with Bricks half alive and Santana mourning over her dead mother. He could have made it upstairs but there was no point in going up there unless he had more guns. Jamal shook the thought. The stick-up boy made his way to the garage.

Darkness filled the large space. A half dozen vehicles lined the wall of the garage. On the other side were an array of cars and car parts assorted much like a mechanic's shop would be organized. Jamal thought to turn on the light but decided against it. There were so many places Slim could be hiding. The last thing he wanted to do was tip the man off.

Jamal tip toed to the nearest car and surveyed the garage. He looked at every single car, searching for something out of place. He didn't see anything. Again, he looked over the vehicles. He was convinced he would see something. On the second pass he still hadn't caught sight of anything. Jamal began to panic. And just then, out the corner of his eyes, he saw a door close to the black Escalade.

Anger and pain fueled the resolve he felt as he moved closer to the SUV. He was less than six feet away from the vehicle. Jamal squatted down so that he couldn't be seen from the windows and moved to the rear of the Escalade. He circled around to the door he saw move.

Jamal took a deep, quiet breath. He wiped the sweat from his hand on his shirt and reaffirmed his grip on his gun. Slowly, he reached up for the door handle. He counted in his head. 3…2…1… Just as he sprang into action and snatched the door open, he felt the all too familiar touch of cold steel pressed against his skin.

"Not this time little nigga," Slim said. "I been doing this shit for too long to let some no name nigga like you take me out. Put that gun down."

Jamal dropped the gun and placed his hands on the SUV. "So you going to shoot me in the back of the head like the coward that you are?"

"Coward?" Slim scuffed. "Little boy, I've done things that would make you shit in your draws. The fuck you talking about."

"Fine, then look me in the eye," Jamal dared.

Slim didn't say anything. But the slight ease of pressure on the nape of Jamal's neck signaled his agreement. Jamal pivoted his right foot and circle slowly on his hips. He caught a glimpse of the smug grin on Slim's face. The anger in the young hustler boiled over.

With all his strength, Jamal spun around, hard, his outward flung hands landing on Slim's back and shoved the drug dealer's head through the window of the driver side door. Jamal grabbed Slim from the back and placed him in a choke hold.

Slim clawed and kicked. The pair went to the ground but Jamal held on for dear life. He was committed to squeezing the life out of the man that had violated him, his friend and the only man he had loved. Tears welled in Jamal's eyes as he tried to rip Slim's head off.

It didn't take long for Slim to start to give up. He wasn't getting air. Small waves of joy began to hit Jamal until he was overcome with elation that the man would finally be dead soon. He beamed as he strangled the man, pressing his rigid bicep and forearm against the man's throat.

Jamal thought he heard the last breath slip from Slim's mouth. Yet the moment was lost. He felt hard steel pressed on the back of his head, again.

"Let him go," Santana demanded. "Knight wants him alive."

Jamal clenched his eyes shuts. Tears welled at the slits. He didn't release the man until she pressed harder into his head. Slim collapsed between Jamal's legs. The stick-up boy kicked him in the side, forcing him on his back. Slim gasped for breath and laughed.

"You can't kill me!" he managed to croak.

"I'm sorry, Jamal," Santana said. "This is bigger than you and me."

Jamal shook his head. He pounded at the ground until he thought his fist would break. And then he saw it. Light. A small sliver of light reflected off of Slim's blade. It was on the ground, just a few feet away. Jamal looked at the blade and up at Santana. She was busy putting cuffs on her uncle.

Jamal scrambled to his feet, snatched the knife and dove for Slim. He brought all his weight down on the man. With both hands, Jamal gripped the blade and plunged the weapon through the man's heart all the way to the hilt.

Jamal gripped the blade and twisted it. He watched Slim's wide eyes twist in pain and then go blank. The young hustler watched as the life left the man's body. Never before had

Jamal felt so satisfied. He looked up at Santana.

"You fucked up," she said. "Knight is not going to be happy."

"You wanted that nigga dead, too," Jamal said.

"I know, but you're going to regret what you just did," Santana warned. "Slim is a bad dream compared to my grand dad. That old man is a monster."

Before Jamal could utter another word, the butt of Santana's gun came down on the bridge of his nose. The world went black. But it was okay. Jamal dreamt of Slim's death over and over again. Whatever horror awaited him was worth it. Jamal had finally gotten his revenge. He got payback for Diego. Slim was dead.

About The Author

BEAST is an author of black, gay fiction. His vast catalog of titles range from pure, salacious erotica to heart pounding romance and nerve wrecking suspense. No genre is off limits for this versatile writer.

Readers can gain direct access with Beast by checking out his website, www.BeastAuthor.com, and joining the online community of folks who enjoy reading his stories. Free stories, giveaways, swag bags and opportunities to read unreleased book await anyone wants them.